# REDEMPTION OF THE PRODIGAL

## A Noir Thriller of Revenge and Redemption

## Michael Caudo

Tasker Morris Ventures, LLC.

For my grandmother
Santa Ruggio


In memory of
Anthony "Radar" Risoli

# Contents


1.  THE BRIDGE  1

2.  DIESEL THERAPY  8

3.  BOOTS ON THE GROUND  12

4.  ZITTI E BUONI  15

5.  THE NOTE  19

6.  THE PINK NUNS  23

7.  AMOR FATI  27

8.  JULIAN  33

9.  UNTO THE BREACH  37

10.  THE GOOD PART  40

11.  THE BAD PART  45

12.  THE DUKE  48

13.  THE CARPATHIAN LYNX  54

14.  THE SAD TALE OF MIKEY FORTUNA  56

15.  CRIPPLED PREY  59

16.  GORGEOUS CREATURES  61

17.  GOOD TIMES  63

18.  NO CALL, NO SHOW                           66

19.  THE LION AND THE STURGEON               71

20.  SUNSET INN                               78

21.  WEEKEND PASS                            82

22.  EMPTY FRAMES                            84

Fullpage image                               86

23.  TWO SHIPS PASSING IN THE NIGHT          87

24.  "YOU GOT A PROBLEM, KID"                91

25.  THE REMBRANDT WHISPERER                 94

26.  HIGH NOON SALOON                        99

27.  HAYWIRE TWIST                           110

28.  ANGELINA'S CLUB TANGIER                 114

29.  SHOWGIRLS                               123

30.  THE ORANGE LOOP                         128

31.  DEAL WITH THE DEVIL                     133

32.  ANDROMEDA                               137

33.  PIMPLE BALLS AND DREAMS                 141

34.  GIRL WITH A HOOP EARRING                146

35.  NO GOOD DEED                            150

36.  THE CALLING OF ST. MATTHEW              154

37.  STRANGER THINGS                         157

38.  SOUTH PHILLY BARBED WIRE                161

39.  BANDO CAPITALE                          164

40.  TOM AND JERRY                           172

41. LOCAL WOMAN MISSING — 178

42. NO SHIESTIES — 182

43. SURFSIDE BAR AND GRILL — 187

44. BABY, PLEASE COME HOME — 193

45. WHITE LIES — 196

46. CHERCHEZ LA FEMME — 200

47. THE SWITCH — 203

48. AMANDA — 211

49. A DIFFERENT SETTING — 213

50. BESPOKE — 216

51. EDEN ROC — 222

52. SPREZZATURA — 226

53. DENROY — 231

54. DMITRY — 234

55. PRODIGAL IN THE TAVERN — 237

56. THE NATIVITY — 240

Fullpage image — 243

57. THE CONVERSATION — 244

58. MIAMI VICE — 261

59. MOON OVER FORT LAUDERDALE — 266

60. MOON OVER SOUTH PHILLY — 269

EPILOGUE — 273

Acknowledgements — 283

About the author — 285

# Chapter One

---

# THE BRIDGE

*"The sum of all human wisdom will be contained in these two words: Wait and hope."* — Alexandre Dumas, The Count of Monte Cristo

A1A was a shitshow. The left turn lane for Commercial Boulevard was backed up twenty cars deep, extending well beyond the confines of the markings on the scorching hot blacktop. When it was finally Nick's turn, he punched the accelerator of the Bentley with gusto, only to be met with the bane of all Fort Lauderdale drivers, a bridge opening.

"Motherfucker." Frankie Stone Crab began to squirm in the passenger seat. "We're gonna be late. I knew we shoulda took Oakland."

Nick laughed to himself, knowing the real reason for his uncle Frank's impatience. The old man was nervously tapping a pack of Marlboro Reds on his right knee as he stared at the bridge rising before him like it was some personal affront. Another rich prick had the audacity to transit the Intracoastal in his Pershing, while Frank had to wait for a smoke and a drink. Lauderdale-by-the-Sea is part of a barrier island, so living near the beach meant crossing over one of the bridges anytime your destination, say a bar or restaurant, was situated on the other side. From Commercial Boulevard to Las Olas Boulevard, the four bridges opened approximately every half hour, causing frequent delays. Nick considered it a small price to pay to reside in paradise.

"Let me ask you something, Unc. How long you been living here?"

"I don't know, twenty, twenty-one years maybe."

"How many bridges have you caught in that time?"

"Feels like a fuckin million. What's your point?"

"Just that every time we run into an opening, you act like it's the first time you've seen one. I mean, look around, what's your rush?"

Frank gazed around at the palm tree-lined street, free of litter, listened to the peaceful background sounds, notably devoid of gunshots. His tapping subsided, and his leg stopped its disco drummer's pulse. The bridge eased down, the barrier arms rose, and still the cars didn't move. Frank's moment of Zen burst like a spring breaker's sun blister.

"Fucking snowbirds. What the fuck are they waiting for?"

"Easy, Unc, we were all snowbirds once."

"Not me. My flight was one-way."

Nick gave him a knowing look, prompting the old man to amend his statement.

"With the exception of that one trip for that thing," Frank added proudly, hinting at something that was not to be spoken aloud.

Nick punched up a playlist on the touchscreen and turned up the volume just a bit on a song he had recently added, "Got To Get You Back" by Sons of Robin Stone.

"Jesus Christ. I haven't heard this since I saw these guys on Steel Pier in Atlantic City." Frank put the Marlboros away for the time and resumed tapping on his knee in time to the rhythm. "Nice, Nicky, very nice indeed. Did I ever tell you what a class act you are, kid?"

"Only about a thousand times, Unc."

"Good. Make it a thousand and one."

They finished the short remainder of the ride like that, pulling up to Roberto's Bayview just as the song ended. They were a few minutes late, and Ralph's Wraith was already parked in its reserved spot, but for the moment, the song made it all worth it.

Nick tossed the key fob to the valet, while another held open a door that was larger and heavier than you would expect for a waterfront café in Fort Lauderdale. It closed with a vacuum *whoosh* behind them, conveying a feeling of dark decadence to the interior, keeping the cool air in and the sunlight out. The bar at the center of the room provided a form of insulation from the touristy rat race lurking just on the other side of those hermetically sealed doors. It was a luxurious oasis free from prying eyes, nosy tourists, and jealous wives. A man could find respite here.

"You're late."

Nick's eyes hadn't quite adjusted from the sun-drenched exterior, but he placed Ralph's voice at the end of the bar; his usual spot, no reservation placard required. Ralph "The Rifle's" bark was directed at Frank even though Nick drove, because... well, because Nick was a few rungs up on their invisible social ladder, and in the end, it was always Frank's fault, even when it wasn't. Frank wasn't insulted. On the contrary, the lighthearted abuse brought some sense of reliability to his otherwise unreliable existence and reminded him this was where he belonged. And that's all Frankie Stone Crab could really hope for at this stage of his life.

"Whaddya drinking, Frankie?" Ralph inquired, indicating the issue of Frank's tardiness had been adequately addressed.

"Stoli Elit martini, blue cheese olives," Frank recited as he walked toward the outside, waterfront portion of Roberto's for his long-delayed smoke. The Marlboro dangled from his lips before he cleared the bar area. He lit the cigarette with a match, a split second before he strode over the threshold that delineated indoors from outdoors, just enough to technically break a minor law. Two fossilized widows looked on in horror from a dockside table as if Frank had lit a stick of dynamite. The more ancient of the two gripped her Shih Tzu close to her chest while snapping her fingers for a waiter. Frank took a deep drag as he took in the intracoastal view. For the duration of that drag, he was at peace with the world, roughly fifteen seconds of harmony in his otherwise tortured existence.

"Frankie." Ralph's good-natured bark indicated today's respite had come to a close. He shot the barely smoked cigarette skyward with a flick of his middle finger, and it made a graceful arc until it was extinguished by the water of the Intracoastal.

"Barbarian," the fossil whispered into the ear of her Shih Tzu as Frank walked by.

He flashed a friendly smile at their table as he passed, giving a seemingly polite tip of an invisible cap. Once he had their attention, his hand dropped to his crotch, and he gripped his junk while giving a quarter turn toward their table. It was executed so deftly, the gesture could easily have been explained as an old man adjusting his pants, as old men will sometimes do.

"You done flirting with the Mayflower twins?" Ralph gestured to a stool with a freshly shaken martini set before it.

"I wouldn't fuck either of them for ten million," Frank mumbled.

"Don't underestimate yourself, you've done worse for free," Ralph said.

Nick short-circuited what usually devolved into an insult fest between the two old friends. "Can we just settle down and get to the point?"

"Sorry, kid," Ralph said. "Whatcha drinking?"

The bartender momentarily abandoned an indecisive couple on the other side of the bar at the sound of Ralph's voice and stood dutifully in front of Nick.

"Just a club soda," Nick said a bit sheepishly, still unsure why he felt as if he needed to apologize each time he demurred.

"What's with the club soda? You sick or something?"

"Nah, just, I don't know, taking a break."

The bartender squirted a club soda from the gun and presented it to Nick with a lemon wedge garnish. It could pass for a Stoli Elit and club, Nick reasoned.

Frank slid up next to Nick. "How long?" he asked, like he was inquiring about a cancer diagnosis.

"I'm not sure; a month, maybe longer." It was the first time Nick had said it out loud.

"So, you're what, sober?"

For some reason, that word sounded even scarier than cancer, and he quickly defended himself. "No, not that, just . . . It's not like I quit or anything. I just missed a day, and the day turned into a week."

"If I knew this was going to turn into an AA meeting, I would have brought coffee and doughnuts," Ralph barked. He put a meaty hand on Nick's shoulder. "Kid, drink, don't drink, God bless, but we have some business to talk about." He nodded toward Frank. "Did he tell you anything?"

"You told me not to say anything," Frank protested.

"I told you not to say anything about Marie Carluccio giving me a hand job at the sixth-grade carnival too, and look how that turned out."

Nick stirred his club soda, contemplating his nascent sobriety, the ice cubes spinning in a vortex that seemed to beckon Nick to abandon this silliness and dive into a warm, fuzzy buzz. He was seconds away from giving in when he felt Ralph's hot breath behind his ear. His words jolted Nick back to his senses.

"We got a little problem, Nicky."

Nick spun on his stool to face him. Ralph was legendary for his stoic demeanor. Nick considered him made of granite. So when he saw Ralph's eyes uncharacteristically darting worriedly to Frank, who was studying the tile floor, Nick got that old sick feeling in his stomach.

"Gary?" Nick gulped as he uttered his old friend's name. His father's trusted right arm and Nick's partner in Caffè Vecchio back in Philly had been suffering from some health problems for quite some time. Nick's racing thoughts were interrupted not by Ralph, but surprisingly, Frank.

"It's Joey."

Nick jolted to his feet. *Not Joey*, he thought. Joey was the closest thing Nick would ever have to a son. Joey's father, Jimmy, was Nick's best friend growing up in Philly, until he was murdered twenty years ago. Frank had settled the score on New Year's Day five years ago, and Nick had stepped in as a father figure.

"Is he . . ."

"No," Ralph said. "We don't think so."

"Well, what then?"

"He's missing."

"That can't be. Tina would have called me," Nick said, referring to Joey's mother.

"She doesn't know," Ralph explained. "She thinks he's off on one of his tears, maybe shacked up with a girl."

"Maybe he is."

"That's what I thought too," Ralph said. "Until I got a call from Andy Boy." Ralph hesitated, knowing what he was about to say would change everything, would be the moment Nick's whole world would shift. Nick's impatience jolted him out of his indulgent silence.

"And?"

"There's no easy way to say this, kid. Joey's been kidnapped."

"What?" Nick laughed. "That's crazy. Who would kidnap Joey? For what?"

Ralph put his hand on Nick's shoulder. "He's being held for ransom."

"Okay, no problem. I'll pay for it. How much?"

Ralph shook his head. "It's not that simple. If it were, I would have paid it myself before you even found out."

"So what is it then?"

Ralph looked at Frank, who knocked back what was left of his martini before responding for Ralph.

"A painting. They're holding him for a painting."

# Chapter Two

## DIESEL THERAPY

Joey tried twitching his nose. There was nothing worse than having an itch and not being able to scratch it. His hands were cinched tightly behind his back with what felt like zip ties. He was seated on a hard chair, ankles secured to the legs, with some type of rough fabric bag over his head. He did his best to contort his face in an effort to rub the itchy part of his nose against the inside of the sack. That should have been the least of his concerns, but he couldn't get a story out of his head that some old-timer around the Caffè had shared while telling jailhouse tales. The one that stuck with Joey, the one dominating his thoughts presently, was a tale of being transported across country in a van, shackled to the vehicle's floor hours on end as it bounced its way west, unable to do something as simple as scratch an itch on his nose. Out of all the dehumanizing experiences during his decade-long stint behind bars, the old-timer confessed to that trip being the worst. Diesel therapy is what he called it. Now, after what seemed like about an hour, but might have only been ten minutes, Joey understood exactly what the old-timer meant.

The first blow came to the left side of his head, just above the temple. It was more than a slap, but less than a full punch. Still, it had his ears ringing. He felt a throbbing begin to develop and set his jaw in anticipation of the next strike. After a few minutes bracing for a second blow that never came, Joey realized a few things. The first was recognition that wherever he was, it was eerily silent. Joey had anticipated some type of questioning or threats to follow, but no voices came after the blow. There was only silence. The second realization was an odd blessing—his nose didn't itch anymore.

Joey did his best to remain calm. Noticing for the first time how fast his heart was beating, he drew a few deep breaths. It seemed to help a bit, and he resolved to use what little time he might have to figure a way out of his predicament. *Start with what I know*, he thought. Joey began to mentally reconstruct the previous night and the series of events that brought him here.

He'd been leaving Stephanie's apartment around 4:00 a.m. when he was scooped up. The two of them had been out on the town. Had dinner at some awful French restaurant in Center City Stephanie found on Instagram, then stopped back at Smokey's for an actually edible late-night bite, followed by more than a few drinks. Joey put on a decent load, and they had closed the place down before walking around the corner to Stephanie's. After a vigorous session in Stephanie's bedroom, which had been preceded by a christening of her new quartz kitchen countertop, Joey had dozed off for a bit.

He'd woken up with a start, quickly gathered his clothes, and headed for the door, not wanting to stay through the night and get caught by the sun. There was no gentle kiss to the top of Stephanie's sleeping head, but Joey did slide three hundred-dollar bills under her keys in the candy dish that served as a valet tray. Stephanie wouldn't thank him or even acknowledge the money. She never asked for it, and it wasn't something they ever discussed. But she would notice if it was missing, and Joey was fine with that. It was only one aspect of the unspoken contract between them. Not fucking anyone in Joey's crew of immediate friends and associates was another unspoken term of the agreement. Not that Joey would be jealous, but it would be a bad look and could possibly lead to messy complications. And messy complications impacted business. *It's better this way*, he thought, *keep it transactional*.

The carjacker had caught him as he was rounding the corner and fishing around his pockets for his key fob. Maybe the night with Stephanie, and all the drinks had left him in a fog. Maybe he was just getting sloppy. Either way, all he could think about was how Big Gary would shake his head in disapproval when he told him the story of how some skinny kid with a ski mask had got the drop on him. Joey's .38, which Gary always preached should be in his hand, concealed within his jacket pocket when he walked to or from his car, was still in his ankle holster. He thought for a split second about reaching for it, but something about the carjacker's behavior made him hesitate. The kid wasn't running up on him for the key fob, and presumably his wallet. He stood his ground, gun raised in a combat stance, aimed at Joey's center mass. Looking closely, Joey observed just enough of the assailant's face through the eyeholes of the ski mask to realize he wasn't a kid, and this probably wasn't a carjacking. That's when a second guy, one he had never seen, stepped out of the van, brought down what felt like a pipe on the back of his head. It was the last thing he remembered until he came to with the hood over his head and a warm, damp stickiness clinging to the back of his head.

*Focus. What would Gary do? Well, for one, Gary wouldn't have been caught stumbling out of some trick's apartment at four in the morning like some fool without a care in the world.*

While this was undoubtedly true, Joey knew beating himself up over what was over and done wasn't going to help him out of this predicament. Instead, though he couldn't see anything, he tried to take in as much as he could about his surroundings using his other senses. *What would Stevie Wonder do?*

He started with the soles of his feet, pressing down against the floor, determining it wasn't carpet. *Probably concrete*, he concluded. His ankles were bound to the legs of the chair, but he jiggled his left leg as best he could, ever so slightly, and felt the holster still strapped tightly to his ankle. It felt weightless. They had found his .38. He allowed himself to draw in a deep breath of cold air. Wherever he was, it didn't feel like it was very well-heated. *A warehouse maybe,* he thought. *Who the fuck would scoop me up and take me to a warehouse, and why?* Joey resolved to solve this riddle and made himself a promise as well. *If I get out of here, I'm gonna find out who hit me on the back of the head and return the favor in spades.*

# Chapter Three

## BOOTS ON THE GROUND

Nick was headed for the door before Ralph had a chance to finish the story. By the time Ralph paid the check, Nick was already at the valet stand. He took the fob from the valet, not wanting to waste time waiting for his car to be brought around.

"Whoa, slow down, kid. Let's not go off half-cocked here," Ralph said.

"Half-cocked? All due respect, but we don't have any time to waste."

"Who's wasting time, Nicky? I've already set a plan in motion. Let's head over to Blaine's, and I'll fill you in."

"That's great, but don't you think you should have told me sooner?"

"Easy," Frank interjected in an attempt to cool things down. He knew how much Ralph loved Nick, but his excited demeanor, while certainly justifiable, put Nick at risk of saying something that couldn't be taken back. And that was territory he didn't want Nick to wade into, love or no love.

"I haven't wasted a minute, Nick. This isn't exactly your area of expertise, and frankly, you're reacting just like I knew you would, which is why I'm glad I waited. So let's all calm down and think this through."

"Look, you're right. This is out of my wheelhouse, but this is *Joey* we're talking about. I might not have been able to save his father, but I'll be damned if I'm just going to sit here while he's tied up somewhere ... or worse."

Joey's father, Jimmy Musante, was Nick's best friend growing up in Philly. His death under suspicious circumstances had been the catalyst that sent Nick to Florida more than twenty years ago.

Ralph didn't doubt that Nick would jump in front of a bullet for Joey—for any of them, if it came down to it—so his response was measured.

"Think, Nick. You know me. Do you really think I don't already have boots on the ground? Besides, if this is what I think, Joey's safe, at least for the time being."

"I don't understand." Nick was doing his best to remain patient, weighing his respect for Ralph against the urgency of the situation.

"Whoever did this is sending a message. Killing Joey doesn't advance their agenda."

"So what's the message?"

"That none of us are untouchable, and if it's who I think it is, families aren't off limits either."

"But how can you be sure?"

"Nothing's a hundred percent, kid, you know that, but I put a call in to Dmitry. He dug around a little, and he's pretty sure they're going to release Joey with a message."

Nick reflected on this for a moment. Calling in a favor from Dmitry was no light affair. Ralph would likely be called upon to return that favor, and he wouldn't have the luxury to say no, whatever that favor might turn out to be. It also wasn't lost on Nick that perhaps Dmitry's 'digging around' was just a subtle way of announcing he was actually behind it and wanted to reinforce his dominance over Nick and the crew. *No*, Nick quickly discounted that theory. They were on good terms with Dmitry, and he wouldn't need to go to these lengths to get their attention. As far as he could see, their interests were aligned. *Still,* Nick thought, *you never really know.*

"So what's their agenda?"

Ralph looked at Frank before responding, and Frank jumped in to take some of the heat off Ralph. He blew out a lungful of smoke before answering.

"You, Nicky. You're the agenda."

Nick suddenly felt like a drink was a good idea, as if his tenuous sobriety was a foolish experiment. He'd proven whatever point he subconsciously believed he needed to prove. Now it seemed like a luxury he could no longer afford, and in his tortured mind, Joey's safe return somehow depended on him abandoning it. These random thoughts flashed in his mind before he recognized a familiar voice. The same voice had visited him in his darkest hours, sounding eminently rational . . . brilliant even. Back then, it had lobbied for him to leave Grace and run back to Angie. The voice had the soothing tone of an old friend showing up to comfort him in his time of need. It was as smooth and silky as a double-oaked bourbon. He would recognize it anywhere.

*The Devil's whispering to me*, he thought as he got into his car and drove to Blaine's.

# Chapter Four

## ZITTI E BUONI

Joey heard a cell phone ring somewhere in the distance. The sound was muffled, like maybe it came from an adjoining room that wasn't very well insulated. The jangly tone was annoying and incessant. Joey imagined its owner clumsily scrambling to mute it, like he was trying to defuse a ticking bomb. Perhaps the man's superior glared at him for neglecting to keep his phone on silent. Joey had been around individuals and situations where such a breach of decorum could eventually prove fatal. Maybe not immediately, but it would be placed on a ledger of offenses that might, one day, tip an invisible scale.

Joey recognized the ringtone tune, an introductory guitar riff from an Italian pop group that had a hit recently with a cover of Frankie Valli and the Four Seasons' "Beggin'." The riff came from a song in the group's native Italian called "Zitti e Buoni." Roughly translated, it meant shut up and be good, or maybe, be quiet and behave. Joey's Italian was minimal, limited mostly to curses and insults, but anyone who grew up in an Italian American household knew the meaning of *state zitto*. (Shut up!)

That's when Joey heard the only words that would be uttered throughout the entire ordeal. They were faint, but the speaker's irritation caused him to raise his voice more than he had intended.

"Gimme that fucking phone."

Joey stored the words away like the combination to a safe. A simple phrase he knew could eventually crack the code that would lead him to his abductors. It wasn't so much the words themselves, but the New York—more specifically, Brooklyn—accent they were spoken in. The authoritarian tone suggested this was the voice of the man in charge.

Joey heard a door open, then footsteps coming closer. He felt a presence behind him. Someone gripped the top of the chair and tilted it forward. He heard the click of a folding knife snapping open. *I heard too much.* He felt a pull at his wrists and then a release as the knife severed the rope binding him to the back of the chair. His hands remained tied behind him, but he could feel they were now untethered to the chair. He was also able to move his feet forward, and he realized they had been bound to his hands in a kind of seated hogtie. Someone gripped him under the armpits from the rear. Not forcefully, more like urging him to stand while providing assistance. His ankles unbound, he attempted to stand, but his legs were rubbery and numb. Mr. X gripped him tighter and lifted him up to a standing position. Joey felt the man's considerable strength, as his feet practically left the floor before he was plopped down ever so gently. Mr. X then placed his hands on Joey's shoulders and spun him so they were facing each other, though the hood was still secured over Joey's head.

*This is it*, Joey thought. His first reaction was one of indignation. *Fuck you, motherfucker. Kill me and be done with it.* When neither gun nor knife immediately followed, his thoughts drifted to the mundane. He imagined everyone at the Caffè coming to his funeral—if they ever found his body. He thought of his Uncle Nick and, oddly, felt guilty, as if getting abducted was something he should feel remorseful about. He thought of his grieving mother. Not only had she buried his father, but now her only son. This made him angry, and he prayed. Not to God, not to the Blessed Mother for her intercession, but to a father he never knew.

*Dad, if you're out there, help me out of this. Help me figure out who did this, and help me take my vengeance.* He felt like he was leaving something out. *I love you, Dad, but I'm not ready to meet you just yet.*

Mr. X thrust his hand into the front pocket of Joey's jeans, jamming something deep in there, then spun him back around and nudged him forward. Holding him by his bound wrists, Mr. X walked him outside as the sound of an industrial garage door retracting echoed throughout the building. *Definitely a warehouse*, Joey noted. He heard an idling truck, and a metal plate clanged under his feet, marking the transition from what he figured had to be a loading dock to the back of the truck. He was made to sit on the floor of the truck bed, and he braced himself as best he could, bending his knees up in front of him and leaning forward at the waist. The ride didn't last very long. Joey sensed only three turns—one right, two left—the last of which nearly sent him tumbling. When the truck finally came to a stop, he heard the two cab doors open and close, followed by the opening of the rear overhead door as it rattled above him.

Getting out wasn't easy. Someone dragged him backward toward the door and swung his legs around until they dangled out of the truck, then pushed him from behind, urging him out over what might have been an abyss for all he knew. What felt like the same hands that had lifted him from the chair now gripped him from the front and deposited him onto the ground. He was pushed to his knees, this time not so gently. He felt weeds crunching under his weight.

*Okay, now **this** is it. This makes more sense. This is how I would do it.*

He felt two playful slaps on his left cheek. Not hard at all. The kind of gentle taps your uncle would give you, affectionate but meant to remind you who was boss.

And then the sounds of the roll door coming down and being locked in place, the driver and passenger doors opening and closing, the engine coughing to life, gravel crunching under the tires, and finally. . . silence. Joey kneeled there for a moment, still not trusting his ordeal was over.

Eventually, he stood upright and tried to walk back in what he believed was the direction of the road. It was difficult to manage with his hands tied behind his back, not to mention the hood over his head. He stumbled a few times, but eventually felt gravel and then smooth asphalt under his feet. He eased back a few steps, not wanting to be run over by a car after surviving his abduction.

Now that he was somewhat free, he began to feel even more anxious and claustrophobic than he had at any time in the warehouse or the truck. He desperately wanted the hood off his head and his hands untied, but what he wanted even more was to see what Mr. X had crammed into his pocket.

# Chapter Five

# THE NOTE

When Nick walked into Blaine's, Connie was pretending to wipe the bar with a mostly clean rag. She looked up for a second, raised her eyebrows in lieu of a more formal greeting, and nodded toward the back room. Ralph and Frank hadn't arrived yet. Nick had floored it out of Roberto's, hardly catching a red light on the way.

The back room looked the same as the last time Nick had seen it—smelled the same too. A lone figure sat backlit by a neon Budweiser light affixed to the rear wall. The only other illumination was an ancient lamp that hovered above a pool table as tendrils of cigar smoke danced above the felt.

Nino Scopa sipped an espresso from a Segafredo cup. It was one of the few mementos he'd allowed himself on his pilgrimage when he and Gloria left Scopa Meats and Cheeses, his shop on Passyunk Avenue in South Philadelphia, over a year ago. He had put a lifetime of peddling soppressata, provolone, and influence in his rearview. At first, he embraced his new home, adapting surprisingly well to the South Florida lifestyle of sun, sand, and early bird specials. Moving to Pompano and marrying Gloria was the best decision he had made in his life, and for a moment, he stopped punishing himself for having waited until he was seventy-seven to finally pull the trigger. Then the worst thing happened.

Gloria, his beloved *Baci*, almost fifteen years his junior, succumbed to breast cancer after a valiant fight. Not a day passed that Nino didn't wish it were him instead. All those years spent hesitating out of fear of saddling Gloria with caring for an old man... *and this is what God sent me. Time makes us all fools*, he thought.

Nino retreated from the tropical landscape he had briefly embraced. Now, the palm trees mocked him. He spent most of his days confined to the dark, smoke-filled back room of Blaine's, safely insulated from the sunshine and fresh air. After a lifetime spent dodging the authorities, he had constructed a cell of his own. Nino went back to what he knew best, re-creating the back room of Scopa Meats and Cheeses, only in Oakland Park. He commenced holding court and doling out advice and small street loans. Ralph jokingly dubbed it *Scopa South*, checking in on him as much as possible. Even stone-faced Connie tried to cheer him up with an occasional sandwich and a joke. She even flashed her tits once, all to no avail.

Now he sat waiting for Nick, having set up an old-school command center focused on Joey Musante's safe return. A beige rotary phone sat on the table before him. He used it to call its avocado-green counterpart over a thousand miles away, situated on a metal desk in the office of Caposecco Fruit and Produce in South Philly, where Andrea "Andy Boy" Caposecco had convened a war room of his own. Nino might have been running the operation, but Andy Boy was providing the boots on the ground.

"Pronto," one of Andy's guys answered on the first ring.

"Is he there?"

There was no response, just the sound of the receiver being placed on the metal desk.

"You must be psychic," Andy said. "Good news. He's okay. A little embarrassed and plenty mad, but none the worse for the wear. Couple a girls picked him up on the side of the road. Lucky son of a bitch. I think they were more scared than he was. He's using my shower now. I don't want him to go home until my guys have a chance to clear it. I'll have him call Nick in a few."

"Good, he'll be relieved to hear— Wait, he just walked in. You can tell him yourself." Nino covered the receiver with his hand out of habit and whispered, "Andy," before handing it to Nick.

Andy repeated the story to Nick, who slumped back into a cushioned folding chair in relief. His mind tried to let go of all the horrible scenarios it had concocted. He insisted on staying on the phone until Joey got out of the shower.

"Hey, Unc," Joey chirped, as if he were routinely picking up the phone at the Caffè.

"You okay?"

"I'm fine, really. Just trying to work a few things out before. . ." Joey's voice trailed off.

"Before nothing," Nick snapped. "You don't make a move until I get there. Understand?"

Joey didn't answer quickly enough.

"Understand?" Nick asked a bit more forcefully, and Joey deferred to his seniority.

"Understood."

"Good. I'll be there tomorrow morning, and we can talk more then."

"There's something else, Unc."

"What is it?" Nick sat up straight in the chair, leaning forward on the felt of the card table, and stared at Nino like he was a blackjack dealer showing an ace. He waved Nino in close and angled the receiver so he could listen in.

"They put a note in my pocket." Joey was feeling Nick out as to the propriety of reading its contents over the phone, but Nick's curiosity overrode his prudence.

"What does it say?"

"It just has a name written on it. Do you know someone named Jerry Salvitti?"

Nino perked up at the mention of the name. Nick paused before answering.

"My father did. I'll see you tomorrow, we'll talk more then. I'm glad you're okay, Joey. Could you hand the phone back to Andy now?"

Joey handed the phone to Andy.

"Yeah," Andy growled.

"You hear that?"

"Sure did."

"I thought he died in jail years ago."

"Well, rumors of his demise seem to have been exaggerated even greater than mine. I heard he got compassionate release last month. He's in a halfway right now, but I imagine he'll be out soon."

"Is there any way you can go see him?"

"Oh, I'm sure I could see him, but I think it would be something of a one-sided conversation."

"What's that supposed to mean?"

"He hasn't uttered a word in over twenty five years."

"Good for him." Nick chuckled.

"I don't think you understand. I'm not talking about just keeping his mouth shut. It's more than that."

"More how?" Nick asked.

"I mean, he *can't* speak. Gennaro Salvitti is a mute."

# Chapter Six

# THE PINK NUNS

*'Love you.'* Those were the last words anyone could reliably recall being uttered by Gennaro "Jerry" Salvitti, a/k/a "The Duke." The setting was the James A. Byrne United States Courthouse in Philadelphia. The phrase was directed to a woman seated in the back of the courtroom, but it could have been construed as being meant for anyone assembled in the crowded courtroom following guilty verdicts across the board in the five-defendant racketeering trial that had lasted almost two months. The bulk of the crimes alleged in the indictment were relatively mundane. For all its sensationalism, the trial turned out to be pretty pedestrian, sprinkled with just enough colorful nicknames to convince the public it was a real effort at crime fighting. More significant crimes were committed daily in the City of Brotherly Love without triggering much more than a paragraph in the *Daily News*. There was one count of murder in aid of racketeering, however, and Gennaro Salvitti was the only defendant found guilty of that count.

The woman to whom Jerry's words were directed wore a large pair of sunglasses that obscured enough of her face to mask her reaction. In place of a response, she blew Jerry a kiss and quickly hustled out of the courtroom. In the years that followed, she would neither visit nor write. She had already received her instructions and readily agreed to the terms.

Although she had attended every day of the trial, listening intently as various witnesses recited the many alleged sins of the Duke, she didn't socialize with the family and friends of the other defendants. She was a familiar figure to them, but none could claim to have actually spoken with her, other than a cordial "Good morning" or "See you tomorrow," in response to which she would politely smile and nod. When the defendants' families would go to lunch together, followed by a phalanx of reporters and cameramen, she would retreat to a quiet hallway, sit on a hard bench, and take dainty bites from a modest peanut butter and jelly sandwich secreted in her bag. Other times, she could be found quietly praying the rosary, her manicured but unpolished fingers moving gently from bead to bead. Perhaps she was praying for a miracle, perhaps she was praying for his soul; the one thing she couldn't be praying for was justice.

She looked like she was pretty once, maybe even beautiful. Her face retained a certain angelic quality, even absent any visible makeup. Her attire was modest and nondescript, and even in the warmth of late spring, she wore a plain overcoat. Her shoes were so sensible, they could have been orthopedic. They stood out by virtue of their utility. Her overall appearance and demeanor were in stark contrast to the other female family members and supporters, who favored more glamorous ensembles. Some appeared to be dressed for tea at the Ritz Carlton, others wore outfits more suitable for a nightclub.

Rita Salvitti's wardrobe looked like something from a nunnery, and with good reason. Every day after court, Sister Mary Rita, as she was known to the other Holy Spirit Adoration Sisters, returned to the Convent of Divine Love, where she had been granted leave by the Mother Superior to attend her brother's trial. She returned each late afternoon to her otherwise cloistered life in time for vespers, and woke at four each morning to complete her chores and perform her adoration of the Blessed Sacrament before attending court. The Sisters wore a rose-colored habit within the cloister, and over the years, the citizens of Philadelphia who would visit to submit their special intentions had come to refer to them as "The Pink Nuns." Twenty-four hours a day, at least one of the Sisters stood vigil in adoration of the exposed Blessed Sacrament. They were permitted to speak when necessary for the advancement of charity or in the performance of work, otherwise, strict silence was expected. Just as in her brother's profession, infractions were dealt with swiftly and sternly.

The Duke served the last ten years of his scheduled thirty-year sentence at FCI Devens, a somewhat experimental medical facility set up to deal with older inmates, many suffering from advanced stages of dementia. That was the diagnosis the Bureau of Prisons had settled on after Jerry had withdrawn into himself and ceased communicating in any meaningful way with either guards or fellow inmates. Devens utilized a system where certain inmates underwent training and volunteered to look after those saddled with dementia or other terminal illnesses. It was a pretty good program and had received accolades, including an article in the *New York Times*, but it had its limitations. It was easy to make the argument the largely octogenarian inmates, many who could no longer even remember who they were, let alone what they did, should be released. After all, what was the sense in punishing someone who had no recollection of the crimes they had committed?

Of course, the next logical question was where these people would be released *to* and who would care for them? In contrast to the modicum of care they received at Devens, this alternative seemed crueler still. Dementia is a subjective diagnosis, and in the Duke's case, it served as a default diagnosis for what bureau doctors and administration had previously referred to as aphasia or selective mutism. Bottom line, as the years passed, the Duke's silence seemed less like a choice and more likely a real medical condition. A doctor at FCI Butner finally concluded he was suffering from Alzheimer's, and off he went to Devens. He was assigned a handler, who decided to help prepare a petition for his compassionate release, even writing to the Duke's sister for help in constructing a home plan. Maybe it was his unique affliction, how long and consistent his silence had endured, or perhaps it was Sister Mary Rita's vocation that swayed the Judge. Whatever the reason, the petition was granted.

Now, after twenty-five years of inconceivable patience, part two of the Duke's plan was finally about to go into effect.

# Chapter Seven

# AMOR FATI

*"Such was my heart, O God, such was my heart. You had pity on it when it was at the bottom of the abyss.... I had no motive for wickedness except wickedness itself. It was foul and I loved it. I loved the self-destruction. I loved my fall, not the object for which I had fallen but my fall itself. My depraved soul leaped down from your firmament to ruin. I was seeking not to gain anything by shameful means, but shame for its own sake."*
*Saint Augustine of Hippo, The Confessions*

Two carry-on bags stood waiting for Nick in the vestibule of his condo when he arrived. He was a stickler when it came to packing, meticulous, superstitious even. So it was a bit of a jolt to see his trusty old Samsonite waiting for him like a loyal golden retriever. For a second, he considered maybe Grace had finally had enough of his shenanigans and had packed his bags for good, except, standing dutifully next to his bag was Grace's own hard-shell spinner. He stood there for a moment, contemplating the meaning of this gesture. Three things came to mind: One, Grace knew about his flight to Philly. Two, Grace had decided she was coming along. Three, if Nick had a problem with that, Grace might not be there when he returned. No questions, no fighting, no ultimatums, just two bags. It was classic Grace.

Nick froze. He wasn't even sure if Grace was home, and certainly wasn't up for a confrontation, especially in his sober state. He had been doing so well, between Grace's gentle nudges toward mindfulness and Dave the philosopher's tutelage on Stoicism, surely, he was equipped to handle this situation. *Amor fati*, he could hear Dave's advice echoing in his head. *Love your fate.* The Tuscan Tiki regular they had come to nickname Plato would undoubtedly have counseled him accordingly.

Nick took one last look at the suitcases standing there like two bookends in search of a story to prop up. *Fuck that*, he thought as he spun on his heel and closed the door behind him as gently as possible.

Sitting quietly in the bedroom, Grace heard the door close.

Nick headed for the Tiki, determined to end his foolish experiment with sobriety. An image flashed in his mind of a long-forgotten memory. The year must have been 1982 or '83. Nick was a teenager spending most weekend nights hanging out in Southwark schoolyard. Nick and his friends would warm up around a fire can, drinking quarts of Miller High Life and blasting music from a boombox. As the night wore on, the fire raged higher, the beer flowed faster, and the music played louder.

A group called C-Bank had a popular freestyle dance track out that year called "One More Shot." After the chorus, the song contained a rousing sound effect of broken glass that was too tempting to resist, and they would all hurl their bottles against the schoolyard wall in unison. The bottles shattered in a beautiful symphony of teenage exuberance and rage.

That's exactly how Nick felt now. He wanted to rage for rage's sake. An immature impulse that made him feel both embarrassed and liberated at the same time. He had imagined he was well past such foolish notions, but wondered, *if God wanted me to be sober, why does he keep throwing these impossible trials in my path when all I want to do is run my little tiki bar and grow old with Grace?*

Except that was a lie. The truth was, he craved the trials and the bittersweet uncertainty that came along with them. Maybe Grace was right, he thought, and we really do manifest what we secretly desire in the core of our being. What he really wanted to manifest right now was a stiff drink.

The voice was back; *I've brought you this far. Haven't I gotten you through every challenge you've faced?*

Maybe. But was it because, or in spite of his basest instincts?

*Joey needs me*, he justified.

*It's too late in the game to switch things up*, he rationalized.

As he walked up to the bar, he'd made up his mind. It was as simple as falling off a rock, easy like Sunday morning, as satisfying as smashing a bottle against a brick wall.

"Makers on the rocks."

*Just start drinking and go wherever the alcohol takes you.* It had never failed him before.

It had worked for his father before him.

*Had it really though?*

Ronnie was his most trusted bartender and confidant. He gave Nick a subtle look of concern, or was it shame, when Nick placed the order. It didn't matter. Ronnie would never question Nick in public, especially from behind the bar Nick owned.

He watched the graceful arc of the whiskey as Ronnie deftly poured it over the ice. It swirled triumphantly in the rocks glass as Ronnie placed it on the bar before him. Nick reached for the drink, feeling the comforting sweat beading on the glass. No plastic cups for the boss man.

"What's up, Nick? Where've you been?"

Nick figured he had finally lost his mind because, for a split second, he thought it was the glass of whiskey talking to him. It took Dave putting his arm around his shoulder to snap him out of the delusion, as he realized it was the Tiki's resident philosopher making the polite inquiry.

"Oh, hey, Dave. You know, here and there. How's it going?"

Nick had confided in Dave things he now wished he hadn't, as Dave glanced at the drink and then back up at Nick.

"How are things going with *you*?" Dave answered Nick with a question.

Nick turned to meet his gaze straight on, recovering from his momentary sheepishness, and wondered how the man always seemed to have it together, never flustered, always exuding a serene demeanor.

Dave had taken on the role of unofficial advisor to Nick, a sort of life coach, sherpa, and confessor all combined. Nick couldn't deny he had benefited greatly from the man's sage advice and calm example, but he occasionally felt a guilty pang of jealousy. It was the type of irrational emotion an addict might feel in the presence of well-meaning, sober compatriots. Nick knew he should be grateful for his friendship, for the interest Dave took in his well-being, and checked himself, ashamed for having these thoughts about a man who had offered him nothing but support.

"Actually, Dave, things are pretty fucked up at the moment." Nick figured the truth was easier than constructing some bullshit. Dave was almost one of the Tiki crew, but they tended to keep him in the dark when it came to some of the grittier aspects of the Tasker Morris business. Tasker Morris was a business entity set up by the Philly expats to pool their resources, acting as a small hedge fund. It was wildly successful. So Nick surprised himself when he blurted out, "Joey was kidnapped. He's safe now, but I'm headed back to get to the bottom of it." It felt good to spit it out like an acidic burn that had been building in the back of his throat. It was meant as a challenge to this self-styled philosopher, but Dave wasn't put off at all.

"That sounds really intense Nick. How does that make you feel?"

*How the fuck do you think it makes me feel?* Nick thought, but settled for, "Honestly, it makes me feel like drinking, which was exactly what I was about to do."

"Yes, I see. Well, don't let me stop you if that's what you want to do."

Nick let that sink in, his hand still wrapped around the sweaty glass.

"Before you do though, let me ask, are you familiar with *The Confessions of St. Augustine?*"

"Can't say that I am, but I have a feeling I'm about to be." Nick turned to face the man who had counseled him through quite a few tribulations with genuine care and concern, arguably making Nick a better man in the process. But instead of gratitude, Nick was filled with anger. He shifted his vicelike grip from the glass to the bullnose of the bar and breathed deeply, peering over Dave's shoulder at a serene ocean. He composed himself, his respect for the man supplanting the immature thoughts he had come to recognize as the remnants of those ancient feelings of abandonment.

"Augustine's early life was filled with the usual indiscretions. He tells a story of how he and his friends once stole pears from an orchard, except they didn't even enjoy eating the pears; they threw most of them to the pigs."

"That's a great story, Dave. Thanks for sharing."

Dave smiled. "Well, there's more. Augustine reflects on this event later in his life, after he had come to make some discoveries about himself. I can't recall the exact quote, but it goes something like this: *I had no motive for wickedness except wickedness itself. It was foul, and I loved it. I loved self-destruction, I loved my fall, not the object for which I had fallen, but my fall itself.* That really resonated with me Nick—*I loved my fall.* So, what do you think?"

Nick nodded at Ronnie and got up from his stool, throwing a hundred on the bar as a tip for Ronnie.

"What do I think? Go fuck yourself, you self-righteous prick, that's what I think." Nick said it without any real malice. It was the kind of quip two street guys could bandy back and forth without rancor, especially at the Tiki.

Except Dave wasn't exactly a street guy, not even close. Despite all the hours he had logged at the Tiki, all the back slapping and rooting in bets, Dave lacked the pedigree that formed a deeper bond among the Tasker Morris boys. And despite all his sophistication and insights into the psyches of others, that was what he craved most. So he gave a satisfied chuckle as Nick gathered his phone and keys.

"Love you too, buddy," he shouted at Nick as he walked out.

# Chapter Eight

# JULIAN

Ronnie smirked as he cleared Nick's untouched drink and wiped away the residue it had left on the bar. He gave Dave a conspiratorial wink.

"Nice work, Plato."

Across the bar, on the patio side, a well-dressed man had listened in on the exchange while feigning rapt interest in a meaningless college game on one of the many screens hanging above the bar. The man had begun appearing once or twice a week, quietly having a drink or two (usually an Aperol spritz) and leaving a handsome tip. Plenty of vacationers and newly minted snowbirds cycled through the Tiki during any given week, so there was nothing especially suspicious about that. Over the years, it took on a comforting rhythm, a way to tick off the months as clientele came and went like the supporting cast in the latest Netflix series.

With this particular client, however, Ronnie had noticed two distinguishing characteristics concerning the man and the timing of his visits. Back in the badlands of North Philly, Ronnie had run a few lucrative businesses back in the day. Even after he'd retired from the streets and sold off the strip clubs, he'd retained his interest in a small chain of check-cashing agencies and pawnshops. He had more than a passing familiarity with jewelry and watches as a result. He could have made a decent living almost exclusively from buying blinged-out Rolexes and Cuban link chains from players in need of bail and lawyer money.

That's why the stranger's watch stood out so much. This was the land of conspicuous affluence. Busboys rocked fake Audemars Piguet Royal Oaks on their wrists on their days off. And that septuagenarian holding court at The Lobster Bar on Las Olas at happy hour? He's not there for the seafood tower. The 350-thousand-dollar Richard Mille he's sporting ever so casually? There's nothing remotely casual about it. It's a billboard flashing an unmistakable message. *"I'm here to play, and I'm willing to pay."* Ronnie had seen every conceivable knockoff, from the dime-a-dozen Hublot fakes to some Rolex Daytona replicas that were so good you couldn't tell the difference unless you removed the case back. Maybe that's why the stranger's timepiece stood out. It was so subtle, so understated, it could have easily been confused for any of a number of perfectly presentable mid-tier dress watches. Ronnie stole a closer look when he last set the man up with his distinctive cocktail.

The Patek Philippe Minute Repeater Tourbillon is not what anyone would regard as a flashy watch. It's a relatively small-diameter timepiece, nothing like the gargantuan Panerai Luminor favored by the Russians. The Patek is a handsome watch, but where it distinguishes itself is on the inside. The complication is a testament to high horology and drives the price north of half a million. It was the epitome of stealth wealth, and that's why Ronnie suspected it was the real deal—no one would bother producing a replica, as its rarity would be lost on all but the most discerning eye. Together with the Loro Piana shirt and Dunhill lighter, Ronnie pegged the stranger as a quiet money megalodon swimming among oblivious great whites, the latter foolishly believing they were the apex predators of South Florida café society. The other thing Ronnie noticed was the timing of the man's visits. They didn't correspond with any particular day, time or sporting events. He could just as likely show up on a Friday night as on a Tuesday afternoon.

"Ronnie, can I get two Pina Coladas, please?"

Kim was one of the newer servers at the Tiki and was struggling to catch on. She took whatever shifts were available, even on short notice, so that helped. Ronnie suspected she was dealing with more than a few demons, but he detected a certain innocence about her that was rare in the industry. Something in her eyes made him feel both sad and protective. Maybe it was the self-conscious way she flicked her hair when she was spoken to. He tried to dismiss it, but he had seen that look before, in his previous life. The look of shame. She had *prey* written all over her face, and the Tiki had no shortage of carnivores. He felt a vague sense of guilt that he knew didn't make sense. His past sins had nothing to do with Kim's plight. He blended up the drinks and decided he would do his best to look out for her as some half-ass penance for his ancient transgressions.

"Thanks, hon." She smiled sweetly as Ronnie put the drinks up on the service bar, but never made eye contact.

Even though it was third and long in the fourth quarter, the score tied, the stranger wasn't showing any interest in the college game. He *was* ogling Kim like she was a wounded seal. That's when Ronnie figured it out; the stranger's haphazard schedule wasn't so random after all. He showed up whenever Kim was working, never when she was off.

"Can I get you anything else, my man?" Ronnie engaged the stranger abruptly, startling the man.

"No thank you." He glanced at his Patek. "I have to be going soon."

Ronnie glanced at his own sturdy Casio. "Well, my shift is almost over. Mind if I cash you out?" Ronnie was eager to have a look at the man's credit card for a name, but no sooner had he rung him up than the man tossed a hundred-dollar bill on the bar as he got up from his stool.

"Thanks, cuz," Ronnie said, reaching over the bar with a hastily wiped hand. "I'm Ronnie by the way."

The stranger gripped his hand with surprising strength for an older guy with a slight build.

"My friends call me Julian."

"Julian it is." Ronnie winked and turned back to catch the game end on a fifty-two-yard field goal.

Julian had already turned and walked away before the ball split the uprights.

# Chapter Nine

# UNTO THE BREACH

*"Once more unto the breach, dear friends, once more"*
  "Henry V" — William Shakespeare

Nick arrived home to find one suitcase where two had previous-ly stood, and Grace nowhere to be found. He wheeled it into the bedroom, flung it onto the comforter, unzipped it, and took a quick inventory. Grace had done a pretty good job packing his bag, but he tossed in a few more dress shirts. A small act of defiance, so he felt a little less like a kid whose mom was sending him off to summer camp.

Nick didn't think it was a good idea to sleep at the condo. He didn't want to have an uncomfortable discussion with Grace that would test his resolve now that he had made up his mind about returning to Philly alone. Part of it was that he really didn't want to expose Grace to whatever was waiting for him there. He knew Grace didn't see the world that way, but the thought of her in the midst of all that ugliness seemed like the greater sin. These were some of the justifications he recited to himself as he zipped up his bag and headed for the door.

It occurred to him that he was on the verge of once again pushing away the single best thing in his life. He took out his phone to text her, but couldn't think of anything worth saying. He imagined he was at the top of a long, dark slide and couldn't see beyond the first twisty turn. And even though he didn't know what waited for him at the bottom, diving headfirst into it seemed like his only choice. He had been here before and knew what sometimes masqueraded as redemption turned out to be an abyss. He hesitated for a moment, one hand on the suitcase, the other on the door, glancing back over his shoulder at the happy home he and Grace had made. He felt a sense of pride in what they had built together and wondered if it would still be the same when he returned—if he returned. Nick looked at the picture of them that hung in the hallway. It was from Christmas Eve a few years back. Grace was sitting on his lap, and they looked like the two happiest people in the world. Nick shifted his focus to his own reflection in the glass and forced a smile. *Once more unto the breach*, he thought. He touched the picture. "Forgive me, Grace." He whispered it like a prayer as he turned the doorknob.

Nick felt the knob turning on the other side and pulled back his hand like he had touched a hot cast-iron pan.

"Forgive you for what?" Grace was standing in the doorway, looking more amused than angry. Nick took that for a good sign.

"Nothing. I was just thinking out loud." Nick knew he should be worried about the conversation they were about to have, but instead, he found himself focusing on her pouty lips. He knew she was messing with him; Grace didn't do the coy act. She was far too mature for that. Still, he stood there mesmerized for a moment, even after all these years.

"Going somewhere without me?" Grace said over her shoulder as she brushed past him. She walked into the bedroom, slipping her shirt over her head and throwing it onto the floor.

Nick felt a bit foolish, frozen there at the threshold, one hand still on the handle of his carry-on. Grace appeared in the bedroom doorway a few moments later, one arm raised over her head, resting against the doorframe, the other hand planted confidently on her hip, wearing nothing but a smirk.

"Well," she said, "if you want my forgiveness, you're going to have to earn it."

Nick loosened his grip on the suitcase and walked toward Grace like he was under a spell, because in fact he was. Grace could have that effect on him.

He left an hour later, doubting he had earned any forgiveness, but hoping he had at least bought himself a little time. Sometimes that was just as good.

They had agreed on a compromise, Grace's idea. Nick would go to Philly first, but if he hadn't resolved his affairs in three days, Grace would follow. Nick really didn't want Grace in the city. He told himself it was for her own safety, but had to admit there were other considerations as well. He resisted her proposal at first, doubting he could wrap things up in three short days. Grace convinced him otherwise. She could be persuasive when she needed to be. She wasn't above using her femininity to her advantage, in spite of her enlightenment, or more likely, as a result of it. Anyway, that was the deal. They sealed it with a kiss, and a good deal more.

# Chapter Ten

# THE GOOD PART

"So we beat on, boats against the current, borne back ceaselessly into the past."

F. Scott Fitzgerald, *The Great Gatsby*

Nick drove to Blaine's and parked around back. He took a moment to book a room at the W on the Hotel Tonight app, figuring he would leave his car at Blaine's and Uber to the airport in the morning.

Ralph and Frank were at the corner of the bar. Ralph stood next to Frank, who was sitting on a stool, hunched over a martini. Nick set up a stool between them, but a few feet back from the bar.

"I heard Dmitry sold a Rembrandt for twenty million," Ralph said.

"God bless," Nick answered. "Doesn't surprise me. Everything the guy touches turns to gold."

"Something called *The Adoration of the Kings*. He paid fifteen thousand for it less than two years ago."

"Fifteen Gs for a fucking Rembrandt?" Frank chimed in.

"Circle of Rembrandt," Ralph corrected. "At least that's how it was attributed when he bought it. Then he did a Dmitry number on it.

X-rays, infrared, a couple of Rembrandt scholars he carries around in his pocket, recited a few magic words, and Sotheby's auctioned it off as a Rembrandt."

"Well, is it or isn't it?" Frank asked.

"You're missing the point," Nick said. "It doesn't matter. There's a 450-million-dollar painting floating around on a Saudi superyacht that may or may not be a Da Vinci. It's real if someone is willing to pay for the privilege of saying so."

Frank took a deep drag of his Marlboro before exhaling his response. "Fucking money goes to money."

"Spoken like a true brokester." Ralph clapped a meaty palm around the back of Frank's neck. "Let me ask you something." Ralph winked at Nick behind Frank's back. "What happened to that hundred K I gave you after that last thing?"

Frank shrugged as he studied his drink for an answer, spinning the toothpick between his fingers. "Is it my fault I can't catch a break?"

"Actually, it kinda is," Nick said gleefully.

"Fuck you, nephew. I liked you better when you were drinking."

Nick was pleased by his uncle's spunk. *Glad to see the old man still has an edge to him.*

Ralph didn't relent. "You still haven't answered my question. Where'd the money go?"

Frank stood, downed the remainder of his drink, and signaled Connie for another. He hiked up his sagging pants as he addressed Ralph. "There's nothing left but rubber bands, my friend."

"That's cute, Frankie. Real cute. Don't tell me, stock market?"

Frank gave a look of indignation that only a man whose vices had been misconstrued could pull off. "Fuck no," Frank protested, before adding by way of further explanation, "I spent fifty on gambling, alcohol, and wild women."

Ralph appeared exceedingly pleased by this answer as he served up the softball. "What about the other half?"

Frank smiled as he started walking toward the men's room. He paused and turned, standing there like an old slugger at the plate.

"The other half I wasted."

The whole bar, including Connie, erupted in raucous laughter as Frank hit another one out of the park.

"So," Nick said to Ralph, "what's the plan?"

"Same as always. We meet Andy at the Caffè and circle the wagons. Something tells me by the time we get there, Andy will have it all figured out."

"That doesn't sound like much of a plan. We're really flying blind on this thing. I've been thinking, though, what if this whole thing isn't about a painting at all."

"Yeah, that's always a possibility. Don't think Andy hasn't considered that angle."

"So what else could it be about?"

"Andy seems to think the whole painting thing could be a ruse, and whoever snatched up Joey was simply setting a trap."

"A trap for who?"

Ralph smiled as he reached over and gave Nick a playful pinch on the cheek. "For you, kid. Who else?"

Nick had suspected as much, but it didn't stop him from looking a bit deflated. "Yeah, that's kinda what I thought."

"Hey." Ralph raised the volume just enough to cause Nick to snap to attention. "I would never put you in danger, you know that. How 'bout you hang back here and let me and Andy handle things."

Nick considered the offer for a moment. "It's not that. I'm not afraid to stick my neck out for the cause, especially when it comes to Joey."

"Well, what is it then?"

"I left that city twenty-three years ago and vowed I'd never return, yet here I am, once again trying to convince myself this will be the last time."

"Did you ever consider maybe it ain't the city you're running from?"

"What's that supposed to mean?" Nick answered, but his mind was already whirring.

"I'm not an idiot, Nick. We all have complicated pasts, I'm no exception. But that's the funny thing about the past."

"What's that?"

"Just because you might be done with the past, it doesn't necessarily mean the past is done with you."

Nick let that settle, then smirked and gave a little chuckle, like Ralph's words didn't touch a nerve. But of course he was right. Trying to dodge the past is like trying to dodge raindrops, and it had been pouring all day. Nick ordered a double-oaked Woodford Reserve from Connie. She poured it a bit less artfully than Ronnie, but this time Nick didn't hesitate. He raised his glass to Ralph as Frankie returned from the men's room.

"What are we toasting to?" Frank asked. He looked gleeful to see Nick with a drink in his hand once again.

"To the most jealous mistress in the world," Ralph answered for Nick.

"Marie Avellino?" Frank inquired sincerely, referencing one of his old flames.

"No, you fucking lunatic," Ralph erupted. "Why the fuck would we be drinking to her?"

Frank was about to answer until Nick gave him a subtle head shake.

"To the past, gents," Ralph continued.

Nick let the toast sink in before adding, "So we beat on, boats against the current, borne back ceaselessly into the past," quoting the last line of his favorite novel.

"You're a strange man, Nick DiNobile," Ralph said.

Nick knocked back his drink before he had a chance to reconsider. *That's that*, he thought. He had expected the long-delayed elixir to be special, like running into an old, trusted friend, but instead it burned in his throat like an ancient grudge. Nick knew how to remedy that and signaled Connie for another. It burned a little less. Old grudges are never really extinguished after all, just quelled for the moment. Eventually, they erupt, usually in a stunning display of vomitous violence.

Connie set them up a few more times before Nick retreated to the jukebox, that warm swirly feeling fluttering around his skull. *This isn't so bad*, Nick thought, feeling foolish for having been on the wagon for so long. *What exactly was I trying to accomplish anyway? This was better.* All his anxieties and worries fell away, and he worked the jukebox feverishly, as if the sequence of songs he chose would solve the riddle of his life. Songs written by other artists; that was the theme he fell upon. He started with Michael Jackson's "I Can't Help It," written by no less a talent than Stevie Wonder. The jazzy groove went well with the early stage of his buzz. He nodded his head to the beat as he punched up a boozy playlist like some dive-bar savant—the Rain Man of R&B, the Sommelier of Soul. When he finished, he turned and walked to the bar. Frankie was all smiles, toe taps, and finger pops as he welcomed Nick back from his strange sojourn in Soberlandia. Nick managed a little shuffle as he strutted over, his inhibitions sliding off him like a winter coat at the airport.

This was the good part.

# Chapter Eleven

# THE BAD PART

Nick was jolted awake by the fear he had overslept and missed his flight. His heart was pounding, and the throbbing in his temples emphasized the previous evening's overindulgence. It took him a moment to overcome the sickening disorientation every drunk knows all too well. *Because that is what you are after all*, the old voice crept up and mocked him, *a drunk*. And no amount of time on the wagon was going to change that fact.

Nick struggled to get his bearings, remembering he had checked in to the W before heading to Blaine's. He couldn't remember how he got there or who had accompanied him. The last thing he could remember was sipping a few bourbons and playing the jukebox, but his head was telling him he had moved on to shots of 1942 at some point. A sick feeling settled in his stomach before he turned over to confirm the other side of the bed was indeed vacant, if a bit disheveled. *Thank God. That's all I need right now.* The pounding in his skull increased as he forced himself to sit upright and limp to the bureau, where he gulped down the complimentary spring water before draining half of the ten-dollar bottle of Fiji.

He stumbled around, rifling through his bag for some ibuprofen. He gulped down two 800 mg tablets, then popped an espresso pod into the machine the W had so thoughtfully provided. It wasn't his treasured Wolf espresso machine, but it would have to do.

The clock radio read 10:26. He had missed his flight. The familiar dread welled up inside him. All the good he had accomplished, his supposed evolution into long-delayed adulthood, everything he and Grace had built together, all that sense of achievement drained out to make room for the bottomless self-loathing that now took its place.

*Slow down. It was just one night. You missed a flight, no big deal. You'll rebook, reset, regroup.* He looked at himself in the mirror. *You've been here before. You've been through worse. You know how to rebound.* He leaned down on the bureau and took in his reflection, flexing his triceps a bit. *You still look good. A little green around the gills, but nothing a hot shower, shave, and a few espressos won't fix.* He rubbed his chin and managed a half smile in honor of yet another roguish night of liquor and song. *This is who I am,* he reassured himself, *I'm a fucking survivor. Grace will understand.*

That's when he heard the shower turn on.

His reflected visage immediately drained of its color. He turned to see the bathroom door open a crack, allowing a streak of fluorescence to slash diagonally across the room. Steam vapor floated through the ribbon of light. Nick's mind fired away, grappling with the events of the previous night, straining to reassemble the pieces he remembered in an effort to come up with an innocuous explanation for this, something he and the boys would laugh about later at Blaine's over a few drinks. Because he had decided in that moment, that's what he needed most. '*Hair of the dog that bit ya,*' some nameless, faceless drunk from Nick's youth, reassured him. There was no turning back now. Nick walked toward the light. His outstretched hand reached for the doorknob, piercing the light beam like some silver screen cat burglar. He nudged the door open.

This was the bad part.

# Chapter Twelve

# THE DUKE



Frank picked Ralph up outside Risoli's Pasticceria on Federal Highway. The Tasker Morris boys would meet there for coffee and gossip most mornings. Anthony Risoli opened the artisan bakery a few years back, after relocating from Philly. It was a big hit with the tourists and locals alike. Risoli was known for his quick wit and sage advice, which he dispensed sparingly, usually accompanied by a ricotta cannolo with just the right balance of sweet and cheesy. Just like Anthony.

Ralph tossed a white bag in the back seat as he got in. "Anthony said to give you this."

"Couldn't you have just handed it to me?" Frank asked.

"It's fucking biscotti, not china. Just drive already," Ralph answered.

Frank shrugged it off and pulled the Civic out onto Federal.

"Let's drive along the beach, Frankie. We need to talk about something."

"Sounds good to me." Frankie made a right onto Commercial, and they soon found themselves driving Northbound on A1A, cruising the Hillsboro Mile. The gates that fronted the beachfront mansions glared at him, reminding him what a failure his life had been, as if he were at risk of forgetting.

"What do you remember about Jerry Salvitti?" Ralph asked.

"The Duke? Not much actually. We kinda moved in different circles back then, and he was a lot older than me."

"Yeah, I figured that. So let me bring you up to speed."

Frank shot a glance over at Ralph. "Any reason for the crash course?"

"Just pay attention, will ya? I'll get to that."

Frank made himself comfortable as they crossed over into Deerfield Beach, and Ralph launched into the tale of Jerry "The Duke" Salvitti.

"The Duke wasn't exactly known as a ladies' man back in the day. To his credit, he was preoccupied with the kind of figures that were preceded by dollar signs. This made him a valuable asset, but more importantly, it made him predictable."

Frank nodded. "A man who worships money is way more predictable than a man who puts pussy on a pedestal."

"Exactly. And the tag team of pussy and unpredictability is unde-feated. Together, they've killed more guys than cancer. So, when the Duke fell for Veronica Gallante, it wasn't long before people started to get nervous. She was way out of his league, and he didn't know how to handle it. Being the oaf that he was, he tried to smother her with attention. Veronica was used to guys falling all over themselves to give her attention, and she usually lost interest quickly. But she had a weak spot. She was nineteen and trapped in a house with a stepfather who made the Duke look like Prince Charming. So when he proposed, she said yes. But she had her eye on the door from the rip. Besides, she was in love with someone else, a guy who didn't give her the time of day."

"Naturally," Frank interjected.

"Yeah, naturally," Ralph responded. "Who's telling this story any-ways, me or you?"

"I'm sorry. Please, continue."

Ralph gave a sarcastic little bow. "Thank you. Where was I?"

"The guy who didn't give her the time of day."

"Right, Mikey Fortuna. Good-looking son of a bitch from the other side of Broad Street."

"They had cable TV before us."

"What the fuck is your point?"

"Nothing, I'm just still not over it, that's all. Should I remember him?"

Ralph shook his head. "Not really. He pretty much kept to himself. Sharp-dressed kid. Came to the gym a little, but mostly to work out, jump rope and hit the bag. I asked him to do some light sparring with me one day, you know, just move around a little, and I'll never forget his answer. He was very respectful, apologetic even. He said, 'I'm sorry, Mr. Cappello, I just don't enjoy hitting another human being.' Can you believe that? It was the strangest thing I ever heard in a boxing gym, but hey, live and let live, right? So he went back to jumping rope, and that's the last I ever spoke to him."

"Jesus, that *is* strange. Whatever happened to him?"

"I'm getting to that part."

They had crossed into Boca, and Ralph gestured for Frank to turn into the Royal Palm Club and Resort, where Frank was a member, but Ralph paid the dues. They pulled up to the front door, handed off the key fob, and the valet parked the lowly Civic on the front line as Ralph and Frank walked in and took seats at the Safari Bar.

"Too fucking hot to sit out there." Ralph nodded out at the beach-front bar.

"Agreed." Frank rapped on the bar with his knuckles and looked to Ralph. "Peroni?"

"Two Peronis," Ralph instructed the bartender. "So, as I was saying, Veronica set her sights on Mikey. He resisted at first, recognizing this was a pretty volatile situation, but eventually, well, you remember Veronica Gallante, right?"

"How can I forget? Looked a little like Raquel Welch, am I right?"

"Exactly my point. And then the worst thing imaginable happened."

"She got pregnant?"

"No, worse. These two fools fell head over heels in love."

"Jesus Christ," Frank said.

"Exactly. Anyway, South Philly being the jealous, backstabbing fishbowl it was—and still is— somebody found out, and that somebody told the Duke."

"Motherfucker." Frank ordered a 1942 on the rocks. "This is getting good. What happened next?"

"Depends on who you ask. Some people say Veronica fell down a flight of basement steps with a basket of laundry."

"What do *you* say?" Frank asked.

"All I know is that gorilla Salvitti dumped her body in front of St Agnes hospital like a sack of potatoes, left her on a bench. A nurse found her. Blunt force trauma. That's what the death certificate said."

"That's a fucking disgrace. Someone should throw him down a flight of steps."

Ralph smiled. "I'm glad you feel that way."

"Oh yeah, why's that?" Frank looked like he already knew the answer.

"Maybe you'll get the opportunity, seeing as you're going to visit him in Philly."

"See? Why do you have to do that?"

"Do what?" Ralph shrugged.

"Tell me a long-winded story instead of just giving it to me straight right from the start."

"I did give it to you straight. I just wanted to give you a little background."

"Speaking of background, whatever happened to Mikey Fortuna?"

"No one ever saw him again. Not all of him at least."

"What's that supposed to mean?" Frank asked.

"They found some bones on a farm out in Potter County. It couldn't be confirmed by DNA or anything, but some informant claimed he heard that's where they buried the poor kid."

"I used to go hunting on a farm in Potter County back in the '80s. Some old-timer from 9th street owned it I think."

"That's the one," Ralph said.

Frank sipped his tequila and stared out at the poolside scene. A little boy with bright floaties on his arms stood at the edge of the pool, crouched hesitantly, his tiny toes gripping the threshold between safety and uncertainty. His father stood in the pool, arms outstretched, assuring that even if he came up short, those two strong arms would be there to catch him. A sensation Frank had never known. The boy leapt . . .

Ralph's meaty palm came down on Frank's neck, causing him to turn away, missing the conclusion of the boy's jump.

"So, are you up for this?" Ralph's voice was different. It had a softness to it that suggested this was less a challenge and more a sincere inquiry. If Frank was looking for a pass, this was his chance. And for the first time in his life, he considered it. He turned to check back on the boy and his father, hoping to see them splashing and laughing, the boy's tiny arms locked around his father's neck . . . but they were already gone. He gulped down the last of his tequila, swallowing hard, and turned back to Ralph.

"Fucking A right I'm up for it," Frank said, knowing there was no turning back.

# Chapter Thirteen

# THE CARPATHIAN LYNX

Nick slipped into the bathroom as stealthily as he could. Which is to say he practically stumbled headfirst into the toilet. A giggle rose up from behind the steamed-up shower door.

"Be a prince and hand me a towel, will you, Nicky?"

That voice. It sent a chill up his spine that threatened to snap him out of his hangover. The fact that he still had a pulse after apparently spending the night with her suggested he was probably safe from Anastasia. As for Grace, well, that remained to be seen.

She slid back the door, revealing a body Nick had once fantasized about. Now, he was hard pressed to remember if he had explored it the night before. Anastasia was Dmitry's most lethal alchemist, but she could also dispense lesser doses designed to incapacitate her targets, rendering them incapable of remembering even having met her. *That would explain a lot*, Nick thought.

She stretched out an upturned palm toward Nick, moving with the grace of a big cat. "Well? Don't look at me like that, Nicky. I know what you're thinking. But you did this to yourself. If I were responsible, you wouldn't be able to stand yet." She waved her hand up and down to emphasize she was referring to Nick's shaky state.

Nick tossed her a towel.

"How did you get in here?" Nick realized how foolish that sounded the moment the words came out of his mouth.

"With *you*. Through the lobby, up the elevator and with your key card. Are you suggesting I broke in? That's not in my skill set, lover. Trust me, you didn't resist."

Something about the way she said lover made Nick's stomach even queasier than it had been, and he barely resisted the urge to dive for the toilet and purge himself of the bile that had been rising within him since the moment he opened his eyes.

"You don't look so good. Why don't you go lie down while I dry off? I'll join you in two shakes of a lynx's tail." Anastasia had a habit of dropping these little sayings that Nick figured came from her native Ukraine. She knew how to play up the sultry accent when she needed to, so her near-perfect English suggested to Nick perhaps they had achieved a level of intimacy that no longer required it.

Nick made his way back to the bed. He didn't have much choice, as his legs were so wobbly, he couldn't manage much else. He fell asleep as soon as his head hit the pillow.

# Chapter Fourteen

# THE SAD TALE OF MIKEY FORTUNA

**South Philadelphia 1989**

He resisted as long as he could. That's what Mikey told himself. He knew Veronica Gallante was trouble from the first moment he laid eyes on her. To his credit, he maintained the platonic charade at first, laughing off her double entendres as nothing more than friendly bartender banter. After all, Veronica had no shortage of admirers and gin-soaked flatterers eager to squander half their paychecks for the privilege of her company, even if it was limited to the width of a bar top. Still, Mikey started to find excuses to stop in the Bamboo Inn more frequently, often staying until closing.

She had married the Duke when she was nineteen years old in a misguided attempt to flee the hellscape of her stepfather's household, figuring it couldn't possibly get worse.

She was wrong.

The Duke was almost thirty years her senior, and he lost interest in his prized acquisition as soon as he broke her spirit. Fresh from the clutches of her stepfather, she had confided her deepest insecurities, and at first, the Duke seemed caring and sympathetic. But what masqueraded as empathy was really just pathological attention to detail; detail he could later exploit, weaknesses he could methodically home in on, old wounds he could gleefully reopen.

In a mercifully fortuitous turn of events, her stepfather died of cirrhosis of the liver, and Veronica found herself the owner and operator of the Bamboo Inn, a run-down South Philly bar favored by slowly dying alcoholics during the day and budding juvenile drunks at night. It was known for the coldest beer in South Philly and a half-decent egg roll. In other words, a goldmine.

The Duke had one of his guys posted there most days, ostensibly to handle the meager sports and loan action, but more importantly to keep an eye on Veronica. Just because his plaything had lost her luster didn't mean he was okay with someone else enjoying her charms. The Duke's guy would usually abandon his post once the crowd switched over and the jukebox music shifted to the soundtrack of the resident young Turks. The Duke himself would barge in from time to time, making a scene and ordering her around. Then he would make a big production of having her come around the bar to sit on his lap so he could grope her and shower her with insincere yet sloppy kisses. Veronica knew better than to resist or exhibit anything other than unbridled joy at being publicly molested by the buffoon she had so tragically married.

Mikey witnessed this display only once. He had walked over to the poker machine, milking his drink and credits at the same slow pace, hoping this *gavone* would tire of the theatrics and go to one of his unfortunate mistresses before Mikey was forced to converse with him.

He was down to his last five credits when he glanced over in time to see the Duke gnawing on Veronica's neck like a bloated jackal. Veronica was facing Mikey, and her stare was unwavering. It wasn't the look of prey. It was the look of a woman in complete control of her emotions. She never averted her gaze from Mikey. If the light had once gone out in those beautiful hazel eyes, a spark had now returned. All it needed was a breath of fresh air to ignite into an inferno.

It was at that moment Mikey Fortuna decided he had to have her, and nobody, not the Duke, not Christ on the Cross, could stop him. He boldly blew her a kiss behind the Duke's back as he slapped the deal button on his last credits. She reciprocated by narrowing her eyes until they were only slits and puffed out her lips in a sultry kiss. The poker machine went off like a firecracker, and Mikey looked down to see he had dealt himself a royal flush. He should have been elated, but was instead filled with an inexplicable feeling of dread, even as the machine rattled off credits at a machine gun clip. Something deep inside told him this might be the last decent hand life would deal him.

# Chapter Fifteen

## CRIPPLED PREY

Nick was awakened by the smell of espresso. For a moment, he imagined he was back at his condo, and Grace was crafting one of her specialty brews. Instead, Anastasia sat on the bed next to him with a cup in her hand. "Feeling better, handsome?"

A different brand of nausea returned to his stomach as Nick recalled where he was and who he was with. Against his better judgment, he sipped the espresso, figuring things couldn't get much worse. Besides, he figured if Anastasia had him in her crosshairs, he would be lying on a slab at the Broward County Morgue by now. To his surprise, the espresso made him feel a little better.

"Don't you have to be getting on a flight soon?" Anastasia poked him on the shoulder with a bright red nail.

*Fuck,* Nick thought as the realizations started to come back to him. It had been so long since he had a hangover, he had forgotten the old routine of reconstructing the events of the night and days preceding a bender.

"I'll drive you to the airport as soon as you shower and get your head together," Anastasia said. "Meet me down at the lobby bar."

The word "bar" made him feel queasy. He checked his phone to see that he had slept through most of the day, and he had a large number of missed calls and texts from Grace, Ralph, and Frankie. The task of calling and texting everyone back seemed as dreadful as a high school exam on a book he had neglected to read.

"I have to book a flight," he responded weakly.

Anastasia looked at him with an amused smirk. She had her hand on her hip, and the image of her standing in the shower came back to him. He had only one thought at that moment, and it manifested itself in what passed for a prayer in Nick's world: *Dear God, please don't let Grace find out.*

"Don't be silly, Nick," Anastasia said. "You're flying private, courtesy of Dmitry. You leave from the executive airport in Boca in three hours, so I think you should get ready." She must have read the look on his face, or maybe he had unintentionally mumbled his silent prayer aloud, because she added, "Oh, and I know you may find this hard to believe, but as tempting as it was, you lying there all vulnerable, I somehow managed to resist molesting you. I don't believe in hunting crippled prey; it's just not, how do you say, sporting. I thought you knew that about me. Believe me, if I make my move, I want you to be fully aware and with all your senses intact. So, until then?" She formed her hand into a gun and pointed her finger at him. She made a little gunshot noise through pillowy lips.

After the door closed behind her, Nick fell back onto the bed, his arms spread out like the crucified Christ as he let out a whoosh of relief.

# Chapter Sixteen

# GORGEOUS CREATURES

*I'm okay, just overslept. I'll be in Philly soon.*

The text bubble popped up on Ralph's phone. Nick sent the same terse message to Frank and Gary. It was all he could manage before jumping in the shower. He would have struggled to explain the events of the night, especially since he could hardly remember most of them. The rain showerhead felt good, but did little to wash away the sticky mixture of guilt and embarrassment that clung to him. Old regrets began to pop up in his mind like a sizzle reel of bad decisions, and no amount of scalding hot water could erase them. It seemed an impossible task to dive in and explore those feelings now, and the predicament he was about to land in made for a convenient excuse not to try. Nick decided that self-exploration, that meditative work, a hybrid of Grace's mysticism and Dave's Stoic brand of philosophy, would have to wait. *Amor fati?* More like *fuck my life.*

If it were true that *the obstacle is the way*, it was also becoming clear the only path through was lined with bottles of liquor. '*What stands in the way becomes the way.'* Wasn't that one of Dave's favorite Marcus Aurelius quotes? Either way, Nick grew convinced the alcohol was an irreplaceable weapon in his arsenal, albeit one that should be wielded sparingly and only in times of great need. He dried off and felt energized by the clarity his newfound resolve had instilled, even if he suspected down deep the journey was calamitous.

Nick had missed the sense of camaraderie that drinking always seemed to engender. His earliest notion of brotherhood was one of shared barroom nights that never seemed to end. They just ran one into another, front to back, like train cars on a nonstop locomotive filled with booze, music, and women. Back then, those nights seemed chock-full of unlimited opportunities. Every time the door swung open, it was perfectly reasonable to expect some gorgeous creature to come sauntering in and make a beeline straight for him. And all those outsized personalities with the colorful nicknames provided nonstop entertainment, fueled by shots of V.O. and egged on by a killer jukebox soundtrack.

Eventually, all those big personalities withered until they had just one thing in common—they were all dead. And those gorgeous creatures? Well, only one of those words was still applicable.

*So then why do I miss those days so much?* Nick asked himself. *Some deluded sense of adventure? A grandiose notion that I was on some epic quest? Maybe it just seemed so much more romantic in the rearview, with all the pain and heartache filtered out.* He was reminded of the old warning: objects in mirror are closer than they appear.

An intense feeling began to rise within him, and Nick realized these questions would have to wait. He vomited into the toilet in a vivid reminder of how so many of those glorious nights had in fact ended.

# Chapter Seventeen

# GOOD TIMES

"He was supposed to be here hours ago." Joey clicked the remote furiously, flicking through channels too quickly to even determine what was on.

Big Gary snatched the remote from his hand playfully but forcefully, flashing a bit of the old hand speed. "You making me dizzy." At sixty-four years old, suffering from a number of ailments, and tipping the scales north of three hundred pounds, little things like stamina had long since evaporated, but he hadn't lost a step in the hand-eye coordination department. "I liked it better when we only had six stations. Something good was always on back then."

"Yeah, like what, *Happy Days*?" Joey snickered.

"Damn straight. *Good Times* too," Gary snarled. "You got a problem with that?" Gary flicked a jab at Joey's chin, stopping about a half inch short.

Joey's father, Jimmy, had died before he was born, and Joey bounced around South Philly, careening from father figure to father figure on the corner bar circuit, until he landed fortuitously at Caffè Vecchio and the relative benevolent tutelage of Gary and his father's best friend, Nick DiNobile. After Nick went to Florida, Gary had taken on the uncle role for Joey. They made for an odd duo, the hulking black uncle and the impetuous Italian nephew. They got the occasional odd look, but nobody was stupid enough to pass a remark. Joey was only twenty-four, but with Gary's failing health, sometimes it wasn't clear who was taking care of who.

"What did his text say?" Joey asked.

"Just that he'd be here soon."

"Well, if he's not here by tomorrow, I'm going to make my own moves."

Gary laughed, seeing through Joey's statement for what it was—a bit of saber-rattling bravado after an embarrassing ordeal. The big man wasn't wholly unsympathetic. He'd been scooped up once himself, back in his Southwark Projects days, before they demolished the towers. And he'd seen quite a few boys tied up too. Neither were pleasant recollections, so he tempered his response.

"Look." He placed a heavy hand gently on Joey's shoulder. "I know how you feel, believe me, I do. But that impulse? The one that's telling you to get strapped up and round up your half-ass crew of misfits? That's the same impulse that got plenty of fools killed. The right move is usually the hardest move; that's how you know it's right. You feel me?"

Joey nodded. In reality, he knew he should wait for Nick. He just needed someone like Gary to put that gentle hand on his shoulder. That's what he had been missing all his life. Otherwise, he was susceptible to a rage that didn't always make sense, a leap into self-destruction, an inexplicable lust for his own fall. Joey would eventually come to identify it for what it truly was—an insatiable desire for revenge against a father who abandoned him by allowing himself to get killed.

Gary moved to the jukebox, confident that Joey got the message. All that talk about seventies sitcoms had his brain firing. He was thinking of the painting they showed during the credits of *Good Times*. It featured people who looked like him, unapologetically black and dancing in a way that made them appear to leap off the screen. In 1976, he would see that same painting used as cover art on a Marvin Gaye album. The painting, *The Sugar Shack* by neo-mannerist artist Ernie Barnes, portrayed a dance hall scene, its subjects absurdly elongated and in perpetually funky motion. Barnes, a retired NFL player, died in 2009. The second of two original prints of *The Sugar Shack* sold at auction at Christie's in 2022 for $15.2 million. Gary walked back over to the bar and poured two Crown Royals. He placed one in front of Joey as a peace offering. They clicked glasses as Marvin's voice washed over them like maple syrup in the oozy opening strains of "I Want You."

"What are we drinking to?" Joey asked.

Gary thought about it for a second before responding. "Nothing. We just drinking. That okay with you?"

Joey raised his glass. "To nothing." But he was lying, because somewhere deep inside, he made a secret toast for reasons he couldn't comprehend.

*To you, Dad.*

# Chapter Eighteen

## NO CALL, NO SHOW

Kim was a 'no call, no show.' She had her fair share of tardiness, but missing a shift completely was unusual for her. Ronnie knew she needed the money, and she was always willing to take a shift from one of the other waitresses. The lack of even a perfunctory text wasn't like her. Whatever hardships she had doubtless endured hadn't managed to impact her manners. Ronnie recognized it as a valiant attempt to cling to some flotsam of humanity in a sea of misfortune. She was unfailingly courteous, even under the strain of the reliably hectic Tiki crowd, always managing a smile even if it was tinged with melancholy. Her hardscrabble graciousness contrasted vividly against the entitled masses clamoring for libations.

Ronnie called to see if she was okay, but the call went right to voicemail. She was living in one of those single-room occupancy hotels on Federal Highway until she could find more stable housing. His next call was to Grace, who agreed to come in to cover her shift. It probably wouldn't be necessary, as the crowd was inexplicably light.

Even regulars like Dave still hadn't arrived. The man Ronnie knew as Julian was also absent. To the best of Ronnie's recollection, it was the first time Julian didn't show for one of Kim's scheduled shifts. It was almost like he knew she wouldn't be there.

"Have you heard from her yet?" Grace arrived and hastily wrapped an apron around her waist. Storm clouds had formed over the ocean; the leading edge resembled an anvil. Ronnie tried to gauge whether the prevailing winds would keep them offshore. A downpour would bring with it a rush of damp sunbathers, their belongings hastily gathered up as they sought shelter from the storm beneath the Tiki's hut.

"Nothing yet, mami." Ronnie gave Grace a kiss on the cheek. "Maybe she's just not feeling well." He wiped at the bar, aware he was trying to convince himself as much as he was Grace. He couldn't put his finger on it, but something about Kim's absence didn't sit well with him. When some of the other girls missed a shift, it barely registered. Sometimes, they came rushing in a half hour late, mumbling an apology, still wearing an outfit from the night before. Ronnie glanced over toward the hotel, half hoping he would see her scrambling down the steps, flipping her hair, eyes downturned. All he could see were a few drunken frat boys strutting toward the pool, caps turned backward, arms flapping comically, masters of all they surveyed, oblivious to how fast it all went. He shook the feeling of dread off for the moment and concentrated on tending to the sparse crowd, striking up a conversation with a nice, first-time couple. That's what Ronnie was best at—making sure new customers soon became Tiki regulars.

As the day dragged along and the temperature rose, those clouds finally broke, and the beach crowd scrambled up, trading their lounge chairs for stools under the shade of the Tiki's roof. Reliably, a few of the regulars bought drinks for the nubile invaders.

Ronnie noticed Dave had arrived and seemed a bit miffed that his usual spot was taken by a horde of college kids. He pulled a Miller Lite from the ice and handed it over the bar to the resident philosopher until a stool opened for him. There was still no word from Kim, and Julian was conveniently missing, consistent with the pattern Ronnie had started to notice.

The day continued in a mercifully comforting pattern. Ronnie's attention focused on tending to the endless cycle of customers demanding everything from the latest craft IPA ("No, we don't carry th at.") to his signature Pina Colada. Little by little, almost imperceptibly, the jukebox music shifted from Top 40 to old school R&B, and by the time Ronnie had a chance to look up, the collective face of the crowd had grown older by a few decades. The kids had mostly cleared out, presumably to prepare for a long night out at one of the swankier spots downtown. The Tiki served them well as a 'pregame' watering hole. Jenna came in a bit early for the evening shift, so Grace got her things together and came over to say goodbye to Ronnie before leaving.

"Thanks for coming in, Grace. I would have been crushed without you," Ronnie said.

"Anything for you, chico." Grace kissed him on the cheek and used it as an opportunity to whisper something in his ear. "This guy gives me the creeps." She thrust her chin over his shoulder. Ronnie didn't turn immediately, just smiled at Grace and gave her a wink that said, *'I'll check him out in a sec.'*

After she left, Ronnie turned slowly. He addressed the couple just to the right of where Grace had gestured. "You guys okay?  Need anything?" They smiled over their full drinks and demurred. Ronnie shifted his attention to where Grace had gestured. "How about you, my friend, what can I get you?"

Julian looked up from his phone and smiled at Ronnie. He must have slid in while Ronnie was busy with the college crowd and ordered a drink from Grace. "I'm good, my man." He stood, reached into his pocket, and peeled a hundred off a substantial fold of its brethren. He knocked back what was left of his drink and checked the time on his Patek. The motion revealed a flash of faded script peeking out from the cuff of an impeccably pressed Brioni short-sleeved dress shirt. Some ancient text that once carried enough meaning to be permanently inscribed on his arm, now just an anachronistic smudge kept in check by the regal fabric. He tossed the hundred on the bar.

"Nah, my man. That's on me," Ronnie said. Julian only had one drink, and Ronnie saw an opening to build a little rapport, maybe learn a bit more about the stranger.

Julian nodded graciously. "Thank you, Ronnie. I appreciate it, but the hundred is a tip."

Ronnie was a little taken aback that the man had remembered his name. By the time he could think of a response, Julian had turned and begun to walk away.

Ralph arrived in time to witness the end of the exchange from the other side of the bar. "What was that all about?" he asked Ronnie.

"Nothing really. Grace just asked me to check that guy out."

"He causing trouble or something?"

"Not at all, quite the opposite, actually."

Ralph watched as Julian walked toward the door. "There's something about that guy that seems really familiar, I just can't put my finger on it."

"Says his name is Julian. You know him?" Ronnie asked.

"Who knows? Maybe in a past life. When you get to be my age, everybody looks familiar."

"Especially around here," Ronnie said.

"Ain't that the truth?" Ralph took off his sunglasses, folding them carefully and sliding them into the breast pocket of his short-sleeved dress shirt. He placed his phone on the bar and reached for a cocktail napkin as Ronnie poured him a Crown Royal on the rocks without asking.

Ronnie felt a sense of déjà vu as he took note of the faded script that peeked out from beneath Ralph's sleeve as he reached across the bar.

# Chapter Nineteen

## THE LION AND THE STURGEON

Nick boarded Dmitry's Gulfstream G600 at Boca Raton Executive Airport. The Russian had spared no expense when it came to outfitting the plane, and the crew was no exception. Tatiana had been headhunted away from Deutsche Bank. She had a Harvard MBA and the body of a Miami bottle service waitress. Dmitry doubled her salary and shielded her from the harassment she routinely batted away in the old boys' club of the high finance world. Her compensation included a generous stock component consisting of shares in the aviation corporation Dmitry created to operate his Gulfstream fleet. She could retire tomorrow, but at the moment, she was serving Nick the best Old Fashioned he'd ever had in his life. The cocktail was served in a Waterford tumbler hand-etched with a lion and a sturgeon, the crest of Waterford City. The single oversized ice cube bore an impression of Dmitry's initials—DI. It looked too perfect to drink. Nick snuck a quick picture and considered sending it to Grace, but decided against it. *I'll just show her when I get back*, he thought before taking a sip.

"Can I get you anything else, Mr. Di Nobile, a pillow or blanket?" Tatiana crouched expertly, knees together, back poker straight as she reoriented his drink so the initials on the ice cube aligned with those embroidered on the linen cocktail napkin. Nick couldn't think of anything else. Well, he briefly thought of one thing, but quickly caught himself. Besides, Dmitry wouldn't appreciate the overreach; Grace even less. "No, I'm fine for now, thanks, he said weakly.

"Well, be sure to let me know. Dmitry insists on your comfort and care."

It sounded like a strangely formal pronouncement, but Nick nodded and repeated his thanks. He glanced at the Seamaster on his wrist, figuring they had about an hour and a half left until landing. He should have been savoring the luxury of the flight, but he couldn't wait to land and get to the Caffè.

At first, he'd thought Anastasia would be joining him and was relieved when she dropped him off at the FBO. Not that he didn't enjoy her company, but he felt like he had a close call the night before and needed to compose himself and have a little time alone. Besides, Anastasia had a way of materializing when he least expected it, sometimes as a blonde, sometimes as a brunette, sometimes wielding the poison, and on occasion, the antidote.

Gary was waiting for him when he landed and deplaned at Atlantic Aviation at Philadelphia International Airport. The sight of the old Fleetwood gave him a nostalgic feeling of comfort. The big man's crushing hug enveloped him like South Philly herself was wrapping him up in a welcoming embrace.

"What's up, killer?" Nick greeted his old friend.

"*You* the killer, pretty boy, way you slayed them skirts back in the day."

"I'm starting to think maybe they slayed *me*, big guy, you feel me?"

"I feel you," Gary answered.

This was the easy banter they fell back into whenever they got together. It was effortless, and there was no other human being on earth Nick felt this comfortable being around. Well, other than Grace, but that was a different type of comfort.

"Where's Frank?" Nick asked. "He was supposed to get in yesterday."

"He did. I got him settled in the room on top of Smokey Joe's."

Ralph kept an apartment above Smokey Joe's for the Tasker Morris boys to use when one of them needed to return to the city. It was the last old-school bar on the avenue, other than Caffè Vecchio, and Frank loved staying there. Nick would have loved to see his reaction to flying on Dmitry's jet. *Next time.*

They didn't talk much for the rest of the ride, and that was just fine with Nick. As long as Joey was okay, he was happy to save the serious talk until they settled in at his father's old restaurant, where he could prop his elbows up on the bar and run his fingers across the weathered surface. *Perhaps,* Nick thought, *some of the old man's instincts would rub off on me.*

*Who am I kidding?* Nick jostled himself out of his reverie and the magical thinking that sometimes went along with it. He struggled to separate nostalgia from reality as Gary pulled open the door and Nick stepped back into the time machine that was Caffè Vecchio. He steeled himself to commune with some old ghosts, but the only spirit that met him was a Maker's on the rocks being poured by Alberto in honor of his return.

"He's on his way. Boy been through a lot," Gary offered as an explanation for Joey's tardiness.

Nick had already factored that in. It didn't matter anyway, because Nick already blamed himself for Joey's ordeal, just like he blamed himself for pretty much everything that went on around him these days. Neither Grace's love nor Dave's philosophy had succeeded in curing him of the state of perpetual guilt that had seemed to plague him since childhood. Nick lifted his glass off the bar and held it slightly in front of him. It led the way to the jukebox like a seeing-eye dog. The vintage black-and-white tiled floor dipped ever so slightly beneath his feet. He ran his right hand along the weathered bar top as he walked, reading the chipped lacquer of the bullnose like some barroom braille. It told the story of an epic novel, the ending still unclear. Above his head, the tin roof firmament that once demarcated the limits of his ambitions, hung in disrepair. A missing corner tile revealed the plaster above, hinting at the folly of his misspent youth, and a slavish loyalty to a neighborhood that didn't always reciprocate it.

Nick stared at the jukebox. He wasn't at that stage of drinking where the machine seemed to play itself. That would come later. For now, he would have to work a little, come up with a theme. He started to feel a low-key rage building inside him. Not the dangerous, violent rage of his youth, but one that channeled some of the old pride he had become nostalgic for of late. The one that tells young men they can walk out into that dark night, fearing no man and finding no woman off limits. The confidence that came with being princes of the city. Back when there was a city worth being the prince of. For the survivors, that pride had morphed into something more useful—experience, and the caution that came with it. Holy Cross Cemetery was filled with those who weren't nimble enough to make that transition. The penitentiary ran a close second. Even so, safe in the bosom of the old Caffè, Nick indulged that rage. It was like going on a sanitized safari in Disney World.

"Love Insurance" by Front Page, a track that channeled some serious post-disco swagger. That's the song the low simmering rage whispered to him to play. He wasn't sure where it was going, but it felt pretty good, and no one questioned the selection. If anything, Gary was giving a subtle, rhythmic head nod that telegraphed his approval. He switched a toothpick from the left side of his mouth to the right. An innocuous enough move, but one that would have sent some pretty serious guys ducking for cover back in the day. The big man retained all that muscle memory and still possessed a capacity for violence that glowed like the dying embers of disco long after it had been declared dead. Nick followed up with "Yearning For Your Love" by the Gap Band. If Gary had a pistol on him, he would have fired a round through the ceiling on principle alone. He settled for taking a healthy gulp of his drink and tapping the glass down just a little forcefully on the bar. He stood up from the stool, hiking up his perpetually slouching pants in the same motion. Gary snapped the fingers of both hands in quick succession, mimicking a double tap from a .22.

"Ooooooooowwwww!" the big man vocalized. It came out like a deep growl that caught even Alberto off guard, judging by the way he jolted to attention, straight-backed and eyebrows arched. Nick caught himself staring at Gary. It had been a while since he had been in his company, and he felt a kind of melancholy awe as he took in the breadth of the big man's undeniable charisma.

"Fuck you looking at?" Gary snapped in a manner a stranger could easily mistake for threatening. "I remember when you was dangerous, slick, before all that sunshine shriveled your balls."

Gary was just breaking his stones of course, but that didn't stop Nick from firing back before he could measure his words. "And I remember when you were under three hundred pounds. What's your point?"

That momentarily stopped Gary dead in his tracks, then he stared daggers at Nick as he walked toward him. He reached for Nick's neck, and in that split second, Nick didn't know whether he was about to be pulled into a bear hug or choked out. He let out a sigh of relief when Gary opted for the former.

"Yeah," Gary grunted, "that's the Nick I was talking about. You was the best that ever done did it." He draped an arm around Nick, his drink dangling carelessly in front of his chest, his meaty hand dwarfing the rocks glass. He leaned forward, using his free arm to brace himself against the jukebox. Nick slumped forward a bit under the heft of his father's best friend. It felt good, safe. It felt like home.

The bell jingled as Joey walked through the door, an amused look on his face. Nick looked over, not even bothering to suppress a goofy grin. This was the Caffè that visited him in his dreams, where he pushed open that front door to unbridled joy and endless possibilities. For that brief moment, it was like he had been transported back, and every shitty thing that transpired since had never happened. It was a bubble Nick knew had to burst, but for the time being, he was content to float around in it, sandwiched between the tile floor and the tin roof, flying among the paintings, soothed by the gentle breeze that seemed to emanate from the jukebox.

Joey joined them at the jukebox. Nick grabbed him behind the neck and pulled him in close for a kiss on the top of his head.

"You okay?" Nick asked.

"I will be," Joey replied, and Nick knew exactly what he meant.

"One step at a time. Let's not be going off half-cocked. You hear me?"

Joey nodded.

"Now tell me everything that happened."

Joey took Nick through his ordeal, starting with the night with Stephanie.

"You trust her?" Nick asked.

"She's never given me a reason not to, but at this point, no, I don't trust any woman. Do you?"

"This isn't about me, Joey," Nick deflected. "Finish the story."

And Joey did, recounting every detail he could remember.

"Where's Andy on all of this?" Nick asked Gary.

"He told me to call when you got in, and he would come over."

"And?"

"And I called, he comin'."

"Alright then."

Nick broke up the three-way hug as they headed back over to the bar to wait for Andy. Marlena Shaw's "Touch Me in the Morning" led the way. They settled in, and Gary proposed a toast to the memory of the recently departed songstress. They drank in silence as the trumpet kicked in at the 3:28 mark, heralding the approaching storm.

# Chapter Twenty

# SUNSET INN

Grace pulled up to the run-down motel where Kim was staying until she could save up enough for a real apartment. The job at the Tiki was her lifeline, another step on her long journey of working the program, making amends, and getting her daughter back. That's why Kim's missing her shift didn't sit well with Grace. She smiled as she walked up to the front desk. The Indian boy sitting behind it looked to be no more than sixteen or seventeen years old. He was playing a video game and appeared disturbed by Grace's approach and interruption of his game.

"Can I help you?" he asked as he took off his headphones.

Grace smiled as she placed her hands palms down on the desk in a gesture meant to put the boy at ease. "I was hoping you could. I'm looking for a friend of mine. She lives here. Her name is Kim."

The boy looked up at her. He was doe-eyed, with gentle features that suggested a kind nature Kim would have responded to. He seemed like he was on the verge of answering her when a large Indian man, presumably the boy's father, emerged from the back. He was disheveled and sweating profusely, and appeared perturbed by Grace's intrusion. A name tag with a smiley face announced him as Sanjay.

"What do you want?" he barked. "We do not give out information about guests; it is against our policy."

By the looks of the place, Grace doubted they had any policies whatsoever, and the use of the word 'guests' to describe its inhabitants seemed out of place. Inmates seemed more appropriate, and the group milling about the entrance where she had parked suggested they had taken over the asylum. The boy put his headphones on again.

"I was just looking for one of my employees. She didn't show up for work today, and I wanted to make sure she was okay. I run the Tuscan Tiki on the beach. You should stop by sometime. Drinks on the house."

"I don't know any Tiki, I don't know any Kim, and I don't drink. Please go away unless you want to rent a room," Sanjay barked.

She hadn't mentioned Kim by name, and the ease with which it rolled off his tongue betrayed the fact he knew her well enough. At least she had the right place.

"Okay, I'm sorry. I didn't mean to intrude. But please, if you see her, tell her to call Grace. That's me." She pointed at herself with her thumb. The awkward gesture made her feel a little foolish. She began to walk away and turned to add, "Tell her that her job is waiting for her." Grace figured perhaps this would incentivize him to pass the message along, in the event she owed any rent.

Sanjay was standing over the boy, glaring at him. He smacked him on the back of his head, sending his headphones flying.

"Please go away," Sanjay said to Grace. "You've caused enough trouble already."

Grace walked to her car. She sat there with the engine idling, trying to gather her thoughts and process what she had observed. Looking around at the seedy parking lot, she felt sadder than ever for Kim. She imagined her trying to get some rest in her shabby room while all this transpired on the other side of paper-thin walls, muffled only by the hum of a rickety AC unit and a borrowed Netflix account.

Grace's head almost hit the roof when there was a sharp knock on the passenger side window. It was the boy; his eyes darted from Grace to the entrance, as he was no doubt keeping watch for his father. Grace hit the button to unlock the door, and the boy slid into the passenger seat stealthily as a cat. He kept his hands on his knees as he looked straight ahead.

"There is a man," was all he said.

The boy's name was Arjun. After some prompting, he told Grace about how Kim would always stop to talk with him. He had taught her to play *Call of Duty* and would sometimes sneak off to her room, where they played together for hours. Kim was the one person who listened to him, more than his family and teachers, certainly more than his father. In turn, Kim had shared her own tales of hardship without a trace of shame. She detailed her long, hard-fought road to sobriety and redemption. He knew on some level, Kim was doing this to make him feel better about his own troubled life.

"She is my only friend," Arjun blurted out while staring at the floor mat.

"Tell me about the man," Grace nudged.

Arjun bit his lower lip. "He is very rich, I think."

"What makes you say that?"

"He has the car with the silver lady on the front."

Grace didn't understand. "The what?"

"The pretty woman on the hood. Her hair blows back, and she has wings."

"You mean a Rolls-Royce?"

"Yes." Arjun nodded. "I think that's what you call it. It says RR in the center of the wheels. The letters stay straight even when the tires turn. He picks her up sometimes late at night. I watch from up there." Arjun pointed to the room above the office.

"You live here?" Grace asked and immediately felt guilty that her tone may have come off the wrong way, as the boy shrank a little further into himself, his shoulders practically covering his ears.

"Yes," Arjun answered, before adding, "For now."

Those two words told Grace that, somehow, the boy was going to be okay.

"Can you tell me anything else about this man?"

"Not really. He doesn't ever get out of the car. Kim plays with her hair a lot before she gets in the car. She does that when she is nervous, right?" Grace nodded in agreement. "And later on, when he drops her off, she looks bad, like she's going to cry, but she never does."

Grace reached over and touched the boy's hand. "Thank you, Arjun. You're very brave. Kim is lucky to have a friend like you." She gave Arjun her number, and he saved it to his phone. "Text me the minute you see her, please. Anytime, day or night. Okay?"

Arjun nodded. "I promise." He slid out of the car as quietly as he had entered.

Grace watched him walk back to the office. He put his headphones back on and shoved his hands deep into his pockets, trying to make himself invisible as he passed by the prostitutes that loitered beneath the overhang.

# Chapter Twenty-One

# WEEKEND PASS

The Duke had quickly settled into an unassuming routine at Kintock, the federal halfway house tucked away on Erie Avenue. It was one of the few neighborhoods left in Philadelphia where such a facility could operate without spurring an uprising. The Duke didn't bother anyone, and no one much bothered with him. In this respect, his mutism served him well. Still, given his dementia diagnosis, the United States Probation Office for the Eastern District of Pennsylvania was eager to approve his reentry plan and transfer him to the care of his sister. The good Sister Mary Rita had obtained special permission to leave the cloister in order to assist her brother in his transition. His probation officer, Jim McMenamin, fast-tracked his home plan and approved a weekend pass within his first two weeks at Kintock. The halfway was ill-equipped to handle an inmate with his diagnosis, and the Duke hadn't bathed since he was released from Devens.

"I'll be stopping by to check in on you, so no funny business," McMenamin recited, more obligatory than menacing. The Duke just stared at him blankly.

For a second, McMenamin thought he detected a faint glint of excitement in those steely pupils, but dismissed the thought at the sight of the string of drool leaking from the corner of his mouth and threatening to escape from his chin. He looked at the box of Kleenex sitting on a metal side table. It was next to a framed picture of him and his wife from a cruise they had taken in the early years of their marriage, back before she put on "the weight." It had sat there for so long, it became like any other fixture you stop consciously looking at. Now, McMenamin found himself staring at it, and it repulsed him even more than the Duke's drool. If he had a shred of humanity, McMenamin would have wiped the old man's face, or at least handed him a tissue, whether the man was capable of using it or not. Instead, he simply stood up, signaling the meeting was over.

The trustee assigned to the Duke nudged him out of his chair, gripped both his hands, and gave him a little tug, helping him to his feet. Even after the trustee released his grip, the Duke stood there with his arms still extended out in front of him like some zombie in an old horror movie. The trustee turned him as he eased his arms down to his side. Just before his face turned completely away from view, McMenamin thought he saw the beginning of a smile form at the corner of the Duke's chapped lips, but just as quickly gave a snort at the silliness of the thought.

He sprayed the office with a generic air freshener, which only served to compound the stale stench of institutional body odor that lingered in the air. He pointed the nozzle at the framed image of his wife's face and sent a blast in her direction that gave him an immense feeling of satisfaction.

# Chapter Twenty-Two

# EMPTY FRAMES

**Isabella Stewart Gardner Museum – Boston**
**March 17, 1990**

St. Patrick's Day was winding down. The last of the drunks had been rounded up, and the festivities were coming to an end. It was a long, tough day to be a cop in Boston. Transgressions that would have been met with the business end of a nightstick on any other day were met with indifference or a mild nudge.

Two officers rang the buzzer at the side door of the Isabella Stewart Gardner Museum a little after 1:00 a.m. on March 18th. One of the two guards on duty observed the officers on the security camera and let them in.

By the time the guards realized something about the officers wasn't right, they were handcuffed and taken to the basement, where they were duct-taped and secured to a workbench.

Rembrandt's *Christ in the Storm on the Sea of Galilee* and *A Lady and Gentleman in Black,* along with *The Concert* by Vermeer, were taken from the Dutch Room, while Manet's *Chez Tortoni* was stolen from the Blue Room. In addition to five Degas sketches, the thieves took a Chinese gu and an eagle finial from atop a flagpole after failing to get at the Napoleonic flag secured beneath it. They displayed some lack of planning and discernment by ignoring priceless works by Michelangelo and Botticelli.

The first man to enter the museum wore a fake mustache and took responsibility for securing the guards in the basement.

In all, thirteen items were reported stolen, including the finial and the gu. The initial reward of five million was upped to ten, and the feds extended an offer of no prosecution for the return of the art.

Theories and wild speculation abounded as the decades passed. Everyone from the IRA to the Italians to a Boston street gang was thought to be responsible. The guards were scrutinized and investigated to no avail. Countless leads and tips poured in over the years. Some appeared promising but were investigated without success. The empty frames remained on display in a show of dwindling hope.

The one fact that all law enforcement agencies could agree on was that the works eventually made their way to Philadelphia. What the same agencies could never figure out was where the works went after that. The hunt for the paintings covered the globe, from Saudi Arabia to Japan to Corsica.

They completely overlooked the possibility that a few of them never left South Philly.

# Chapter Twenty-Three

# TWO SHIPS PASSING IN THE NIGHT

Sister Mary Rita had petitioned and received special permission from Mother Anna Cornelia to take a leave of absence from the cloister. Her sabbatical was for the limited purpose of assisting her brother in what was represented to be his final months on earth. She had spent the previous week cleaning the old rowhouse she had grown up in. It was an ancient affair, hermetically sealed in the South Philly Seventies, but well preserved thanks to a monthly visit and cleaning by one of the neighborhood ladies still living on the block. Anything for Sister Mary Rita.

The good sister had provisioned the pantry and refrigerator with all the essentials. The trusty green Kelvinator had kept humming reliably throughout the decades of the Duke's incarceration, the compressor cycling on and off, ticking away at the years of his sentence. Sister Mary Rita still had a few larger items remaining at the convent that would require some assistance with their transport.

The Pink Nuns were beloved for their gentle eccentricity, and they consistently received generous donations from benefactors in the Philadelphia region and beyond. Most came in the form of small financial contributions, but they occasionally found themselves named as beneficiaries of substantial estates. In this fashion, the Holy Spirit Adoration Sisters had accumulated a substantial portfolio of stocks, real estate, and occasionally, art.

Sister Mary Rita did a wonderful job of cataloguing, storing, and preserving the many artifacts. The inventory consisted primarily of religious statues of saints and paintings depicting divine events. The nativity was especially popular, and the storeroom held more than a dozen depictions of the birth of Christ. Many years ago, Sister Mary Rita had logged in a damaged but lovely reproduction of Caravaggio's *Nativity with Saint Francis and Saint Lawrence*. The donor was listed as anonymous, and the large canvas had been rolled up for more convenient storage. Since the theft of the original from the altar of the Oratorio de San Lorenzo in Palermo in 1969, there have been countless reproductions commissioned, including a hi-tech facsimile by Factum Arte that hangs in the previously empty frame in the Oratorio. It is faithful to the original in every detail and is virtually indistinguishable from it.

As for the original, theories abound as to its whereabouts. Some say it was left in a barn and eaten by pigs. Another theory is that it was sold off to a Swiss buyer. Various turncoats have offered information on sightings, a recurring theme being that it had occasionally been displayed at certain high-level meetings in Sicily convened by the man known as Diabolik.

Maurizio Messina Denaro, the man known as Diabolik, had been a fugitive since 1993, and the mystery of the Caravaggio was eclipsed only by his legend. Sightings were called in from time to time, but he remained as elusive as the painting he came to be synonymous with. As long as Diabolik remained a ghost, hope for the recovery of the *Nativity* was dim.

In January of 2023, more than a hundred members of the Carabinieri and assorted Italian armed forces converged on a private oncology clinic outside of Palermo, where an unassuming man—now known to have been Maurizio "Diabolik" Denaro—suffering from colon cancer had been receiving chemotherapy. They took the man into custody and transported him to a prison hospital, where he eventually fell into a coma and died. It is rumored that in his final days, he was given last rites by a priest from his hometown of Castelvetrano. The priest beseeched Denaro that true absolution could only be granted upon a genuine act of contrition. He urged him to reveal the whereabouts of the *Nativity* as his final penance. It cannot be verified, but Denaro's final gesture to the priest was said to be one that was less than contrite, wherein the now withered Denaro smiled weakly, mustered all his remaining strength to bring his lone uncuffed hand to his chin, and with a flick of his fingers, gave the priest a Sicilian gesture that loosely translates as *fuck off*. And with that, Denaro took his last breath.

With the death of Diabolik, the hopes of recovering the *Nativity* dissipated like his ashes, which were spread over the Tyrrhenian Sea.

At the convent, Sister Mary Rita readied the last of the items to be moved to the rowhouse, including a large oriental rug the Sisters had generously donated to her geriatric brother. They had no use for it, and it had been sitting in the corner of the storeroom collecting dust for decades. She had arranged for a neighborhood handyman to assist her by loading the last of the items into a van and unloading them back at the rowhouse. There was never a shortage of helpful volunteers from the neighborhood ready to lend a helping hand to a Pink Nun. The handyman had arrived early, and the van was already backed up to the gate leading to the convent's makeshift loading dock in the alley behind the old building.

Sister Mary Rita turned to the page in the inventory log that listed the *Nativity* reproduction and tore it out. She glanced at the column alongside the entry titled E.V., for estimated value. She had logged it in over thirty years ago at $500.00. She chuckled to herself as she calculated how many zeroes she had left out. She crumpled the page and shoved it into a pocket beneath her habit. Now, the painting sat wrapped in the oriental rug, awaiting its journey back to the Duke, who had made a deal with certain New York associates before he was incarcerated. They had a Sicilian friend who wished to transport a painting to the United States for safekeeping, free from the prying eyes of the Carabinieri Art Squad. But the man known as Diabolik required collateral for this transfer. That's where the Duke had come in. He just happened to have a stolen painting of his own that needed to disappear for a while.

And that's how a Caravaggio set sail for the Port of Philadelphia, while at the same time, a Rembrandt stolen in the Gardner Heist, *A Lady and Gentleman in Black*, made its way across the Atlantic, bound for Palermo, farther away from the scrutiny of the FBI's Art Crime Team. Two masterpieces, one Dutch, one Italian, passing in the night. It was the perfect arrangement... until it wasn't.

# Chapter Twenty-Four

# "YOU GOT A PROBLEM, KID"

The Caffè was empty except for Nick and the guys. Frank arrived and lost no time in retreating to the kitchen to retrieve a basket of locally baked bread. He sat at the bar, and Alberto brought him a plate of extra virgin olive oil.

"Can't get this bread in Florida," Frank lamented.

"You said the same shit last time you came back," Gary said as he slid the half-curtains closed, covering the bottom section of the front windows.

Joey took great pleasure in hanging the "Private Club, Members Only" sign on the front door, something Gary hadn't allowed since... well, since the last time Nick had returned. So, when the little bell affixed to the front door jingled, they all turned in unison to see who had either the familiarity or the audacity to enter. They were way past the point of caring, and locking the door would have been an admission of concern that was simply unacceptable. Joey was situated behind the bar, his right hand resting on the shelf beneath the cash register, scratching the diamond grip of a Smith & Wesson with the fingernail of his index finger.

A guy about Joey's age stood on the top step, holding the door without stepping into the Caffè. He reached down to offer his hand to an older man who was taking his time on the steps, placing two feet on each landing and favoring his right side. Andy "Andy Boy" Caposecco slapped the hand away, reaching instead for the brass rail on the door. "Fucking hip," he groaned as he pulled himself up the last step and limped into the Caffè.

Gary pulled out a chair at the head of the table. Nick stood out of respect, but knew better than to offer any assistance. Alberto stood by dutifully, ready to take Andy's drink order. Andy pinched Nick's cheek and smiled. He took his seat and nodded to Alberto. "V.O. and water."

Alberto walked briskly to the bar, where Joey was leaning forward in anticipation of hearing the old man's take on events and hopefully, a plan for revenge. When Alberto returned, Andy proposed a toast to Nick's father. He may have been dead for a few years, but in Andy's view, this was still his place, and the first toast was rightly in his honor. He looked over his shoulder and raised his glass toward the reproduction of Rembrandt's *The Prodigal Son in the Tavern* above the jukebox. Virgil Corrado, the "Mad Painter of Rittenhouse Square," had lovingly depicted his old friend in the role of the prodigal, so that even in death, Tony DiNobile raised his glass in a perpetual toast.

Andy was big on following rules and was frequently called upon to adjudicate on matters of street etiquette and underworld protocol. The assembled crew followed his lead and echoed the toast. Andy gently placed his glass down after taking a sip and tapped his right palm on the table so softly that it didn't make a sound. Still, it had the effect of a gavel, as the assembled crew straightened their backs and gave the man their undivided attention. He turned to Nick and, in a gravelly voice, confirmed what they had all suspected.

"You got a problem, kid."

# Chapter Twenty-Five

# THE REMBRANDT WHISPERER

Andy filled them in on the story of Diabolik and the Caravaggio, the Duke and the Gardner painting, the swap, and the double-cross that had been revealed only after Denaro's death.

"When Denaro died, his successors decided they wanted the *Nativity* back, but the Duke turning into a vegetable complicated things."

"So why kidnap Joey? How does that help?" Nick asked.

"It got you here, didn't it?"

"Okay, I'm here. What makes them think I can find their painting?"

"Not for nothing Nicky, you did find two Rembrandts," Frank spoke up, referring to the two paintings, *The Return of the Prodigal* and *Christ in the Storm*, Nick had indeed played a part in recovering.

"Come on, Unc. You know better than anybody, I got lucky stumbling over those paintings. If they're counting on me, they're even more fucked than they think."

Andy held up his hand, cutting them off. "Don't sell yourself short, kid. You actually have quite a reputation on the other side."

Nick laughed. "Oh yeah? What do they think I am, some kind of art detective?"

"Not exactly." Andy gestured toward Alberto with his glass and made a circular motion with his index finger, the universal signal for drinks all around. Alberto returned with a tray of drinks, and Joey finally came out from behind the bar to join them. Andy raised his glass to Nick. "Sussurratore di Rembrandt." They clinked glasses.

"Care to translate?" Nick asked.

"Sure, kid. It's what they call you over there—the Rembrandt Whisperer."

Nick let that sink in. It felt like he was standing outside of himself, witnessing someone else's life. He was overcome with the worst kind of impostor syndrome, the kind that develops when other people see you completely different from your internal, truer self. Some embrace it. They start to believe their own press, living an outward life that conflicts with their truth. Some even prosper. But Nick had no intention of living a lie. He had come too far, overcome too many demons to give in to self-deceit. He felt like he could really use Grace's calming presence now, as well as Dave's sage advice.

"Let me ask you something," Nick said. "Why the sudden urgency, kidnapping Joey and all that? It all seems a little desperate if you ask me. I mean, I get they want their painting back and all, but they're still sitting on a priceless Rembrandt."

"Nicely done, kid. Maybe they're right about you after all," Andy answered. "That brings us to the second problem. The Rembrandt's been with Denaro all these years. Hardly anyone has set eyes on it, except for a few instances when he would display it on some special occasion. That's what they had previously done with the Caravaggio for decades before the swap."

"So what's changed?" Nick asked.

"Technology. That's what changed. That and some healthy curiosity. When the Duke was granted compassionate release, our Italian friends decided the time had come to switch the paintings back. After all, the *Nativity* was revered like a religious relic, which it kind of is."

"Funny how many people tend to get killed in pursuit of religious icons. Kinda ironic, isn't it?" Nick said.

"Irony or not, the Italians made preparations. To their credit, they wanted to return the Rembrandt in good condition, just like they expected to receive the *Nativity*. Both paintings had been cut out of their frames, as you well know. So they had a light restoration performed on the Rembrandt. They commissioned a well-known art restorer to do the work, and he had some tests performed, infrared something or other. Well, you can imagine what happened next."

"Reflectography." The voice came from a man who stood in the doorway to the kitchen. He looked like a homeless person who had wandered in after rooting through the dumpsters.

"What the fuck." Andy's guy moved toward the man and was about to tackle him when Gary moved in.

"Whoa, take it easy." Gary stepped between them, then turned to address the newcomer. "Yo, Virgil, why you sneaking through the kitchen like that?"

Virgil stared down at his feet. "I'm sorry. I saw the sign."

"What sign?" Gary asked.

"You know, Member's Only."

"Yeah?" Gary asked.

"Well, I'm not a member."

That relaxed everyone, and even Andy's guy let out a chuckle.

"You more than a member, Virgil. You family." Gary put his arm around Virgil and led him to a seat at the table. "Alberto, get Virgil a drink. What you drinking?"

"Tequila," Virgil answered.

"Get him a 1942," Nick spoke up. "Have a seat, Virgil. You're always welcome at Vecchio. Finish what you were saying."

Virgil took a sip of his 1942 and let out a long, satisfied *aaaahhhhhh.* "Infrared reflectography," the Mad Painter of Rittenhouse Square explained. "That's the test you were talking about. It looks beneath the surface of a painting, penetrates the pigments, and reveals the underdrawings."

"Sounds like something I'd like to use on a few people," Andy quipped, and everyone laughed… except Virgil.

"You can't use it on people," Virgil said.

"We know that, Virgil," Gary said. "It was a joke. Sorry, Andy, he don't mean no harm."

"No offense taken." Andy raised his glass, sensing that Virgil was on the spectrum. He had a nephew with autism and was sensitive to the signs. "Thank you for that clarification, Virgil."

Virgil raised his glass back to Andy and smiled.

"So the Duke gave them a fake Rembrandt?" Nick asked.

"Eh, I'm not so sure about that. I mean, the Duke was a slimy son of a bitch, and he was capable of some fucked-up shit—like what he did to his wife and that poor Mikey Fortuna kid—but I doubt he had the sophistication, and more importantly, the balls to fuck over the Italians like that. He's lucky Denaro didn't discover it before he died. No, I don't think the Duke was in on it. More likely, someone had switched it out from under him before he made the trade."

"So why don't they go right to him then?" Nick asked.

"I'm pretty sure they tried. They had guys on the inside at Devens, and they reported back that it was a lost cause. That's where you come in."

"How's that?"

"Well, they figure the original is still around South Philly somewhere, so who better to track it down than the Rembrandt Whisperer?"

Nick shook his head and retreated to the jukebox.

Virgil leaned over to Gary and asked, "Who's the Rembrandt Whisperer?"

# Chapter Twenty-Six

# HIGH NOON SALOON

**South Philadelphia - 1979**

Little Mikey Fortuna looked out the window of his sixth-grade classroom. There were exactly six minutes left in the school year, but it may as well have been six hours. His classmates were getting rowdier by the second, and Sister Teresa had given up on trying to maintain any semblance of order. Mikey passed the time by looking out the window and counting the planes that passed by in the distance. They took off from Philadelphia International Airport, and he imagined the wealthy and glamorous passengers on board, bound for exotic places he could only dream of. He had never been on a plane, but imagined himself inside one of the cylinders, hurtling toward some tropical paradise where everyone spent their days strolling on the beach, instead of dreading whatever threat lingered around each street corner. He looked back at the clock. Only one minute had passed. He made a bargain with the universe; if he counted at least two more planes before the bell rang, it would be a good summer, if not . . .

One plane passed. Mikey tucked his sketchbook under his arm. The classroom was boiling hot, and he was sweating through his parochial uniform dress shirt. The sleeves were too long, and the cuffs were turning black along the edges from rubbing against the charcoal pencil pictures he drew in the book—faraway places he only read about, places with palm trees and mansions on the beach, sketches of his sports heroes, sketches of that girl in the seventh grade. He didn't know her name, but she made a bug-eyed face at him once when she caught him staring at her in the arcade. He'd tried but failed to capture the way her lips shimmered from the tube of balm with the image of cherries on it, the one she seemed to apply constantly. Mikey imagined it must taste like cherry water ice. He imagined she would be kissing a boy later that night in the alley behind the arcade. Mostly, he imagined that one day he would be that boy.

When the bell rang on the last day of sixth grade and the second plane hadn't passed, Mikey made a new bargain; if he could run home and get through the door before three o'clock, it would still be a good summer. Maybe not as good as if the second plane had passed, but not a disaster. He bolted out the door and raced down the hall. His school shoes slipped a bit on the hallway floors the janitors had already begun waxing with the machine that spun in circles, but somehow remained in place. His shoelaces had broken off a few times over the school year, so now they were only long enough to cross over twice. He had resorted to tying one giant double knot that barely kept them on his feet. His heels slipped out a bit as he took the stairs two at a time, and he leapt down the last four and hit the sidewalk in a full sprint.

The candy store and the arcade whizzed by. He cut the corner hard at the High Noon Saloon, his shoes almost losing their grip as he skidded toward the curb. The sign for the High Noon was a picture of three cowboys. Mikey had no idea who they were, and the whole cowboy thing in the heart of South Philly made no sense to him. Besides, no one in the neighborhood called it by that name. Mikey and his friends just called it *The Bar*. He was in the process of switching his sketchbook from his right arm to his left as he turned the corner and prepared for the straightaway portion of his run home—*I'm going to make it by three*, he thought, *it's going to be a good summer*—when he ran into a brick wall. Well, it wasn't exactly a brick wall, but it may as well have been.

Four older guys, maybe twenty or so, were standing between a cellar gate and a telephone pole. The cellar gate was opened in an upright position as a beer truck was about to unload a delivery. Mikey had nowhere to go, and as he tried to stop, one of his shoes flew off into the street, while his sketchbook skidded across the sidewalk. Mikey fell to his knees. He felt his pants tear and then a hot burn where the skin on his knees peeled off. His momentum carried him straight into the biggest of the crew, who managed to catch him before he slid into the back of the beer truck.

"Whoa there, Flash, where's the fire?" The man had a cigarette dangling from his mouth, and it danced up and down as he said the words. He was gripping him under his arms, and Mikey felt ashamed because he knew they were wet with perspiration. He was certain the man would say something mean and the others would start to tease him, maybe make up some cruel nickname for him like 'Mikey Armpits' that would spread around the neighborhood and stick with him for life.

He tried to squirm away. "I'm okay, I'm okay," he repeated as he tried desperately to get to his sketchbook. One of the other men was bending over to pick it up. *Please God, don't let him open it.*

He opened it. "Hey, did you draw these?" The man was laughing. He seemed a little bit older than the others, but not as smart as the man who caught him. Something told Mikey that the man who caught him was the leader, and the one with the sketchbook answered to him. Even at twelve years old, Mikey was good at picking up on things like that. It turned out he was correct.

"Give me that." The man Mikey would come to know as JR snatched the sketchbook from the other man. "Hey," JR said, "you're bleeding."

Mikey looked down at his legs. His knees were torn up pretty badly, and he felt the warm blood running all the way down to his ankles.

JR put his arm around Mikey's shoulder. "Come on. Let's go get you cleaned up."

Mikey was feeling a little woozy and allowed JR to guide him. He figured the man was taking him to a hose or maybe a fireplug to wash off. The fire hydrants in the neighborhood were opened almost daily. The old ladies used them to clean the streets, and the neighborhood kids stayed under 'the plug' for hours. So he was more than a little surprised when JR led him to the door of the bar instead. Mikey froze as JR reached for the door. He'd passed this corner at least twice a day for as long as he could remember, but he had never glimpsed the inside. None of his friends had either. The door was heavily tinted and was surrounded by a metal frame. Sure, he had been close by when people went in or stumbled out, but it was pitch-black inside, and he could never make out the figures within. The door would close with a whoosh and sealed like Tupperware, swallowing up even the few musical notes that had managed to briefly escape. Sometimes, Mikey would stand on the opposite corner and watch the people come and go, playing a secret game of name that tune. He would tell himself, if he could name three songs before his eight o'clock curfew, one day he would be rich and marry that girl in the seventh grade. Now, he stood in front of the big black door and couldn't move.

"What's wrong, kid? It's okay, really, this is my uncle's bar. You'll be alright."

Mikey gripped the railing as JR tugged on the door, a gush of ice-cold air rushing out and caressing his face. It was barely three o'clock, but the jukebox was already blaring like it was midnight. Martha and the Vandellas announced they were "Ready for Love." Mikey blinked at the cool darkness. JR led him along a narrow pathway between the patrons standing at the bar on the right and the men seated at cocktail tables on the left. Red candles dotted the tables and lit a path to an unknown destination. In the far rear corner of the bar, a larger table was set off from the others.  A hulking figure sat with his back to the corner, enveloped by a red upholstered booth. Mikey couldn't see the man's face, but somehow, he sensed the man was looking at him. JR continued to guide him into the kitchen. A bow-tied cocktail waitress appeared with a wet bar towel and crouched gracefully to tend to Mikey's scraped knees. She had hair like Farrah Fawcett and wore black pantyhose beneath a short black skirt. When she knelt beside him, the hose stretched across her knees and became somewhat see-through. As she patched him up with a few Band-Aids from a first aid kit, her hair brushed against his face. The sweet smell of her shampoo made his head swim. He hardly felt the sting of the alcohol wipes. That smell, together with the song and the luxurious cold darkness in the middle of a hot sunny day, caused the earth to shift beneath his feet, and he knew his life would never be the same.

JR led him back out from the kitchen, and they sat together at one of the cocktail tables. He sipped on an ice-cold Coke with bright red cherries skewered by a tiny plastic sword. Even the ice cubes were fancy, with holes through the center, and Mikey tried but couldn't figure out how you made such a thing. His eyes began to adjust, and he looked over to see the man at the corner table. The man was smiling at him. Mikey felt like the man knew exactly what he was feeling—as if he were reading his mind.

"Vieni qui."

Mikey didn't speak Italian, but every young boy in the neighborhood with an Italian grandmother knew what the phrase meant. The man waved him over, and Mikey noticed the man's other hand was resting on his sketchbook. The man patted it gently and gestured toward an open seat. Mikey looked at JR.

"Go ahead, kid. That's my Uncle Sal. He won't bite." JR walked behind him, nudging him gently with a hand on the small of his back.

"You're Domenica's grandson, right?" Sal was bald, with thick glasses and teeth that seemed too bright for his weathered face.

Mikey just nodded. Most people called his grandmother Minnie, so he figured this man must really know her. The waitress was at the service bar, waiting for the bartender to make her drinks, and she smiled at the sight of Mikey sitting at Sal's table.

"I looked at your drawings while Julie was fixing you up. You've got real talent, young man." Sal slid the sketchbook across the tablecloth. Mikey took it and gripped it with both hands as he placed it on his lap. "It's nothing to be ashamed of, kid. You should be proud. Some of the world's greatest artists were Italian." Mikey shrugged. He felt his ears getting hot and wondered if they were turning red. "You play halfball?" Sal asked. Mikey nodded, not yet having found the confidence to speak. "I figured you did. I used to play too. I was pretty good until my high school baseball coach told me it would ruin my swing."

Halfball was a South Philly staple. A 'pimple ball,' a rubber ball with stars and bumps on its surface, was cut in half along its equator.

The pitcher would throw underhand with enough spin to deliver across the street to a batter wielding a broomstick bat. Hits to the first floor of the building opposite the batter were a single, second floor a double, third floor a triple, and over the roof a home run. The defenders could also make a catch off the wall for an out. It was a pretty basic game, but it possessed its own mythology and was almost a religion in the neighborhood. Mikey cut his finger with a razor blade once while trying to cut a pimple ball in two. He wasn't very good at halfball, or any other sport really, but he liked the ritual of it. He enjoyed calculating the angles of the objects in flight; he just wasn't as good as other kids at making his body move in the ways his mind told him it should.

Sal produced a pimple ball as if by magic and held it up before him. His hand practically swallowed the ball, and the light from the candle made a shadow on the wall that looked like a python devouring an apple. "I want you to take this ball home with you, but it's not what you think. Don't have a catch with it, don't bounce it on the sidewalk, don't even show it to anyone. This ball is magic."

Mikey must have smirked a little. He was old enough to know there was no such thing as a magic pimple ball.

"Don't believe me?" Sal arched one eyebrow as he gently gripped Mikey's hand, which he had balled up into a small fist. Sal unfolded Mikey's hand and placed the ball in it. Then he took his other hand and put it on top, enveloping Mikey's much smaller hand. He held it softly but firmly and gave it a shake as he said, "Bring this ball back to me tomorrow, and I'll turn it into twenty dollars. How's that sound?"

Mikey shrugged and muttered a soft "okay" that could barely be heard above the jukebox, which was now playing some song about the lights going out in New York City.

"Okay then, kid, it's settled. Just remember, no matter what you do, don't lose that ball."

JR walked over and stood next to the table. Mikey understood that meant it was time for him to leave, and JR put a hand on his shoulder. "Hey," Sal said. "Aren't you forgetting something?" He was holding up the sketchbook.

JR took it from Sal and handed it to him. He tucked it under his left arm and gripped the pimple ball in his right hand until he felt it compress. He stood there for a second in front of the table and locked eyes with Sal for the first time.

"What is it, kid?" Sal asked.

Mikey hesitated a moment, then blurted out what he was thinking. "This is a test, right?"

Sal smiled, and Mikey could hear JR chuckling over his shoulder. Sal rocked forward, not quite standing up, but leaning toward Mikey with an outstretched hand, pushing the table forward and causing it to make a low rumbling sound as it slid over the tile floor. He pinched Mikey's cheek between his thumb and forefinger. "Smart boy."

They walked toward the door but had to pause, as a man in dress slacks and an elaborate collared shirt was spinning Julie in a twirl that lifted her skirt. The man stopped for a moment, bowed, and swept his arm as he bent over at the waist, gesturing for them to pass. JR led the way, and Mikey trailed close behind. This man also pinched Mikey's cheek, which was starting to hurt more than his knees.

"Can I buy you a drink, kid?" the man said.

A few guys started to laugh. JR was already at the door, and Mikey desperately wanted to follow.  The man smiled at him. His hair was perfectly blow-dried in a style Mikey had only seen in the movies. Mikey thought he looked like John Travolta, but a little bit older. He put out his hand for Mikey to shake and introduced himself as Frank.

Mikey shifted the pimple ball to his left hand and wiped his hand on his pants, as it felt moist from gripping the rubber ball. Frank's teeth gleamed like pearls, and Mikey felt something placed into the palm of his hand as the man shook it.

"Mikey Fortuna," he mumbled, not wanting to be rude.

Frank burst out laughing. "Mikey Fortuna! I love it. That's a lucky name!" He tousled Mikey's hair as he walked past him.

Mikey put the twenty-dollar bill in his pocket as JR pushed open the door. They stepped out into the white heat of the outside world, and the door made the whoosh sound behind him. Before it shut, Mikey heard Frank singing a little improvised song to Julie. Mikey recognized the tune from the movie *Grease*, except instead of "Beauty School Dropout," the man replaced the lyrics with the five syllables that made up his name: "Mik-ey For-tu-na." He sounded pretty good.

"Hey, kid," JR said, "you know who that was?"

Mikey nodded. He hadn't quite figured it out until the man sang his name.

"You okay getting home?"

Mikey nodded again.

"Okay then, see you tomorrow." He said it like it was the most normal thing in the world, like it was preordained. He handed him his schoolbag, and Mikey walked toward home. His pants were a wreck, and his shoes had finally given out. Thankfully, school was over. He kept playing the events that took place in the bar over and over in his head like they were scenes from a movie. As he walked through the front door of his rowhouse, his grandmother was in the kitchen cooking, as usual. He put his schoolbag down on the floor, but never let go of the pimple ball. He placed the twenty-dollar bill in the candy dish on the kitchen counter without giving it a second thought.

His grandmother looked at him out of the corner of her eye and said, "What happened to your pants?" Then added, "And who gave you twenty dollars?"

Mikey wasn't about to tell her the whole story, but he didn't want to lie either, so before he even thought about it, he just blurted out, "Frankie Avalon." She smacked him lightly on the back of his head, never suspecting that he was telling the truth.

Mikey went upstairs, washed up a bit, and threw his pants and shoes into the bathroom trash can. He lay on his back on the bed, throwing the pimple ball up in the air, just short of the popcorn ceiling. He caught it with the same hand and kept doing it over and over as he thought about the bar, JR, and Sal. For all his young life, he had passed by that door nearly every day, never really knowing of the magical world that existed on the other side. He was like Dorothy strolling into Oz for the first time, and his narrow world had suddenly widened and burst into Technicolor. He watched the ball soar up, seeming to defy gravity for a moment, suspended in time. He no longer thought of his pants, or his pathetic shoes, his stupid friends, or even that girl in the seventh grade. He could only focus on the rising and falling of the pimple ball, certain that life as he knew it would never be the same.

His trance was finally broken by his grandmother calling him down for dinner. "Wash your hands," she added.

Mikey placed the pimple ball carefully on a shelf and braced it with his clock radio. He finally remembered his sketchbook and sat there for a moment with it in his lap. He ran his hand over the black, pebbly surface and felt an indescribable sadness; a melancholy nostalgia for something he hadn't yet lost but felt certain he soon would. He gently placed the sketchbook in the bottom drawer of his dresser, beneath his winter sweatshirts. Mikey told himself he would only keep it there for a while. He simply needed a break from his silly sketches while he focused on more practical things, like making money... and the pimple ball.

He never touched the sketchbook again.

# HAYWIRE TWIST

Sister Mary Rita had packed her meager belongings in anticipation of joining her brother. Aside from a duffel bag and an antique reading lamp, the largest item was an oriental rug bound up by twine and duct tape. The rolled rug was upright next to Sister Mary Rita on the small loading dock at the rear of the convent, where she stood at the top of the loading dock steps, gripping the railing with one hand and balancing the rug with the other. She was wearing a gray habit, as the sisters only wore the rose-colored habit within the confines of the cloister. The stairs led to the rear parking lot, which was surrounded by a razor-wire-topped brick wall. A metal roll gate protected the parking lot from a neighborhood that had become increasingly sketchy of late. Sister Mary Rita hit the button, raising the gate to allow the van to enter. It maneuvered in reverse, beeping rhythmically.

There were always a few unemployed, involuntarily retired barflies available and eager to pocket some drinking money for fixing a light switch or assisting in a move. One of the parishioners had referred just such a character to help Sister Mary Rita, and a price of two hundred dollars was negotiated—clergy discount. The man had even arrived an hour early, which was fine with Sister Mary Rita. He was dressed in drab blue coveralls, probably left over from his last official employment with PECO or PGW, no doubt, and some twenty years old from the looks of them. He had a non-branded ball cap pulled down tight over his head. From Sister Mary's elevated position, she could only see the bottom part of his face, covered in a predictable scruff. He gave a weak wave as he alighted from the van. He shuffled to the rear, a rolling gait betraying a long-delayed hip replacement, put off due to a reluctance to take a break from the demanding schedule of an 8:00 a.m. drinker.

Sister Mary waved back and silently gestured toward her belongings. The man nodded and walked around to the passenger side, opening the door as an invitation for her to take her seat for the short ride to South Philly. He pulled a hand truck from the van and pushed it up the ramp to retrieve her belongings as she pulled herself up into the van. The handyman had thoughtfully left the radio on, tuned to an easy listening station he figured the sister would enjoy, in spite of the fact she was technically prohibited from listening to secular music. He noticed she left it on, and it pleased him immensely.

He had spent the previous day preparing for the move, requisitioning the hand truck and moving blankets. He had also constructed a few custom tools for the job, cutting two four-inch sections of a broom handle and drilling a crossways hole through each. The handle's diameter was a bit larger than he preferred. Still, he thought it was unnecessarily risky to buy a dowel from Home Depot. He would have preferred a 49-strand shark rig cable secured to the dowels with a loop and double crimps, as he had fashioned many years ago, but settled instead for a single-strand, 86-pound-test wire finished with a trusty haywire twist. It was a bit susceptible to kinking, but would be serviceable for the application.

After he finished loading the van, the handyman lifted the hand truck and flipped it over to keep it from rolling around during the ride. He took great care in securing the Oriental rug, mindful of its value. He closed the rear doors from within, opting to make his way up to the driver's seat that way. He crouched a bit as he made his way forward. Sinatra's "Put Your Dreams Away" was playing low, and the handyman recalled it being the last song played at the crooner's funeral. Sinatra was fond of saying at the end of his concerts, "May you live to be a hundred and may the last voice you hear be mine." The handyman had always loved that line, and today, he loved it a little bit more.

"Hello, Rita," he said as he slipped the wire over her head. He hadn't accounted for the coif and veil that covered the back of Sister Mary Rita's neck, but still felt confident the garrote would do its job. He cinched it just tight enough to gain control of her, as there was something he needed to do first. He pulled her out of the passenger seat, into the space between it and the driver's seat. She instinctively clawed at the wire as the handyman positioned her in line with the rearview mirror and pressed his face against hers. Her eyes stretched open even wider and bulged out from the combination of the tightening wire and recognition of the man's face. He noticed the look and realized she had put it together; this thought gave him great pleasure. Sinatra's song had come to an end.

"Remember me, you fucking cunt?" He tightened the wire with renewed vigor as her mouth gaped open and she struggled to scream. "This is for Veronica." Tears streamed down his face as he added, "And my child."

Sister Mary Rita kept her vow of silence to the end. The last voice she heard on this earth wasn't Sinatra's, but Mikey Fortuna's.

# Chapter Twenty-Eight

# ANGELINA'S CLUB TANGIER

*Fate leads the willing, and drags along the reluctant.*
*Letters from a Stoic*, CVII, Seneca


Nick needed to get away somewhere and think. The whole "Rembrandt Whisperer" business was a lot to digest. He excused himself from the Caffè and the guys under the pretext of needing some rest after the flight and all the excitement. They all agreed to meet back up the next day, at which time Andy would have hopefully formulated a plan. But Nick had an ulterior motive. He borrowed the Fleetwood from Gary and headed over the Walt Whitman Bridge to the Atlantic City Expressway. Someone else had heard he was back in town, and the boldness of her text was rivaled only by its brevity. *Angelina's 3:00 p.m.*

There's a certain melancholy romanticism that can be found only in a dying city, where the sense of abandonment is so exquisite, one senses a morbid exclusivity upon entering its grid. Imagine being a VIP at a once-popular nightclub no one goes to anymore. The city holds you to her withered bosom, and despite yourself, you suckle on her dried-up teat. A final tepid kiss in the dying embers of yet another failed relationship.

A desperate welcome sign hung from an overpass above the expressway, declaring Atlantic City the "Entertainment Capital of the Jersey Shore." It made Nick sad to think of the well-meaning office drone who came up with the slogan and pitched it with a straight face to a portly bureaucrat.

At 2:45 p.m., Nick stepped over the threshold into yet another dark bar. He considered that he could chronicle his entire life as a series of moments just like this one, leaving the real world behind and stepping through portals of outrageous possibilities that just as often resulted in soul-crushing regret. Maybe, he thought, this time would be different.

Angelina's had closed for a time, and the new owners decided to bring it back as an homage to its original incarnation, Club Tangiers, which predated the heady '80s version Nick associated with his youth. It had undergone what could best be described as a reverse renovation. The décor seemed to have been sourced from the advent of the passage of casino gambling in Atlantic City, that magical moment in time when AC stood alone on the East Coast, and even the New York elite flocked here for a slice of the new hedonism. Nick had caught the tail end of the heyday, a fleeting rise that preceded yet another inevitable fall.

It was a quarter to three, but unlike Sinatra's version, it was afternoon. Nick found the afternoon every bit as magical as closing time and remembered a time when he sauntered into taprooms in the early afternoon to escape the sun, prying eyes, and his own conscience. It was also a good time to have the jukebox to yourself. The lunch crowd had vacated, the "first call" morning crew had sauntered off home for some fitful sleep before they returned for the second shift, and the happy hour people had yet to arrive. You might catch a few union construction workers coming off work at 2:00 p.m., grabbing a shot and a beer before heading home for dinner.

The place was empty except for the bartender and a lone figure at the end of the bar. Even in the shadows, she was beautiful, her face dramatically illuminated by neon like she had been painted there by Caravaggio in the style known as tenebrism. Angie was sipping her drink from a straw, and it made a slurpy noise as she got to the bottom of the glass. She patted the top of the red Naugahyde stool set next to her. It was newly upholstered and gave off a sharp crack like she had slapped a bongo. Nick leaned over the bar and ordered a Crown Royal on the rocks.

"Remember this place?" Angie smiled. It was a question meant to break the ice, not elicit a response. Nick must have met her here at least twenty times over the years, in all seasons.

"Something seems different," Nick quipped.

"My hair?" Angie flipped it as the bartender set down Nick's drink. He tossed a hundred onto the bar.

"No," Nick answered, like it was a serious question. "That's not it." Nick took in her scent as he kissed her on her cheek. He scooted the stool back a hair, making a screeching noise as the legs dragged across the tile floor, not yet committing to taking a seat. Angie must have arranged them like that before he arrived.

"I don't think anything's changed at all," Angie said. "In fact, that's why I asked you here."

That got Nick's interest, and he chuckled. "Care to explain?"

"I've been thinking about what you said to me once, about not ever stepping into the same river twice."

Nick took the bait. "And?"

"And I'm calling bullshit on that, Nick."

Nick took a sip of his drink, rearranged his coaster, and his eyes darted toward the front corner of the bar like he was looking for a trusty friend to bail him out of this conversation.

"Nick." She grabbed his hand with both of hers. "Look at me. It's gone." She was referring to the space where the old jukebox used to be. "There's no musical escape hatch from this conversation." Nick knew she was right.

"The answer isn't in some dusty jukebox, Nicky. It's sitting right here in front of you. A lot of water may have flowed by over the years, but it's always been the same river, the same force that causes it to flow. The same sensation when it rushes by your skin, envelopes your body."

"What are you saying, Angie?"

She stood and draped her arms on Nick's shoulders. "I'm saying what you already know, Nicky, what you've always suspected." She paused until she caught his gaze, and they locked eyes. "It's always been me."

Nick felt like he had lost his balance and edged backward until he found a seat on the stool. Angie followed and stepped forward between his legs until her face was inches from his. Nick thought about kissing her and wasn't sure what stopped him. Instead, he put his arms on her shoulders and eased her back gently, careful not to convey an outright rejection.

"Let's talk about this." That was the most innocuous phrase he could come up with in the moment. "Are you drunk?" he asked.

"I don't know, Nick. Are you? Okay, yeah, sure, I'm drunk. Maybe I've been drunk all my life. Maybe that's the only time I can face the truth . . . and maybe I don't ever want to be sober again."

"Look," he said, "I get it. I've been standing exactly where you are right now. You think I'm not tempted? Falling into your arms, ending up in bed, that would be incredible. I must be nuts for resisting. But then what? Where would that leave us? When the sun comes up, we're right back where we were all those years ago. How long before the novelty fades and all the fucked-up ugliness of the city consumes us?"

"I'm no fucking novelty, DiNobile. Take that back."

"I know you're not. It's not you and it ain't me. It's this whole sordid fucking world."

"So? Life is ninety-nine percent suffering and one percent ecstasy."

"What the hell is that supposed to mean?"

"You tell me. You're the one who said it. Remember? A long, long time ago. And I'm starting to believe you were right all along. I remember exactly where we were when you said it. If I close my eyes, I can picture you back then, your shirt off, looking out the window of my bedroom. The lights of the avenue on your face. You looked like some movie star." She closed her eyes. "I still see you like that."

"Angie. Please. Don't do this."

"Don't do what, Nick, speak the truth? I remember you once told me the only happiness you felt in life was the time we spent like that together, you inside me. It can be like that again."

That hit him hard. No matter how outrageous the notion was, Nick couldn't deny it sounded pretty fucking tempting.

"Even if that were true, and I'm not saying it is, there are other people involved here. What about Grace? She's innocent in all this."

"Really, Nick?" She raised one eyebrow while taking a sip of her drink. "Nobody's innocent in this ugly world. Besides, 'sometimes the innocent need to suffer.' That was another one of your cute sayings back in the day."

*Jesus Christ. Was I really that fucked up of a person to have said these things?* Nick thought. *Worse yet, have I even changed?*

"Did I really say all those things? What the fuck was wrong with me?"

"Nothing. You were just trying to survive at a brutal time and in an unforgiving place." Angie edged forward, closing the space between them. "I love you, Nick. It's always been you. I've never been so sure of something in my entire life. Maybe that love will devour us both, burn us to a cinder, but that doesn't make it any less real."

Nick measured his next words. Angie was in a fragile state. He knew this because twenty-five years ago, he had been in the same position, hoping, praying, pleading for a chance. It had almost killed him. He didn't want to hurt her, but he didn't want to give her false hope either. Besides, Grace was his life, his partner, his soulmate. . . if there was such a thing.

"I have to think about this, Angie," was the best he could come up with. It would buy him some time, and it wasn't entirely a lie. He was starting to feel a lot like Atlantic City; his life had been a series of dramatic rises and precipitous falls. His phoenix had risen so many times, he doubted it had the strength to fly once more. He looked around the bar at all the reconstituted memorabilia and wondered if a flightless phoenix could instead make a new life out of the ashes.

"Okay, Nick, I can do that for you. But there's something you have to do for me in the meantime."

"What's that?" He barely got the words out of his mouth when she leapt at him, wrapping her arms around his neck and kissing him. She pressed her body against him hungrily.

He thought about resisting, but Angie pushed him back on his stool and draped her arms around his shoulders. He momentarily indulged the silly notion that she had overpowered him and the convenient belief that this was where the universe had placed him. He knew that's what Dave would tell him. *Even Grace would—*

The thought of Grace brought him to his senses, and he gently, ever so gradually, nudged Angie away.

"Sorry, Angie. I can't do this." He excused himself to use the men's room. "I'll be right back." It was a convenient excuse and not entirely untrue.

He saw the disappointment in her eyes. She looked timeless, like she had been transformed along with everything else in Angelina's. Nick half expected to walk into the bathroom and see a thirty-year younger version of himself reflected back at him, and wondered, if given the choice, would he go back? But there was something else about Angie's look that gave him pause, something he had glimpsed in her eyes only once before, many years ago.

She looked vulnerable.

Nick made his way to the men's room. He stood at the sink. The vintage mirror possessed no magic. For a minute there, he had hoped perhaps the spell that had transformed the place had the same effect on him. *No such luck,* he thought, as his somewhat weathered visage stared back at him. He washed his face and realized he really did have to take a piss. Even the toilet was circa 1982. He flushed with his foot, not wanting to touch the handle, washed his hands, and reached for the door, but something made him pause. An eighties-era push-button telephone sat on the sink like a movie prop. For a fleeting moment, he entertained the thought that the bathroom was actually a time machine. If he could only get a dial tone and punch in the right sequence of numbers, he would walk out into another decade, preferably one before life had become so complicated, before Angie had slipped away. He took the phone off the cradle and placed it to his ear.

The silence was deafening.

He took a deep breath and steeled himself for the tough conversation he needed to have with Angie. Not so long ago, he would have sold his soul for a moment like this; Angie laying everything on the line and risking it all for another chance. Now, he couldn't help thinking that God or the universe or whatever the fuck there was out there had protected him from getting the things he had once so desperately desired. He wasn't sure where this was going, but he thought of Dave's advice—*amor fati*; love your fate. Here was a rare opportunity, he thought, a real-life opportunity for a second chance. The universe doesn't provide them often, and well, Nick had been burned enough to suspect that while he contemplated a plan to go back in time, the universe was laughing at his folly. He placed the phone back on its cradle.

He moved forward, stepping into the breach, and as he had done so many times in his life, vowing to surrender to this latest wrinkle in his journey. Nick turned the doorknob, eager to escape from the kitschy tomb and step into the present, whatever it held, like some dime-store Marcus Aurelius. But as his eyes adjusted to the relative darkness, he struggled to track fate's latest curveball.

Angie was gone.

He walked around the bar to where they had been seated. Her drink was still there, still sweating on a coaster. Maybe she had simply gone to the bathroom, but something didn't seem right. Angie would never have left her drink unattended, let alone the hundred-dollar bill Nick had tossed onto the bar. Maybe she had read through his bullshit once again and spared them both the heartache. That was the story of their tortured, decades-delayed relationship. One of them was always hanging on while the other pulled away, until they reunited a few years later, and by then, the roles had reversed.

"Excuse me." Nick waved to the bartender, who was wrestling with a VHS tape like Indiana Jones with an Egyptian relic. "Did you happen to notice where the girl went?" Nick had almost slipped and said, *my girl*.

"I think she left with your friend," he said.

"Friend? What friend?" Nick's voice had an edge to it, and the man snapped to attention. He put down the tape and walked over to Nick.

"The gentleman who was sitting back in the lounge before you guys came in. I just figured you guys were together. They walked out in a hurry. I thought they went out for a smoke, and well... I'm a bartender. I learned a long time ago to mind my own business."

"I'm sure you did, my man. Anything else you can tell me about my new friend?"

"Well, he had an accent too."

"What do you mean, too?"

"Like you and the girl. Maybe a little different. You're from New York, right?"

"Not even close," Nick snapped. He pushed the hundred toward the man and headed for the door.

He stood on the corner beneath the retro neon sign. It promised passage back to a nostalgic past that perhaps never really existed. His eyes darted up and down Arctic and Georgia Avenues.

Angie was nowhere in sight.

# Chapter Twenty-Nine

# SHOWGIRLS

Ralph flew into Philly and arrived at the Caffè the next day. Gary had called and told him the story Andy relayed about the Caravaggio and the forged Rembrandt. Ralph thought it best that he was on-site. If things went south, he would have to explain to Dmitry. Besides, Nino would hold down the fort at Blaine's while he was away, just in case there were any further developments down south.

They had all assembled at the bar by 1:00 p.m. and were waiting on Andy. Frank was already half in the bag and was going on and on about some bullshit story from 1982. Ralph groaned but couldn't help listening. Finally, he realized the only way to shut Frank up was to launch into a story of his own.

"This is the part I don't understand. You got this painting for years, decades, it's on the wall of a museum, and people flock to see it. Okay, some people have a look, they think it's nice, and keep moving. Some other people admire it, they study it, talk about the technique, and how brilliant the painter is. Still others are moved to tears; they fall in love with it. They write songs and books about it. Then one day, it's supposedly discovered that the picture wasn't painted by the artist after all. What now? All those people were wrong? All those emotions and smiles and tears, they weren't real? I don't buy it." Ralph paused to take a sip of his Crown Royal.

Frank leaned back in his stool, arms folded, gazing at his shoes. He took a cocktail napkin, spit on it, and pretended to buff something off the tip of his loafer.

"What? You got an opinion on this?" Ralph snapped.

"I didn't say anything," Frank said.

"Exactly. I know how you work, Stone Crab, I can practically see the wheels turning in that cement head of yours."

Frank took a drag of his Marlboro and used the time to craft his response. "Gina Gershon," he stated cryptically as he exhaled an impressive plume of smoke.

"Yeah. What about her?" Nick asked. He just knew this was going to be good.

"I was obsessed with her ever since that movie with the girl from *Saved By The Bell*."

"Elizabeth Berkley?"

"Yeah, that's her."

"*Showgirls*," Nick answered. "A real cinematic masterpiece. I didn't realize you were such a film buff, Unc."

"I didn't say it was *Citizen Kane*, Nicky. It was a real T&A fest for sure. But that Gina Gershon, *Madone*, I couldn't get her out of my mind."

"I felt the same way about Rita Hayworth in *Affair in Trinidad*." Ralph got up and walked toward the kitchen. "But if this is headed where I think it's headed, I think I'll take a pass."

"Anyway," Frank resumed, "I see this girl in the liquor store on Federal one afternoon. A real knockout. She was standing in front of the wine section, and I could see she was struggling to pick something out. She was holding a bottle of Barolo and reading the label.  So, I say to her, 'What are you serving, leg of lamb?' She turns to look at me and laughs. That's when it hit me. For a minute, I thought it was really her."

"Elizabeth Berkley?" Joey asked.

"No," Frank snapped indignantly. "Pay attention. Gina Gershon."

"Sorry," Joey said.

"Anyway, we get to talking. I recommended a Brunello di Montalcino."

"Real fucking sommelier this guy. I remember when you drank Ripple in a paper bag in Southwark schoolyard." Ralph had wandered back. Truth be told, he wanted to hear Frank's story. The Stone Crab still told a great tale.

Frank ignored the interruption and continued. "I asked her if she had plans for the bottle. She said no. I said I know a great BYOB on Federal Highway. She smiled that toothy smile with the sneering lip, just like Gina Gershon in *Showgirls*. I was mesmerized. I grabbed two more bottles, a Tignanello and a Gaja Barbaresco, figuring we would have us a little tasting."

"You sprung for Tig and Gaja?" Ralph asked.

"I had a good week. Let me finish my fucking story for Chrissakes."

Ralph shrugged and smiled, indicating he wouldn't interrupt anymore.

"I took her to my buddy Radar's restaurant on Las Olas. He put me on Broadway, as usual, laid out quite a spread. Fuckin charcuterie board would have choked a horse. Made me out like I was the Sultan of Brunei."

"He was a great kid," Ralph said. "I miss him dearly."

"Fucking prince," Nick added. "Sorry, Unc. Please continue."

"It's okay, I miss him too." They all raised a glass, pausing the story to acknowledge their old friend. "So, dinner was amazing. She's loving the wine and my stories, and it occurs to me."

"That you're broke?" Ralph said. Everyone chuckled.

"I thought you weren't going to interrupt. No. I was flush, like I said. Plus, there *was* no check. I told you our boy gave me the royal treatment."

"There it is." Ralph couldn't resist.

"As I was saying. It occurs to me that here I am, sitting with this beauty who happens to be a dead ringer for Gina Gershon, and we're drinking wine in my buddy's restaurant, and the food is amazing, and she's laughing at all my jokes, and I think to myself, what's the fucking difference?"

"I don't get it," Ralph said.

*I think I do*. Nick thought.

"I could have been sitting in the Beverly Wilshire, drinking Cristal with the real Gina Gershon, and I wouldn't have been having a better time. So to answer your question, Ralph, it's all a fucking illusion and nothing really matters except the way it makes you feel."

"So what happened with her?" Joey chimed in.

"My usual." Frank smiled. "I took her back to my cabana at the Royal Palm and nature took its course."

"You mean you took her back to Rochester Benny's cabana, and whatever did or didn't take its course had less to do with nature and more to do with Viagra and all that wine you poured down that poor girl's throat."

"Thanks for the kind words, Ralph. But for your information, she only had three glasses, one from each bottle. But my point remains, sometimes a knockoff is just as good, if not better than the real thing."

Ralph cupped his hand to his ear and squinted. "Did you hear that?"

"What?" Joey responded.

"I think I just heard Gina Gershon sighing in relief."

The room erupted in laughter, but even Ralph would have to later admit that the old man had made his point in classic Frankie the Stone Crab style.

# Chapter Thirty

# THE ORANGE LOOP

The man had a distinct Brooklyn accent, adding Rs to the end of words that should have concluded in vowels. It was a phenomenon known as "intrusive R" and ironically grew out of the non-rhotic accent, which drops the R sounds after vowels. Angie knew it well. Her grandfather, Biagio, had arrived from Italy and settled in Brooklyn before moving to Philadelphia in the seventies. She wasn't precisely sure of the reason for the move, but she had heard whisperings over the years about another family he had in Palermo and a vague reference to a *vendetta*. He held on to the accent as stubbornly as the grudge.

"Relax, no one's going to hurt you." The man sat in the back seat of a sedan Angie had been guided to ever so gently; the barrel of a gun, resting gingerly against her ribs, had obviated any show of brute force.

"Maybe I'd believe you if your flunky hadn't jabbed a gun into my back and forced me into the car."

The man was pleased by Angie's reaction and chuckled like she had lived up to his expectations. She stared daggers at him as she sat opposite in the back seat.

"Look, Angie, we need your help, and whether he knows it or not, so does Nick."

Angie jumped a bit at the mention of Nick's name. The man was probably more than eighty years old, and he had a gentle face that smiled easily. This made Angie even more concerned. A man of that age, so soft spoken yet able to direct a goon to snatch her so efficiently, was no doubt an apex predator.

"I can see you're a bit doubtful." The man raised a liver-spotted hand and gestured rhythmically, like he was conducting an invisible orchestra. "If you weren't Biagio Romano's granddaughter, you'd have a hood over your head right now. And your boyfriend? If he wasn't Tony DiNobile's son, he'd be chained to a fucking radiator in a warehouse so remote that only the rats would hear him scream. So forgive me, but can we dispense with the bullshit?"

"He's not my boyfriend." For some reason, that was the first response Angie thought of.

"Really? Now it sounds like you're bullshitting yourself."

"Well, maybe I was working on that until somebody pulled me away so rudely. If we're all being so cordial, and you had even a shred of respect for my grandfather, you would have simply introduced yourself, and we could have discussed all this over drinks. Which, by the way, I didn't even get to finish."

The man nodded a bit as Angie was speaking and rubbed his chin when she finished, seeming to consider her words. "No," he said finally. "That would have been too risky. This works better." Then added with a broad smile, "Believe me, this is how your grandfather would have done it."

Angie folded her arms in resignation. She wasn't going to be able to negotiate with this old scorpion.

"Look," the man said after a minute of silence. "Maybe you're right. I'm just saying, you don't get to be my age, troubling yourself with etiquette. But if I came off a little rude, allow me to start over. My name is Angelo." He reached out a bony, arthritic hand, and against her better judgment, Angie unfolded her arms and gripped it gently.

"How did you know my grandfather?" she blurted.

Angelo appeared caught off guard by her boldness and had little choice but to answer.

"Eh, it was a long time ago. I looked up to him. He was ten years older than me and kind of took me under his wing."

"And?" Angie pressed him.

"And then shit happened."

"What kind of shit?"

"What kind of shit? The same shit that Italians have allowed to divide us for centuries, while other nationalities stuck together and became collectively rich. Perceived slights, jealousy, gossip, stupid fucking grudges."

"You won't get an argument from me about that. South Philly's even worse than New York in that respect."

Angelo coughed a little. "Very true. These maniacs would practically kill each other over two words."

"What two words?"

Angelo looked at her like the answer should have been obvious. "Sauce and gravy."

Even in her present circumstances, Angie had to snicker at that.

"Your grandfather taught me everything. I emulated him, loved him even." He caught himself. "Who said anything about New York?"

"Please." Now it was her turn to give '*the answer should be obvious*' look. "There's something you're not telling me."

"You hearing this?" Angelo shouted over the headrest to the goon who had snatched her. "Pay attention, you could learn something from this girl." He turned back to Angie. "You're right, beautiful. I left something out." He looked away from her and gazed out the window as vacant buildings, low-budget hotels, and the occasional cannabis dispensary whizzed by. They were moving at a pretty good clip, and it seemed the driver was pacing himself to time the traffic lights. They hadn't come to a complete stop since they pulled away from Tangiers. Angie considered making a dive out the door and onto the sidewalk, but that option was fraught with complications. She decided her chances were better inside the car.

They turned onto Tennessee Avenue and entered an area known as the Orange Loop, after the Monopoly game. It was just off the Atlantic City Boardwalk and bordered to the south by New York Avenue. Like most other areas of Atlantic City, it was once something glamorous but now mainly consisted of vacant lots and dilapidated buildings. Some intrepid developers had nonetheless embarked on a noble mission of revitalization, resulting in a few successful businesses, anchored by a beer hall and a beloved cigar lounge. Angelo had jumped in and scooped up a few old, boarded-up rooming houses. They were surrounded by presumably vacant buildings and abandoned parking lots.

"It was over a girl," Angelo said after a while, as he continued to stare out the window. It appeared to Angie that his eyes had become misty. She felt it was the first thing he had said since she'd been in the car she could trust to be true.

She let out a breath she had seemingly been holding since Nick walked into the bathroom at Angelina's. The admission made the man seem a bit more human. Still, she'd had more than her share of manipulative men pretend to share confidences in furtherance of their sinister schemes. Still, her sense of self-preservation suggested the only way out of this situation was to negotiate with him. Her mind began to race with ideas. Maybe a deal could be struck.

"Isn't it always?

"It usually is." Angelo nodded in agreement. "Except sometimes..." He turned away from the window to look her in the eyes. "Sometimes, it's over a painting."

That's when Angie saw her opening.

# Chapter Thirty-One

# DEAL WITH THE DEVIL

*"Who holds the devil, let him hold him well, He hardly will be caught a second time."* Johann Wolfgang von Goethe

"I can help you get the painting." It was a risky gambit, but Angie figured it was the only leverage she had, so she took a shot. She had no idea whether she could deliver on the bold statement, but she announced it with a certainty that got the old man's attention. She needed to get him thinking she was more than some pawn in this game he had been playing before she was born. The damsel in distress role didn't suit her, so she reverted to what she knew best. He may be old, but he was still a man, and Angie had never failed to deliver when it came to bending men to her will. If he had even one milligram of testosterone still coursing through his calcified arteries, she would find a way to take full advantage of it.

At first, his left eyebrow raised just a little. Then he started to nod as a smile began to form on his weathered face. Soon enough, he launched into a combination chuckle/cackle that caused him to wheeze and cough as he slapped his knee in satisfaction.

*The power has shifted*, Angie thought.

"You really are your grandfather's granddaughter," Angelo said. "Biagio would be proud of you." He paused. "But please, beautiful one, don't doubt for a second that I'll slit that pretty throat if you try to fuck me over."

Angie smiled like his threat had no effect on her and put out her hand confidently to shake on it, but it chilled her to the bone. Angelo took her hand in his. She may as well have been shaking the hand of a corpse thrusting from beneath the soil.

"You got a deal," Angelo confirmed their Faustian bargain, and Angie felt a little bit of her soul leaking out of her body and transferring to this devil's bony appendage.

They pulled into a weed-strewn lot, and the driver positioned the passenger side so close to the wall of the adjacent building, Angie had no choice but to wait for Angelo to exit before she was instructed to slide over and get out on the driver's side. She sensed she was still at gunpoint, albeit through her captors' jackets. Either way, she wasn't making any mad dashes. She felt she could navigate this situation on the strength of her wits and abundant charm.

The driver opened the back door to the rooming house and pulled on a chain to a bare bulb that illuminated an ancient stairwell. He gestured for her to enter first. She started up the stairs, with the goon and Angelo close on her heels. The stairs groaned audibly as the three of them ascended. Angelo lagged behind, gripping a worn railing and placing both feet on each tread, pausing briefly at each step. A cane draped unused over his bony forearm. The goon unlocked a door that had been painted over so many times, the beveled panels were practically smoothed over. The door swung open, and he gestured for Angie to enter.

A musty odor of ancient wood combined with mothballs filled her nostrils. Light filtered in through a kitchen window with a view of a red brick wall. Dust swirled in the ray of light, and Angie caught her first glimpse of an old iron radiator. In the low light, there appeared to be a snake coiled around its base. As her eyes adjusted, she realized the body of the snake was in fact a chain, and its head a padlock. She remembered Angelo's comment on the ride over and suddenly felt drunker than she was, as the room began to spin.

Angelo had finally made it to the top of the stairs. She turned to face him as he walked through the door. She forced a weak smile as she fought back the urge to vomit.

"Nice place you got here," she said, trying to sound confident, as if being abducted were an everyday occurrence for her.

"I'm glad you like it." He was breathing hard and paused before adding, "You might be here for a while."

He pulled out a chair for her and took his own seat at a kitchen table that must have been around since the bicentennial. He collapsed back into the chair in a huff, basically falling the last six inches. Angie made a mental note that it would probably take quite an effort for him to get back up without assistance.

"Richie," he barked at the goon. "Make us some coffee."

Angie took a seat, crossed her legs, and folded her hands on one knee as casually as she could, given she was essentially a hostage. She spun a tale about star-crossed love, forgery, and betrayal. She sprinkled it with truthful anecdotes she had heard whispered over the years—some from Nick, but mostly from her grandfather—about the Duke, the

Bamboo Inn, a painting, and a ghost who once roamed the streets of South Philly and went by the name of Mikey Fortuna.

# Chapter Thirty-Two

# ANDROMEDA

Grace saw Arjun as he dashed across Federal Highway and made his way to the Chick-fil-A where she sat waiting for him with a twelve-piece nugget meal. She was pleased to receive his text asking to meet and relieved he wasn't with his father. He looked a bit more disheveled since their last meeting, and Grace could swear he was wearing the same clothes.

"Hello, Arjun, how are you?" she said as he slid into the booth and scooted over to the window.

"I'm okay, I guess." His eyes were darting from the window to the nuggets and back.

Grace pushed the tray and drink over to his side. "It's okay, I'll keep lookout. Why don't you have your nuggets and we can talk when you're done?"

He reached for them but paused to take a napkin, which he placed six of the nuggets onto. He slid them over toward Grace.

"Thank you, Arjun. That's very sweet. I'll just have one if you don't mind."

Arjun wolfed down the other eleven, and Grace wondered when was the last time the boy had enjoyed such a small treat. Not two blocks away, crowds lined up at the latest sushi sensation for omakase at $200 per person. South Florida was nothing if not a study in contrasts. Outrageous wealth brushed up against abject poverty like they were old classmates meeting up at a high school reunion.

Arjun folded his napkin diagonally, dabbed at the corners of his mouth, then used it to sweep up any crumbs into his hand, depositing them on the tray. Grace watched him and marveled at his poise. Home life must have been hell for the boy, yet he maintained a quiet dignity that Grace decided would serve him well in life. Soon, he would break free from the gravity of the seedy motel and embark on a life more in keeping with his intellect. Grace was certain of it. She reached for his hand and held it gently, causing him to look up and make eye contact.

"You said you had something to tell me. Is it about Kim?"

Arjun shook his head and took the last sip from his Coke.

"No, it's about the man with the Rolls-Royce."

"Has he been back at the hotel?"

"Not exactly." Arjun began to fidget with his straw, and it made an irritating sound as he nervously jiggled it in and out of the cup's opening.

"Arjun." Grace addressed him gently but firmly. His dark eyes rose up tentatively to meet hers, still uncertain whether to trust her. She smiled a little, and she was now holding his hands in both of hers. She considered that to the few customers seated near them, she probably appeared to be a concerned teacher or perhaps a social worker, not wanting to push the boy away, but not willing to risk losing him. Maybe she was a little of each.

"I was out on the balcony Thursday night. I had my telescope set up to view the Andromeda Galaxy. The sky was cloudy, so I had pretty much given up. My uncle Vijay owns the motel across the highway, and I noticed the car outside the office."

"How can you be sure it was the same car?" Grace considered for the first time that maybe he had just invented an excuse to see her and get a free Chick-fil-A meal. Not that she cared. She liked Arjun and, frankly, would be fine meeting up with him weekly to check in on him and make sure he was doing okay.

"It's possible it wasn't, but I don't think so."

"What is it, Arjun? You can trust me," Grace assured him.

"There was a girl. She got out and walked in front of the car before going to a room. For a second, I thought maybe it was Kim, but I'm sure it wasn't. This girl had much longer hair and was older. By the time I swung the telescope around, she was already in the room."

"What about the Rolls-Royce, did you see the man inside?"

"No, he pulled away while I was trying to focus on the girl."

"Okay, Arjun, thank you. Can I get you anything else?"

Arjun shook his head.

Grace had resigned herself to the idea that Arjun had an active imagination and likely welcomed the opportunity to sit with her for a dose of normalcy in an otherwise chaotic life. "Anytime you want to meet up, just give me a call or text. I really enjoy seeing you." She thought she saw the beginning of a smile on his face, but it receded as soon as it appeared. They started to gather their things, and Arjun neatly stacked his tray and trash for disposal.

"One more question, Arjun. You said that at first, you thought maybe it was Kim. Why did you think that?"

Arjun shrugged. "Well, she had the same kind of shirt on that Kim used to wear to work."

Grace considered the implications of Arjun's observation. Someone, presumably the same man who had accompanied Kim at the Sunset Inn, was now shuttling another Tiki waitress to an even seedier motel on Federal Highway. Kim had been missing and unreachable since she no-showed two weeks ago. What was the simplest explanation? Grace didn't want to acknowledge the darkest possibilities.

*This sweet, sweet kid*, Grace thought. Here he was, straining for a glimpse of a galaxy two and a half million light-years away, anything that suggested his current predicament was only a temporary aberration in his cosmic destiny. She wanted to scoop him up and hug all the hurt away. Of course, the world doesn't work that way, and she needed to get back to the Tiki to tell Ronnie Cruz everything she had learned. Perhaps he would have a better read on this development. Maybe he would have some idea about the second Tiki waitress, and the man behind the wheel of the Rolls-Royce.

She wanted to kiss the top of his head, but squeezed his hand instead. He got up from the table, dutifully disposed of their trash, and skittered back across Federal highway, cautious as a scrub lizard.

# Chapter Thirty-Three

# PIMPLE BALLS AND DREAMS

**South Philadelphia – (1979-1987)**

Mikey brought the pimple ball back to the bar the next day. He wore his best shirt, a striped Chams de Baron tee his grandmother had bought him for his birthday, gelled his hair with the last remnants of a rolled-up tube of Tenax, and splashed his face with Aqua Velva from a dusty bottle he found in the hall closet. He was still afraid to walk in by himself, so he stood by the railing waiting for someone to notice him lingering. He had the strange sensation someone was watching him from the other side of the tinted glass. Per Sal's instructions, he didn't bounce the ball. His friends looked on from the northeast corner of 9th & Morris in a mixture of jealousy and concern. They were free to hang out on three of the corners of the intersection, but the northwest corner, where the bar was located, was strictly off-limits.

Their concern turned to amazement when JR opened the door, put his arm around Mikey's shoulder, and led him into what they imagined to be some South Philly version of Disney World. He was led to a table, and the waitress from the other day brought him a Coke. She bent forward and lit a candle that barely illuminated the cozy darkness. The candlelight flickered off her cleavage, anointing Mikey with its reflective glow. A man with two days of stubble and a *Racing Form* rolled up in his left hand pulled on the handle of a cigarette machine; it sounded like someone racking a 12-gauge. This, he decided, was yet another step in the initiation that had begun when he first fell outside.

He would retain that belief for the rest of his life—that sometimes misfortune preceded the most improbable series of events, and theretofore unimaginable adventures. The cocktail waitress punched in some numbers on the jukebox she apparently knew by heart, and a bluesy saxophone blared the opening notes of Evelyn "Champagne" King's "Shame." Mikey had watched that girl from the seventh-grade dance to the song at the St. Nicholas of Tolentine school dance and had imagined himself swirling her around, but instead, he remained leaning against the safety of the water fountain. He thought she caught him staring at her, so he pretended to crouch down for a sip.

He wished she could see him sitting there now. Perhaps some strange twist of fate would cause her to appear at the door with a scraped knee of her own, and after the cocktail waitress patched her up, she would sit at the table with him. He would order her a Coke, and she would look at him the way the waitress looked at Frankie Avalon. He considered this for a moment before deciding it was a silly thought and could never happen, except in the movies. No, he decided, she wasn't allowed in here, but he, Mikey Fortuna, was.

*Fuck her*, he thought, and at that moment, he made a resolution. He would do whatever Sal and JR asked him to do. He would follow their instructions to a tee. Because he was never leaving *this*. His friends, he concluded, were wrong.

This was way better than Disney World.

Turns out, what they asked him to do was simple—carry the pimple ball from one place to another. And so he did. Mikey shuttled the pimple ball between the bar and the many corner stores, delis, and cafes that populated the neighborhood. Weeks turned into months. Somewhere along the way, he discovered the slit along its equator that permitted items to be stashed within, and he occasionally peeked inside. Sometimes the contents were light: pieces of paper with numbers on them. He would squeeze the ball gently, just like Julie squeezed the lime wedges into the Beefeater and tonics he started drinking at the age of thirteen after hearing David Ruffin extol its pain-soothing powers on "I Miss You (Part 1)." The slit in the ball would pucker up like two thin lips, and the unmistakable scent of money escaped from within.

Months turned into years. The twenties became hundreds. He filled a duffel bag in his bedroom closet with the hundreds, reserving the smaller denominations for his living expenses. With JR's guidance, he opened a corner video store, a beeper store, a detail shop, and eventually, a café of his own. Sal and JR conducted business at each location.

It was a midsummer day, indistinguishable from any other day of the long, hot summer of 1985, when he walked in to find JR seated alone at the corner table. No one said much about it. One day, Sal was there, and the next day, he wasn't. Mikey wouldn't learn the details of his hasty departure until some twenty-five years later.

As the years passed, the pimple balls became heavier... and riskier. JR recruited another boy from the neighborhood to shuttle them around. When the young boy first strolled into the bar on a blazing hot afternoon in his parochial school uniform, Mikey readily recognized the familiar look of wonderment on the red-cheeked urchin's face. Mikey moved behind the bar. It was the perfect vantage point to observe the daily travails of drunken humanity, the hugs and kisses that preceded the inevitable betrayals. He took it all in with hardly a word, poured drinks, made his collections, and filled the duffel bag until the zipper broke from the strain.

On his twenty-first birthday, after blowing out the candles on a rum cake from Termini's Bakery, he decided his fortune ultimately lay outside the confines of the bar. What once possessed all the possibilities in the universe suddenly felt suffocating. The music became repetitive, and even Julie's beauty began to fade, the lights of the jukebox revealing a new frown line or two on her still beautiful visage. Nonetheless, the bar continued to hold a nostalgic spell over him. God knows he wouldn't shake it for years. Maybe he never did. The wistful yearning for a time and place that had given him a way out, albeit in exchange for the loss of his childhood. He only knew one thing for sure—he had to get out, or eventually he would die there.

But he underestimated how deep his roots had grown, how intertwined they had become with an ecosystem that rewarded blind obedience and punished evolution. It would take him years to extricate himself. Each new effort to escape found him slipping and skidding to an inglorious fall, not unlike that first tumble, except the consequent injuries became a great deal worse than scraped knees.

The years passed, and his efforts to transcend the neighborhood sputtered along a cycle of momentary liberation quickly followed by some crisis that demanded his return. Nonetheless, he continued to prosper, adding real estate and stocks to his diverse portfolio. His net worth swelled, and he plotted a move to the West Coast.

It was on a nondescript day filled with the mundane tasks that comprised his utilitarian existence when everything finally changed. Like all truly life-altering catalysts, this one came without warning and in the absence of any forethought on his part. He had a meeting scheduled for 3:00 p.m. at the Bamboo Inn, one not unlike any number of appointments he attended on any given week: an introduction; a favor requested or returned; a benediction sought or bestowed. It was all a stealthy subterranean soap opera that mimicked the daytime serials, except with better acting.

# Chapter Thirty-Four

# GIRL WITH A HOOP EARRING

**South Philadelphia**

**Summer 1987**

It was July of 1987. Jody Watley was "Lookin for a New Love," and U2 still hadn't found what they were looking for. Mikey Fortuna walked into the Bamboo Inn from the blazing hot afternoon streets and was stopped dead in his tracks by a vision standing behind the bar. She turned her head at the sound of the opening door, her face side-lit by the harsh glow of the beer box as she gazed over her shoulder at the visitor. They locked eyes, and in that moment, the universe composed a three-act play, sealing their fate. Like all narrative works, however, whether it would be comedic or tragic depended largely on where in the timeline the tale would conclude. So for the time being, like Schrödinger's cat, both potentialities existed simultaneously.

She wore a headband, and her mouth was slightly open. Eyes, lips, and the one earring he could see formed a triangle whose vertices vied for his attention. His eyes darted from one point to another in a doom loop. She was not unlike Vermeer's *Girl with a Pearl Earring* in this respect, except her earring was of the hoop variety.

Mikey realized he was standing there motionless. The door had closed behind him what seemed like an eternity ago. Mercifully, a drunk stumbled out of the bathroom, distracting Veronica. Otherwise, Mikey might still be standing there today, such was the strength of the spell. He took a seat at the far end of the bar, where he could possibly compose himself before she came over for his drink order.

His appointment, a masonry contractor from the neighborhood looking for a bridge loan to acquire and renovate a triplex in Queen Village, walked in soon after. He took a seat on a stool next to Mikey. His presence only slightly deflected Veronica's luminance, but Mikey was able to get out his drink order when she approached them.

The man introduced himself as Carlo in a comforting broken English. His cadence was soothing, and his inflections connected the harsh English words together in a lyrical style that was pleasant to the ear. He shook Mikey's hand. The texture was rougher than cinderblock, and Mikey knew right then and there Carlo was good for the loan. Not that it mattered. The collateral was so secure Mikey couldn't get hurt. Still, something about this guy's humble demeanor had him rooting for his success. Veronica returned with a Beefeater and tonic, along with a Bud for Carlo. They clinked glasses as Veronica walked back along the length of the bar. Mikey watched her through the barback mirror.

The terms of the deal were ironed out and sealed with a handshake and a shot of sambuca. Mikey added the anticipated revenue to the invisible ledger he maintained in his head. He would incorporate it into the calculations he performed obsessively each morning. The sum of these calculations added up to the trajectory of his anticipated journey. On that day when the numbers aligned, his rocket would ignite, and he would lift off to a destination far removed from the taprooms of South Philly. But for the present, ignition was delayed indefinitely by the face and figure of Veronica Gallante.

Carlo left soon after knocking back his sambuca, and Mikey did his best to blend into the wallpaper of regulars, tinkering with the jukebox and sipping on his drink. He strived to come up with a song that captured the precipitous moment he found himself on the edge of. He suspected his life was about to change, but instead of fear, he found himself exhilarated by the prospect of having his destiny altered by something as seemingly innocuous as the choice of a song. He hadn't felt a sense of magic so intense since he was twelve years old and first walked into the High Noon Saloon with scraped knees. He was still nursing his Beefeater and tonic and decided to play the tune that inspired his first cocktail all those years ago. David Ruffin's angst-ridden vocal on "I Miss You (Part 1)" soon filled the room with an ooze of heartache, and Mikey wondered how it was possible to miss a girl he hadn't yet kissed.

It was the perfect song.

Veronica came over to check on his drink, and so began a series of playful conversations that would continue over a series of months. Mikey did his best to emulate the snappy banter of a 1940s leading man, maintaining what he was sure was an enticing air of indifference. Veronica saw right through his act but was nonetheless charmed by the effort. Besides, it was all unnecessary; there was a chemistry between them that required neither artifice nor pretense. It was simply a matter of time before opportunity entered this volatile equation of sexual attraction they both imagined to be the burgeoning of romantic love.

Opportunity came knocking at closing time on a slow Tuesday night. Mikey had been staying late every night for the past two weeks and waiting for Veronica to lock up, a courtesy that could be interpreted as chivalry but was in truth a desperate longing masquerading as gallantry. Of course, Veronica wasn't fooled for a moment, as evidenced by her silence as she took his hand in hers after turning out the neon lights in the windows. She led him to an upstairs apartment usually reserved for drunks who had lost the ability to walk home or been put out by a wife who had finally had enough. Fortuitously, neither of those classes of short-term tenants was presently occupying the crash pad, and they fell onto an unmade bed that consisted of a thin mattress on the hardwood floor.

Mikey would stay in quite a few luxury suites in the years to come, but none would ever eclipse the memory of that night. More than once, he would find himself in a penthouse, on a bed of 1500-thread-count Egyptian sheets. He would close his eyes while attempting to conjure up the memory of the glorious night in that squalid apartment.

# Chapter Thirty-Five

# NO GOOD DEED

**South Philadelphia**
**Summer 1987**

When the slight man took a seat at a table at the far end of the High Noon Saloon beneath an autographed black and white photo of Joe DiMaggio, he was virtually invisible to the clientele preoccupied with drinking themselves to an early grave. Mikey was behind the bar, pretending to be busy washing a glass, but observed, assessed, and categorized the man as a non-threat. His name was Scotty, and he stopped in occasionally, always ordering a White Russian. Were it not for his somewhat odd drink of choice, Mikey would have hardly remembered him. Still, as he favored a cocktail he'd first heard of in an obscure R&B song, he could hardly judge. He recognized the small but dapper man as a denizen of the neighborhood, someone who was *from* but not really *of* the South Philadelphia Italian American diaspora.

Over the following months, Scotty would keep a predictable schedule of Tuesday afternoons for the precise duration of two White Russians. He would occasionally play a song on the jukebox when it went silent, careful not to interfere with someone else's playlist. Occasionally, he would snicker good-naturedly at a regular's joke or something on the television that was suspended by chains above the beer box. Mostly, he did his best to remain invisible and stay out of the way of the regulars. Once, someone tried to engage him in conversation, inviting him to a friendly game of cards, but he politely declined and seemed to shrink even further down into his seat. He was a good customer, tipped the cocktail waitresses well, and Mikey hoped he wasn't scared off by the intrusion. Mikey was happy to see him return the following week and sent him over a White Russian on the house. When the waitress told him the drink was comped, he looked up at Mikey with a weak but good-natured smile and raised his glass, nodding in appreciation. Mikey nodded back.

Mikey went about his business, tending bar and answering a phone that never seemed to stop ringing. When he next had a chance to look up in Scotty's direction, he noticed he appeared to be drawing in a sketchbook, and Mikey had the distinct impression he was the subject. It was an odd sensation, and while not entirely uncomfortable, it caused him to glance in the mirror to verify his hair was reasonably coiffed. His reflection did not disappoint. He walked over to Scotty's table, took a seat, and asked to have a look at the drawing. It also didn't disappoint.

Neither of them mentioned their previous encounter.

Mikey had been making his rounds the week prior, stopping in a few center city bars to settle up the poker machines he and JR had scattered around a few taprooms on the periphery of South Philadelphia. It was a wildly profitable business, and the bars and clubs just outside of South Philly proper were particularly lucrative. A few of the spots they serviced were in an area around 13th and Locust that catered to a gay clientele, which didn't bother Mikey. In fact, they were some of the spots that caused the least trouble for him. It was the bars in the neighborhood that were a constant pain in the ass and a source of endless rancor. Somebody was always trying to move in, and the owners were always trying to steal. It was the subject of perpetual wrangling, and occasionally a bit more serious intervention.

It was in one of those bars around 13th and Locust that Mikey spotted Scotty in a corner booth. He was alone and sipping a White Russian, just like at the High Noon. Mikey sort of nodded in his direction, and in the dim lighting, he thought Scotty nodded back. Mikey didn't think it was necessary or even appropriate to walk over. After all, Scotty seemed like a pretty private guy, and maybe he just wanted to be left alone. Even so, as Mikey was about to leave, he leaned over to the bartender and asked him to send a drink over. He thought he saw the man snicker just a bit. Before he could catch himself, he reached over the bar and grabbed a fistful of the man's shirt collar, pulling him toward him and stretching it out in the process.

"Did I say something funny?"

The smirk, if it was there in the first place, had disappeared. Mikey loosened his grip and pushed an envelope containing the house's take across the bar. He turned and walked briskly out of the bar. "No good fucking deed," he grumbled under his breath as he brushed past the doorman.

A few minutes after Mikey left, the bartender brought a White Russian over to Scotty, plopping it down unceremoniously. A few drops splashed onto the table but spared Scotty's open sketchbook. The bartender looked down at a hauntingly lifelike image of Mikey Fortuna. The eyes blazed with a fire that threatened to ignite the page.

So accurate was the sketch, the man couldn't help but mutter an apology for spilling the drink.

For the first time in his life, Scotty felt the strangest sensation; the sensation of another man's fear, and the modicum of power that came along with it.

He had to admit... it felt good.

# Chapter Thirty-Six

# THE CALLING OF ST. MATTHEW

A few days later, Mikey was bartending at the High Noon, and Scotty was in his usual spot. Mikey had been thinking about their encounter, and a crazy idea had begun to take shape in his mind. It was a longshot, but so was Mikey's whole life up to this point.

"Mind if I have a seat?"

Scotty hadn't noticed Mikey's approach and jolted upright, slamming his sketchbook closed in the process.

"It's okay." Mikey pointed at the sketchbook. "I don't mind."

Scotty rested his hands protectively on the marbled cover. He drummed his fingers on its surface, considering whether he should show Mikey his drawings. He had no reason to trust Mikey, but his intuition told him perhaps there was more to this man. He struck Scotty as being somewhat above the usual neighborhood thuggery, a creature who managed to roam and navigate the jungle without allowing himself to become *of* the jungle. Scotty spun the sketchbook around and slid it over to Mikey, who had taken a seat across from him.

Mikey leafed through the pages, turning them delicately and taking in the images. They were a mix of portraiture and sketches depicting Biblical scenes, but set in the present-day neighborhood. He recognized a few barflies and local characters in the compositions.

"This... this is incredible," Mikey said. He'd stopped at a drawing of Christ among a group of individuals assembled in a bar that looked an awful lot like the High Noon. Christ was pointing at a man seated across the room. The look on the man's face suggested he was uncomfortable to have been singled out by Christ. It was a twist on Caravaggio's *The Calling of St. Matthew*. Scotty had transposed the scene to the modern-day saloon, a practice Caravaggio himself had revolutionized in his time, using the common people of Naples in lifelike Biblical scenes. Mikey was transfixed by the sketch, especially the face of the man Scotty had drawn as St. Matthew. It was in the unmistakable likeness of Mikey himself, and was more lifelike, more honest than a mirror's reflection. A man looks at his reflection in a mirror, and his mind interprets it, but this portrait was divorced from any such interpretation. There was no hiding from its truth. It saw right into his soul, just as Mikey suspected Scotty did.

That was Mikey's first indication that he and Scotty were more alike than he could have imagined. He began to think up uses for Scotty's considerable talents, and an idea began to take shape in his mind. It involved the Duke, Veronica, a mythical painting she had described to him, and some hairbrained deal the Duke had allegedly struck with some guys "from the other side." Mikey didn't know what to make of it at the time, but now the path appeared, and if everything went right, it would lead to untold riches, Veronica's liberation, and the end of the Duke.

Mikey knocked back what was left of his gin and tonic and locked eyes with Scotty. "I have a proposition for you."

Scotty didn't hesitate. "Whatever it is, I'm in," he replied with the certainty of someone who had been waiting all his life for a man like Mikey to utter those words to him. They shook hands, and the strength of Scotty's grip caught Mikey a little off guard. Scotty must have noticed; it was the first time Mikey had seen the man smile.

# Chapter Thirty-Seven

# STRANGER THINGS

**Caffè Vecchio**

**South Philadelphia – Present Day**

"Don't make it obvious. You're just paying a friendly visit. Nothing unusual about two old hoodlums catching up." Frank was seated on a barstool, and Ralph rubbed his shoulders like he was working his corner.

"I'm no hoodlum," Frank protested.

"No? I'm sorry, Dr. Valleto, my mistake."

Joey liked that one. "Why not just send me?" he said.

"Because," Ralph replied, "we just want to have a look inside the Duke's house, see if we can learn anything. If I send you, I have a feeling things might not end so peacefully."

"I'll bring him some biscotti," Frank said. "Everybody likes biscotti."

"He might not even have teeth anymore," Joey said.

"I'll dunk it in fucking espresso for him."

"Let me just go there with a shiesty and a .38 and be done with it," Joey volunteered.

"Hold that thought," Ralph said. "It's a kinda ski mask," he added in response to Frank's puzzled look. "We need to find this thing *before* anybody goes in the ground."

Frank nodded in agreement.

Ralph palmed a piece of paper into Frank's hand. "That's the address. It's on Juniper Street between Tasker and Morris. Three houses off the corner. The backyard faces Watts, so check that out too, just in case we have to come back without ringing the bell. *Capisce*?"

"*Capisce*." Frank unfolded the paper, stared at it for a second, and then lit it on fire with a lighter. He tossed it in an ashtray and lit a Marlboro in the flame before it turned to ash.

"Oh, and one more thing. I heard that crafty cunt sister of his has been staying there with him, so watch what you say in front of her."

"Isn't she a nun?" Frank asked.

"Sorry, *Sister* Crafty Cunt." Ralph made the sign of the cross reflexively, more out of superstition than contrition.

"I'm just saying, I heard she took a vow of silence."

Ralph took a deep pull on his bourbon and deposited the empty glass down firmly on the bar before answering. "So did a lot of people, Frankie. So did a lot of people."

Frank let that sink in, considered the seemingly countless number of guys who swore unending loyalty, only to play that ace when their luck had finally run out. A lifetime of vilifying others didn't stop them from joining their ranks when the alternative was dying in jail. Some caved in for far less.

"Okay, so I get in. Maybe have a coffee with the old mute. I doubt the painting is just gonna be hanging on the wall, and I can't imagine he'll spontaneously regain his voice. I heard he's half a vegetable."

"Who knows, Frankie, stranger things have happened. The two of you go back a while. Maybe it will stir something in him. Keep it light and breezy; maybe he'll let his guard down. Sit with him and watch fucking *Jeopardy* or something. Either way, you'll get a look around the place in case we have to return heavy."

"And if the sister's there?"

"I don't know, improvise. As I recall, she wasn't a bad-looking woman before she went in the convent. Who knows? Maybe she'll be looking to break a different vow."

Frank blew out a cloud of smoke in disgust. "What do you think I am, some fucking degenerate?"

"Yeah, I do. Aren't you the same guy who took a priest to a massage parlor on Christmas Eve?"

"That was different," Frank snapped defensively. "It was for his own good. Besides, it was just a hand job."

"Good luck making that distinction to St. Peter."

"I gotta believe it's a shade better than diddling an altar boy."

Joey had been leaning over the other side of the bar, taking in this exchange. He slowly shook his head in disbelief. "Are you guys fucking serious? I can't believe what I'm hearing. You guys are joking. Right?"

Ralph looked at Frank for a moment. "I don't know, Frankie, are we?"

"Yeah," Frank answered after taking a drag of his Marlboro. "It's all just one big fucking joke. Don't worry, kid, you'll get there soon enough." Frank put on his jacket and headed toward the exit. Ralph walked close behind and slipped a .38 in Frank's jacket pocket as he held the door for him.

"I thought you said this was a friendly visit," Frank remarked at the sudden heft.

"It is, but this guy's a fucking wild card. Nobody's seen him in years. He could be faking the whole vegetable act. After all, it did get him sprung. We've seen stranger things in our time."

"I guess you're right. Besides, you know the old saying."

"Which one? I got an encyclopedia up here." Ralph tapped his head with two fingers.

"Better to have and not need . . ."

Ralph nodded approvingly, a smile spreading across his face as he finished the phrase. "Than to need and not have."

Frank turned right as he walked out of the Caffè, headed down Passyunk Avenue.

"Yo, Frank," Ralph hollered after him. "You're going the wrong way."

Frank turned. "No I'm not. I'm going to Termini's first."

"The bakery? For what?"

Frank smiled as he tapped a finger against his head. "For biscotti. Remember?"

"Nice, Frankie," Ralph answered, then walked back into the Caffè. "Very nice indeed," he said to himself as the door closed behind him.

# Chapter Thirty-Eight

# SOUTH PHILLY BARBED WIRE

The two tree-lined blocks of Juniper Street between Dickinson and Morris are still firmly entrenched in South Philly, yet close enough to the Broad Street subway to entice professionals desiring easy access to Center City and hipsters looking to tap into the nouveau South Philly vibe. Frank knew the area well. That is, he used to, long before the advent of two-hour parking and the ubiquity of Ring doorbells. He considered a light cover disguise, an Amazon Delivery jacket and cap, but Ralph ruled against it. This was ostensibly a friendly visit between two old acquaintances after all.

Frank took an exploratory stroll down Watts Street first. It was more like an alley, with barely enough room for a car to pass. As a result, there was little traffic, either vehicular or pedestrian, and it was favored for both sex and drug trafficking back in the day. By the looks of the scattered condoms and broken beer bottles, it appeared that some customs remained intact. The west side was composed of roll-gate garages for the homes and businesses on Broad Street, while the east side consisted of cinderblock walls that fenced in the backyards of the houses on Juniper. The walls were about six feet high, and a few were topped off with the jagged edges of the bottoms of broken bottles cemented into the surface. It was an old-school security system, the South Philly version of barbed wire. Frank had been counting off the houses as he walked and figured that one of the fences led to the Duke's backyard.

A tattered coat draped over the top of one of the glass-topped walls stopped Frank in his tracks. It was the first sign that someone else had paid their respects prior to his visit.

Frank went around the block and climbed the front steps cautiously, peering through the blinds as best he could. The interior of the house was dark, with just a narrow strip of light slashing across the portion of the interior visible from his vantage point. He was about to ring the doorbell, but his finger stopped short when he noticed the front door wasn't fully closed, like someone had left in a hurry, dragging the door behind them but not turning to close it completely. He used his left arm and shoulder to nudge the door open. His right hand remained in his jacket pocket, and he was grateful for Ralph's last-minute addition. Unlike the previous visitor, Frank closed the door behind him.

He found himself in an aged vestibule. The door in front of him was frosted in a sickly opaque orange that resembled a cough drop that had fallen between the cushions of an ancient sofa. Frank turned the knob and entered a living room frozen in the seventies. The couch was hermetically sealed in nicotine-stained, vinyl upholstery. An ornate, freestanding ashtray was situated next to a recliner. The sole strip of light leaking in from the front window blinds continued along the wall until it intersected with the face of the figure slouched in the chair. The effect was not unlike a Caravaggio.

The Duke's eyes were wide open, and his mouth was unnaturally agape, his bottom jaw extended well beyond its natural limits, almost touching his chest. His mouth was filled with a white, viscous fluid with blood-red swirls and speckles that poured out onto his shirt. Frank's first impression was that the Duke had choked on cherry vanilla ice cream. Then he noticed an open gallon of white paint on the floor, and a piece of bloody meat that could only be the Duke's tongue resting in the ashtray. Whether he'd been faking it or not, Frank could only conclude the Duke had stayed silent to the end.

Frank did a cursory walk-through. He was sure whoever composed this little piece of performance art had done a thorough search. Moreover, he didn't wish to linger too long in a crime scene not of his design. After a lifetime of close calls, he wouldn't be able to deal with the irony of getting pinched for a murder he didn't commit. He backtracked to the vestibule but couldn't resist turning around to take in the scene one last time. *Man reclining sans tongue.* Frank smiled, pleased that the title came to him so quickly. *Maybe I'm not going senile just yet*, he thought as he slipped out the door as quietly as he had entered, closing it carefully behind him.

As he hustled down Juniper Street, he considered tossing the biscotti into a trash can, but thought better of it. *It would be a sin to waste a good box of biscotti.*

# Chapter Thirty-Nine

# BANDO CAPITALE

"Scratch a lover and find a foe."
Dorothy Parker

Nick tried calling and texting Angie a bunch of times. The calls went straight to her voicemail, and the texts went unanswered. *Just like the old days*, Nick thought. It was so easy to fall back into the old patterns. Sometimes it felt like the two of them had been having different versions of the same disagreement for years, with a few years off here and there. He convinced himself it was for the best she ran out of Angelina's, that she wasn't there when he emerged from the bathroom, ready to cast her spell again. *I was right to resist*. Maybe he had dodged a bullet.

He could still feel the shrapnel embedded from all those years ago, the fragments lodged in a location that caused the occasional ache but were too risky to remove. Old flames could be problematic like that, too hot to touch, but even more painful to fully extinguish. So you occasionally rub the burn, comforted at least by the notion you can still feel *something*. Maybe he was simply soothed by the knowledge that the scar remained, proving it hadn't all been a dream. In any event, he had to put the Angie drama aside for now. He still had a painting to recover, and Grace was growing impatient back home. If he didn't wrap things up by the end of the week, she'd be on a flight to Philly, and that was a complication he couldn't handle right now.

When Nick walked into the Caffè, Joey was behind the bar. He was leaning forward on his elbows, his head inches away from Ralph, who rested his hand on Joey's shoulder as he whispered something in his ear. Frank was at the next stool, swirling the blue cheese-stuffed olives in his martini and staring at the smoke-like tracks they left on the surface while he pretended not to hear anything. Nick took in the scene.

"What do you call two Italians talking on a street corner?" Nick quipped.

Joey looked up and shrugged. Frank just smirked as he stirred his olives.

"I don't know, what?" Joey answered.

"A conspiracy," Nick answered.

"I'm glad you're here," Ralph said. "There's been... a development."

"From the look of things, not a good one. Joey, why don't you play us a few?" Nick said, nodding toward the jukebox.

Joey wiped his hands on a bar towel. "I don't get it," he said.

"Don't get what?" Nick answered.

"How is it a conspiracy?"

"Just go play some songs," Ralph interjected. "I'll explain it to you when you get back."

Frank slid up a few stools, leaving one open for Nick next to Ralph.

"Should Gary be here for this?" Nick said.

"He's on his way," Ralph said. "Frankie will give you the short version until he gets here."

Frank draped an arm around Nick's shoulders as Joey fired up the jukebox. Frank began to fill him in on what he had discovered at the Duke's place as Teddy Pendergrass sang "The Whole Town's Laughing at Me."

"What about the nun? Any sign of her?" Nick asked.

"Nothing so far," Frank answered.

"Who knows? Maybe she was in on it. I never bought the whole Sister Mary Rita act. She was always a twisted cunt, even back in grade school," Ralph said.

"The paint, the tongue—someone was sending a message," Nick said.

"Granted," Ralph said, "but what message, and to who?"

"I'm thinking maybe us." Frank pulled a cigar from his pocket and handed it to Nick.

"No thanks, I've been giving the sticks a break."

"I didn't mean for you to smoke it, Nicky. I took it from the Duke. It was in his breast pocket."

"So the Duke was about to enjoy a smoke before someone rudely removed his tongue. It doesn't mean anything," Ralph said.

Nick picked up the cigar, rolled it around in his fingers a bit. "I'm not so sure."

"Whaddya mean?" Ralph asked.

"I don't know. It just seems a bit off. Frank, was there a lighter or a cutter nearby?"

Frank shook his head. "Not that I recall."

"How about the house? Did it smell like smoke?"

"No, definitely not. Matter of fact, I didn't think of it much a the time but it kinda smelled like cologne."

"Oh really?" Ralph snapped. "What are you, a fucking bloodhound now? Don't tell me, was it woody, with hints of citrus?"

"Fuck you." Frank turned in a huff and went back to swirling his martini.

"I'm just saying, it seems a little staged, that's all." Nick spun it around, studying the band. "It's a Montecristo. That mean anything to you?"

"Not really," Ralph answered. "I've smoked plenty of them. Not my favorite, but a decent brand. Unless it's a Cuban, they're pretty special."

Nick studied the cigar. It had a double band. The top band was understated, brown with what looked like a fleur-de-lis embossed in the center. The brand name, Montecristo, along the top, *Habano* along the bottom. The secondary band, closer to the foot, was a bit more flashy and intricate—yellow and gold, with the words *Wide Edmundo* printed around it.

"You think the Duke was smoking Cubans?" Nick asked.

"Nah," Ralph answered. "He was a real *gavone*. Smoked cheap stogies, if I recall correctly."

"So the cigar is a message then," Frank added.

"Maybe," Nick said. "What do you make of the name Edmundo?" Ralph shook his head.

"I know," Joey volunteered. Nick hadn't even noticed him return from the jukebox.

"Go ahead, kid," Ralph said.

"It's from the book *The Count of Monte Cristo*. I heard they used to read the book to cigar rollers in Cuba to make the time go by as they worked."

"Good movie," Frank offered.

"The main character is—" Joey began.

"Edmond Dantes," Nick finished for him.

Nick reflected on the possible significance. *The Count of Monte Cristo* had been one of his father's favorite books. He had bought it for Nick for Christmas many years ago. Nick had left it to collect dust for decades. It served as one of many painful reminders of their strained relationship. He suddenly found himself lost in a familiar spiral of depression as he fed resentment and anger into the growing vortex. Ralph's booming voice and snapping fingers pulled him back moments before he fully dove into the whirlpool.

"You still with us, kid?" Nick nodded as Ralph guided him down onto a stool. "You were having one of your spells." Nick rubbed his eyes and attempted to blink away the small dots of light darting around the periphery of his vision.

"Get him a drink," Ralph said to Joey. He reached for the beer box before Ralph stopped him. "Not a beer, a real drink."

Joey poured Nick a Maker's Mark neat. Nick took an exploratory sip before knocking it back. Joey opened a Peroni chaser and put it in front of Nick, just in case.

"Okay," Ralph said after Nick took a sip of the Peroni. "So what does all this tell us? The Duke's tongue, a mouth full of white paint, a cigar."

"Well, the paint seems obvious," Frank said. "It's about the painting. That makes me think it's gotta be the Italians."

"I don't know," Joey chimed in. "The tongue seems like a Philly thing." All three men looked at him. "I'm just saying, it sounds like something I heard of before."

"You've been watching too many movies," Ralph said. "The Duke was a lot of things, but I seriously doubt a rat was one of them. Unless that's what someone wants people to think."

"Why would they want that?" Joey asked.

"To throw everyone off the trail, I guess," Frank answered.

"It can't be that simple. This seems more personal," Nick said, staring off in the direction of the jukebox.

"Personal how?" Frank asked.

"Personal like someone wanted to get revenge for something deeper than money."

"What's deeper than money?" Frank asked.

"The other thing," Ralph answered quickly, getting Nick's point.

"What other thing?" Joey asked.

"Love," Frank said. "Right, Nicky?"

"Maybe, Unc. I might be reaching. It all seems a little too convenient. I can't help it, that's the way my mind works. Sometimes I hear hoofbeats, and the first thing I think of is zebras."

"Don't be so hard on yourself, it's served you well. But what about the cigar? What the hell does that mean? A Cuban Montecristo we can all agree probably wasn't the Duke's, so what's the significance?"

"Well, you know the old saying," Nick answered.

"Sometimes a cigar is just a cigar?"

"No, I'm thinking of another one. Remember the story of *The Count of Monte Cristo*. The Count isn't really a Count. He's just a man in love with a woman, Mercedes. A woman who is unfairly taken away from him."

"Revenge," Joey said. "It's a dish best served cold. That's the saying anyway."

"Maybe, Joey. But this guy staged the scene very carefully. Revenge isn't all that complicated. I think maybe he was after something even more gratifying."

"I don't know, Uncle Nick, there's not much more gratifying than revenge, hot *or* cold."

"The way the light was coming in from the window, it was like one of those paintings your father loved," Frank said.

"Like that one?" Nick asked, pointing at a Caravaggio reproduction hanging on the wall at the far side of the Caffè. It was *David with the Head of Goliath*, in which David's arm is outstretched, holding the giant's decapitated head by its hair. Both of their faces are illuminated brilliantly on one side, creating beautiful shadows of contrast on the other. It is widely believed that Goliath's face is a self-portrait, serving as Caravaggio's commentary on the *bando capitale*, or death sentence, issued against him by Pope Paul V for the murder of Ranuccio Tomassoni, the alleged Roman pimp of Caravaggio's muse and frequent subject, the courtesan Fillide Melandroni. The death sentence hung over him throughout the bulk of his tumultuous life, and he painted numerous beheading scenes as a commentary on his plight.

"Exactly like that," Frank answered.

"I used to think of *The Count of Monte Cristo* as a book about revenge. I know that's how Hollywood portrayed it. But eventually, when I reread it later in life, it became about something deeper. Funny how you can carry something around with you all your life, but it doesn't fully reveal itself for years, sometimes decades."

"I'm not sure what you're getting at, kid," Ralph said.

"This whole thing can't only be about revenge. I mean, I'm sure that's part of it, but I feel like it's about something more spiritual. It's the whole reason my father wanted me to read that book in the first place."

Frank eased up closer to his nephew. He spoke softly, sensing Nick's fragile state. "What is it, Nicky?"

Nick's voice began to crack a little as he answered, and he had to clear his throat. "It's about redemption."

The Chantels' "Maybe" blared from the jukebox.

"The guy we're looking for, he's more than just a killer—he's an artist."

# Chapter Forty

# TOM AND JERRY

Angie awoke with a start, not sure where she was. She had fought off sleep as long as she could, but eventually passed out on the flattened cushions of a threadbare sofa. Light poured in, filtered through a window covered in yellowed newspaper touting sales at long shuttered stores. She sat up and blinked as her eyes adjusted. She made out a figure seated at the kitchen table. Richie, Angelo's goon, was looking at her in a way that suggested he had been staring at her for some time. The idea made her uneasy, but she did her best to force a smile and feign nonchalance, like there was nothing unusual about waking up in quasi-captivity. She felt Richie's eyes running all over her, and the smirk on his face made her sick to her stomach. She made a mental note—he would be the first one she got back at for this predicament. That is, if she got out of there in one piece.

Her ruminations, and Richie's smirk, were interrupted by the flushing of a toilet. Angelo shuffled into the room. A smile spread on his face as he took her in.

"*Che bella*, you're awake."

It caught her off guard for a moment. It was a phrase her grandfather would frequently use when speaking to her. It was jarring how much the two were alike. Her grandfather, for all his bluster and old-school machismo, was, at heart, a gentle man. She couldn't yet discern what parts of this man's demeanor were an act. Whether he was truly sincere, or luring her in with a grandfatherly act.

"How did you sleep?" Angelo stopped and stood up as straight as his old vertebrae permitted. "I'm sorry. That was insensitive. I'm sure you didn't sleep well on that old couch. Please, I hope you'll forgive me for this whole ordeal, but as I said before, it couldn't be helped."

"That depends," Angie replied. "Am I leaving here?"

Angelo lifted a dented percolator-style coffee pot from the stove and poured two lukewarm cups. He placed one in front of Angie. It had an old cartoon image of a cat chasing a mouse. The image was beginning to fade, like it had been washed a thousand times before being retired to the back of a cabinet for a few decades. Angie spun the handle clockwise, and Tom chased Jerry around the perimeter of the cup.

"That depends," Angelo answered.

Richie's smirk returned, and he folded his arms in front of him.

"On what?" Angie tried to force a smile, but only managed to make one corner of her mouth twitch a bit. She hoped Angelo hadn't noticed the small tell of fear. Oddly enough, it was the first time during her ordeal that she felt genuinely scared.

"On your performance." Angelo reached into his pocket and tossed her the phone he had taken from her handbag the previous day. "Call him. Tell him you need to see him. I'll handle the rest."

Angie called.

No answer.

She tried again.

No answer.

She took a sip of her coffee.

"Sorry, I wasn't sure how you take it," Angelo apologized gruffly. "Besides, we're fresh out of cream and sugar." The grandfatherly mask was beginning to slip.

Angie put the cup down. She remembered a silly thing Nick had said once, many years ago. *If Tom ever catches Jerry, the show is over.*

She tried again. Nick answered, and she breathed a sigh of relief. She launched into an improvisation about how she had to run out of Angelina's because she loved him too much to make him feel trapped, but now she had given it more thought. If she ever meant anything at all to him, she practically begged, he would meet her at the old Bamboo Inn to hash it out for good, one way or another.

Nick bought it. She nodded at Angelo to indicate as much, and he nodded back in approval.

"I love you, Nicky," she said as the call disconnected on his end.

"And the Academy Award goes to . . ." Angelo clapped slowly, a cane in the crook of his thumb and forefinger.

"So?" Angie said.

Angelo looked at Richie the goon for a moment before turning back to her.

"And now, beautiful..." He paused for a painfully cruel interval. "You can leave. He'll drive you back home."

"If you don't mind, I'll call an Uber."

"Suit yourself," Angelo handed her phone back. "But no funny business."

"Thank you," Angie said as she powered up her phone.

"Would you like to use the facilities first?" Angelo gestured toward the bathroom.

As much as she truly wanted nothing more than to run out of there, she really did need to pee, as well as a moment alone to get her head together. She would never make the trip otherwise. She walked past Angelo and closed the bathroom door behind her. She slid a paint-caked lock over as far as it would go and turned to look at herself in the cracked mirror of the medicine cabinet. She strained to recognize the face that Nick had fallen in love with all those years ago. That girl seemed to be missing of late, but she vowed to find her. She splashed her face with some cold water. A generic tube of toothpaste was rolled up in the corner of the sink. The cap was missing, and it looked like it had been squeezed at least three times since it first appeared empty. A toothbrush was lying flat on the porcelain, its bristles mashed down into oblivion. In the opposite corner, a coating of grime coated the fossilized sliver of what may have once been a bar of Irish Spring. She considered wiping her face on the crusty towel draped on a metal rod, but it looked like it had serviced at least a dozen poker games, and Angie thought better of it.

She walked out of the bathroom, thankful that Nick had bought her story. It wasn't exactly a lie. She did love him, and she did want to be with him, but she couldn't ignore that some of what he said to her in Angelina's made sense. How long before they would just go back to the old ways? The old grievances, the petty jealousies. Maybe he was right, as she had always suspected. They were too much alike, identical even, in many ways. And being in a relationship with a version of yourself never works out well.

She walked down the rickety stairs and was never so happy to breathe in the urine-drenched "fresh" air of the Atlantic City morning. Her Uber arrived, and they drove in silence onto the Atlantic City expressway. She counted off the mile markers in her head and began to nod off. She was jolted awake by the driver's voice.

"Is this good?"

They were pulled over on the corner of Passyunk and Moore. Her apartment was just a few buildings away. She got out and was in the process of tipping the driver on the Uber app, so she didn't see the man approach at first.

"You look like you could use a drink." The man startled her, but she felt safe, standing outside Smokey Joe's, less than a half block from her home. She peeked inside the crowded bar. It was busy and likely filled with people she knew, including the bartender. The man was tan and exceptionally well-dressed. He smiled broadly as he extended his hand in an old-world gesture of chivalry. He was older than her, and unlike Angelo, had a gentleness about him that gave her the confidence to respond in the affirmative.

"You know what? I could," she said as he escorted her to the door. "I'm Angie, by the way."

"I know."

"And your name?"

"That's not so simple," the man said as they took a seat at the bar. He eventually introduced himself, and once Angie overcame her shock, he launched into a conversation that spanned hours. They continued like that well into the afternoon. He told a mesmerizing tale. She cried, she laughed. Then it was her turn, and the strangest thing happened. Somehow, she found herself telling this man things about herself she had never shared with anyone. Not even Nick.

* * *

At the Caffè, Nick sipped a double espresso. He dunked a biscotti from the bag Frank had left on the bar the previous day, careful not to let it soak so long that it broke off in the cup.

He smiled as he reflected on Angie's call. Her gushing manner, the urgency in her voice,  like if he didn't agree to see her, she would die. Something was off; he had sensed it straight away; Angie would never beg. He would meet her at the Bamboo Inn like he promised.

But he wasn't buying it for a minute.

# Chapter Forty-One

# LOCAL WOMAN MISSING

Ronnie had two blenders whirring at the same time. It was 1:00 p.m. on a sunny Saturday, and the Tiki was packed with an eclectic mix of the usual locals and tourists seeking refuge under the hut. He garnished one of his signature Pina Coladas with a pineapple wedge and placed it before Dave.

"You heard from Nick?" Dave asked as Ronnie topped off his drink with a rum floater. Dave was one of the only regulars who indulged in the touristy cocktails, and Ronnie could never recall him drinking more than one or two drinks.

"Not since he left, but Grace said he should be back by Monday."

He barely finished the sentence before Grace came strolling in, her arms full of bags. Ronnie smiled at her, and her face lit up. She never seemed to show up without bearing some gifts or supplies. She plopped down the bags of lemons and limes on the bar, and Ronnie signaled for one of the barbacks to carry them to the walk-in box.

"Hey, Ronnie. How's it going?"

"Much better now that you're here, chica."

Grace stood on her toes and leaned over the bar to kiss him on the cheek. She had a special place in her heart for Nick's oldest and most loyal friend from back home. Neither of them spoke much about how they came to know each other, an Italian from South Philly, and a Puerto Rican from the badlands of North Philly, but she got the sense the two of them had been through some trials together.

A news alert flashed on the TV screens above the bar.

*Local Woman Missing*

The story provided scant details, but showed a photo of a smiling, attractive woman that might have been lifted from social media. She was last seen leaving her job as a cocktail waitress at Robert's, a waterfront bar and restaurant in Pompano, not too far from the Tuscan Tiki. A chyron crawled along the bottom of the screen, displaying a telephone number for tips on her whereabouts. Grace studied the photo on the screen; something about it caused her heart to ache. There was a sadness in her eyes that was at odds with the smile. There was something else too. Something that made Grace sick to her stomach. The missing woman looked an awful lot like Kim.

Ronnie made an abbreviated sign of the cross and kissed the crucifix hanging from a chain on his neck. "Poor baby." He said it like a mini prayer, tucked his chain back in his shirt, and returned to pouring drinks, leaving Grace in Dave's company for the moment.

"How's our boy?" Dave asked.

"Good," Grace answered. "He should be back soon."

"Well, tell him I was asking for him. Things aren't quite the same here without him."

Grace considered it for a moment before responding. "No, they're not, Dave. Not even close. I'll be sure to pass that along. Thanks." Grace gazed out at the ocean. Her view of the beach was framed by pillars on either side, palm fronds above, and the bar top along the bottom. Nick would call it his movie screen, and the thought made her smile. Were it not for a lone, wispy cloud scooting along from right to left, the scene could be mistaken for a painting. She squinted, and the image blurred just enough for her to begin to conjure an image of Nick entering from stage left.

"You know," Dave said, interrupting her fantasy, "Seneca once wrote, 'A gem cannot be polished without friction, nor a man perfected without trials.' I shared that quote with Nick, and it really seemed to resonate with him."

Grace considered it. Perhaps she was just perturbed by the interruption, but she took issue with their resident philosopher's simplistic quote. She turned away from the beach scene and looked Dave straight in the eye. "Did Seneca ever consider that maybe the gem doesn't need to be polished, that maybe it's just fine the way it is—imperfect?"

"I'm sorry, Grace. It's . . . it's just a stoic quote Nick and I discussed once," Dave stuttered. "I didn't mean to offend you. I'm sorry if I did. I can imagine how much you miss him."

"That's okay, I'm just feeling a little sensitive, that's all." Grace forced a smile, but harbored a suspicion that Dave was incapable of feeling genuinely sorry for anything he had done in his life. And she was quite certain he couldn't imagine how she felt. After all, that would require empathy, an emotion he appeared to be devoid of. Grace had had just about enough of his pseudo-stoic bullshit and was considering having Ronnie bar him from the Tiki.

Grace looked at Ronnie, who had been watching and listening, certain he was reading her mind. She shook her head ever so slightly, deciding to wait until Nick returned before making that call. By the time she turned back to the cinema of the oceanfront scenery, it was like trying to slip back into a dream after being rudely awakened. She turned away, fearing that if she didn't, the credits would begin to roll.

# Chapter Forty-Two

# NO SHIESTIES

**Bamboo Inn – South Philadelphia, Present Day**

Angie ordered a Tito's and club with lemon. She got a Smirnoff and tonic. No lemon.

"We're fresh out of lemons," the bartender said without a trace of an apology. In this case, fresh out meant not since 1985.

*Welcome to the Bamboo Inn,* the sign above the bar read without apparent sarcasm.

"That's okay." Angie slid a crumpled twenty across the bar. Three barflies were scattered around the room. She speculated that at least one of them had to be Angelo's guy.

It might have been the rancid tonic, but Angie started to feel a sickness building in her stomach. Something was off. Angelo had given his assurance he wouldn't harm Nick, that he just wanted to talk to him, share some information, and work together to recover the painting. He had sworn on his friendship with her grandfather, on the soul of his mother.

*Bullshit*, she thought.

She made a snap decision and texted Nick hastily.

*It's a trap.*

There was no response.

Across the street, a black BMW idled. Angelo sat in the back seat and peered out through a tinted window. A beer delivery truck pulled up to the corner, parking in the loading zone and blocking his view of the front door. The delivery driver exited on the street side and walked up the two steps to the entrance.

"No shiesties." The bartender pointed at a sign that recited the establishment's rules.

*No Gambling*

*No Drugs*

*No Credit*

*No Fighting*

Below this list was another line, written in black magic marker; it appeared to have been added recently.

*No Shiesties*

The delivery driver had a plain trucker cap pulled down tight on his head, and a pair of Wayfarers that met the mask referred to as a shiesty on the bridge of his nose. He took a seat next to Angie, put his sunglasses on the bar, and pulled off the shiesty. It was only then that Nick responded to her text by whispering two words in her ear.

"No shit."

One of the barflies Angie had noticed earlier stood up and began to walk over to them. That's when Gary came through the front door and covered the ground between the barfly and Nick in two seconds flat. He didn't need to say a word. The barfly sat back in his seat.

"Hey," the bartender chirped, pointing to the line of the sign that said *No Fighting*.

Angelo had followed Gary through the door. "Don't worry," he said, leaning on his cane, "there ain't gonna be no fighting."

A fourth "barfly" Angie hadn't noticed emerged from the bathroom; he must have come in through the back door labeled *Ladies Entrance*.

Ralph wiped his hands on a paper towel, tossed it on the ground, and hiked up his pants. "Agreed," he responded to Angelo's proclamation, and with a sweep of his arm, invited all assembled to the back room, where a table and chairs had been arranged for a meeting that hadn't appeared on Angelo's schedule.

They took their seats around the table. Nick told Angie to go to the Caffè and he would meet her in a bit. She squeezed his hand and held on.

"I know," Nick said softly as he eased his hand out of her grip. "It's okay, go sit with Frank until I get there, then we'll talk." Nick kissed her on the cheek and tucked the folded shiesty into her palm. "Hold this for me, will ya?"

"You're still full of surprises, DiNobile, maybe that's why I can't quit you." Angie held the folded shiesty to her face, then turned and walked away.

Joey had arrived and opted to lean on the pool table instead of taking a seat. Introductions were made all around, and drinks were ordered. The bartender must have finally recognized Ralph and snapped to attention, rushing to the bar for the drinks. Angelo's guy, Richie, sat on his right side, and when he spoke, Joey thought he recognized his voice. But it wasn't until his phone rang with that stupid song that any doubt Joey had was removed. Richie was the guy who had tied him up in the warehouse.

"Turn that damn thing down," Angelo snapped.

*Dirty motherfucker*, Joey muttered under his breath.

Ralph and Angelo did the bulk of the talking. Gary occasionally contributed a sucking sound he made with his toothpick, and Joey continued to mutter low-key profanities. They noted initially their mutual friends, which lent some assurance to their negotiations. Both men regarded one another as equals; honorable men who kept their word . . . most of the time. The unspoken caveat being that self-interest and subterfuge sometimes required honor to take a back seat.

Ralph shared what Frank had discovered at the Duke's, and Angelo was either genuinely surprised or turned in an Academy Award worthy performance.

Now it was Angelo's turn to deliver.

"Mikey Fortuna," he said.

"What about him?" Ralph asked. "Nice kid. Sad fucking story. Now that I think of it, he used to hang out in this very bar, until that thing happened."

The years had passed, but the legend would never fade. If anything, it grew more intense, even more so after Veronica turned up dead, her body dumped unceremoniously outside Saint Agnes Hospital.

It was never proven, but it was generally assumed the Duke had attacked her in some jealous rage and, not being certain she was dead, had someone drop her body off outside the emergency room. When Mikey Fortuna disappeared immediately thereafter, there was little doubt out on the street as to what happened to him.

Angelo smiled. He liked knowing something Ralph didn't. He savored it for a moment and paused to take a sip of his Chianti.

"You mean that femur, or whatever they found on that farm? After the Duke's wife *fell* down the steps." He made a sarcastic gesture with his hand to mimic Veronica's unfortunate tumble.

"Yeah." Ralph jutted out his chin. "*That* thing." He was beginning to become impatient, and the old man must have sensed it, so he just blurted it out.

"I'm not sure what poor soul those bones belonged to, but it sure wasn't Mikey Fortuna." "How can you be so sure?" Ralph asked.

"Because he's very much alive, and unless I'm sorely mistaken, he's the key to finding the paintings, or at least one of them."

Ralph considered what Angelo was saying. It wasn't impossible. The details on Mikey's disappearance were always a little sketchy, and the bones found on the farm in Potter County, well, it was before all the DNA stuff. And it was always a little too convenient, based solely on the testimony of some low-level junkie informant.

"Okay, so assuming that's all true, that the kid somehow got his hand on one of these paintings before he pulled a disappearing act. How the hell do we track down a guy who's been missing for over thirty years?"

Angelo lifted his cane from the middle and pointed the handle at Nick, who appeared to be just as surprised as Ralph at the gesture.

"Ask *him*," Angelo said as he settled back in his chair.

# Chapter Forty-Three

# SURFSIDE BAR AND GRILL

**Deerfield Beach, Florida**

Mia stood at the service bar, arranging the drinks on her tray. She was grateful for her new job and had been so happy to get the call that she cried for ten minutes after. Terri, a sweet, blue-haired girl she met in rehab, had encouraged her to apply. It was a good thing too, because her rent was due in five days and she was fresh out of options—good ones at least. The man who interviewed her suggested she purchase a white skirt from lululemon, and Surfside would supply the branded tank top. She was shocked to discover the skirt cost $100, and thankfully, Terri helped her find one for $19.00 at Ross.

She half expected Stu, the nerdy little manager, to demand some sexual favor when she arrived for her shift, and was shocked when he simply tossed her an apron and turned her over to Shena for training. He smirked at her as he slithered away, conspicuously sockless in his attention-seeking loafers, khakis hemmed two inches too high for even European standards. But this wasn't Milan, and the whole getup conveyed an affect masquerading as 'style.'

Mia had made plenty of mistakes in her young life, but the one upside was that she had come away with a pretty good understanding of men, and she could tell something was causing this one to try way too hard. She steeled herself for the possibility he was simply saving his pathetic demands for another time. A feeling of shame washed over her because she knew she would likely comply in silence. That's what happens when you're out of options. But she was safe for the time being, so she tucked away her feelings of low self-esteem and put a brave, cheerful smile on her face as she shouldered her tray.

Surfside wasn't a fancy place, but it was on the beach in Deerfield and had a loyal following of locals, with the sun-seeking tourists sprinkled in during the season. Most of the crowd this afternoon was on the mature side. Shaena gave her a quick tutorial on the ordering system and a few insider tips. Her coworkers were welcoming, and she was actually pulling in some decent tips. One customer in particular was especially kind and helpful.

"Don't worry about him," the customer said as Stu passed by. "He's a creep, but he's harmless."

Mia laughed louder than she had intended and covered her mouth in a girlish way that made her feel self-conscious. The man gently touched her arm, easing it away from her mouth. "You look so beautiful when you laugh."

He was handsome for a man his age and very well dressed. To her surprise, Mia didn't recoil from his touch. She thought she sensed a sincerity in him that caused her to let her guard down just a little bit. Things had been going well for her since she had been clean. *Maybe my luck is finally changing*, she thought.

She could hardly contain herself when he closed out and tipped her two hundred on a forty-two-dollar check. She held the bills in her hands and stared at them in the privacy of the ladies' room stall. Three months ago, she knew exactly what she would do with her good fortune. Now, she was clean, but she would have been lying if she said she didn't feel a gnawing pang in the pit of her stomach. She considered calling her sponsor, but instead splashed her face with cold water, clenched her fists, and took a deep breath before stepping back out onto the deck.

When she clocked out, there he was, waiting at the valet stand, having a cheerful conversation with one of the attendants. He waved at her casually, like he was surprised to see her—like he hadn't timed the end of her shift perfectly. A Rolls-Royce Spectre pulled up to the entrance. Mia expected some celebrity to exit the car and was shocked when her new friend walked to the driver's side and palmed a bill to the driver. He looked over the top of the roof of the vehicle toward Mia and said, "Can I give you a ride?"

Like an actress in a silly romantic comedy, Mia looked over her shoulder to see who he was talking to. He laughed and didn't wait for an answer. Good thing, because she was unable to mouth a response. He walked around and opened a massive door for her that was hinged in the opposite direction. The whole production threw her off kilter. She somehow managed to gather her composure enough to smooth down her Ross skirt with her hands as she slid into the plush interior. It was more spacious than her shared rented room and more comfortable than any bed she had slept in since... well, since ever. When she leaned back, she noticed the headliner sparkled with countless points of light that looked like a star-filled sky from her childhood in Oklahoma. As they pulled away, she absentmindedly placed her left hand on the console. An electric shock travelled up her spine when she felt his hand gently cover hers.

She didn't pull it away.

Mia was feeling sweaty and grimy from her shift, and sitting in the passenger seat of this monument to opulence only accentuated her discomfort. She wanted nothing more than to get to her room, hide her earnings (which felt like a king's ransom to her), and since the air conditioner had been groaning to keep up with the stifling heat, jump into a cool shower for relief. Still, she was ashamed to have her customer drop her off at her low-income housing development. She asked him to drop her off at the Cuban sandwich stand at the corner of her street instead.

"You must be starving after your shift," he said. "Why don't you let me take you somewhere nice for dinner?"

She hadn't had a decent meal in weeks, mainly subsisting on cheese crackers from the Dollar Store, not even the name-brand ones. Even the Cuban stand would have been a stretch up until a few hours ago. The events of the day had her thinking that maybe what they preached in recovery was true, that if she worked the program, good things would start to happen. That maybe she wasn't some disposable person, that she had worth. She dreamed of going back to school and training for a real job, perhaps even something in the medical field. She would wear scrubs on her way back and forth to work, and people would look at her like she was normal. She felt a strange sensation welling up in her. For the first time since she could remember, she had hope.

"Okay," she suddenly answered, afraid if she thought about it too long, she'd change her mind. "I'll go to dinner with you, but I need to stop home and freshen up first. Is that okay?"

The man laughed a friendly laugh. "Of course it's okay. Just tell me where you live."

"Down there." Mia pointed down the pothole-speckled road that ran behind the sandwich stand to a one-story cinderblock structure painted a sickly approximation of seafoam green.

The Spectre glided down the weed-lined road, the suspension smoothing over every crater without so much as a jostle. They came to a stop, and the man got out to open the door for her.

"I'll only be a few minutes," she said cheerfully as she walked briskly to her front door.

Mia was well past the point of being embarrassed. The man made her feel... unjudged. Besides, what was he expecting from a struggling, beachfront cocktail waitress? *Wait.* Just then, it hit her—she had a job, belonged somewhere. She was *needed* and would be missed if she didn't show up. She touched the Surfside name tag with 'Mia' inscribed on it, as if it were a treasure. It was proof she existed, that she had responsibilities. She placed it proudly on top of a plastic two-drawer file cabinet she was using as a dresser. It contained all her earthly belongings.

And now she had a date, a real date, with a rich guy who seemed genuinely interested in her. She cried a little in the shower, then threw on her best outfit, borrowing a cute little red top from Terry. *She won't mind.* She put on some makeup. Not as much as when she used to do that other thing, but just enough. *Like the ladies wear in Palm Beach.* She chuckled at the thought, as if she knew what ladies in Palm Beach wore or did.

When she walked outside, she was half surprised he was still waiting, that it hadn't been some dream, and she had hallucinated the whole thing. She crunched over the gravel in some old wedges she had retrieved from a Rubbermaid bin and got into his car, this time a bit more graceful—like it was no big deal; like it was something she did every day; like it was the first of what would be a series of similar trips.

Like it wouldn't be her last.

# Chapter Forty-Four

# BABY, PLEASE COME HOME

**South Philadelphia**

**Christmas Season**

**1990**

The High Noon was decked out in tinsel and garland. The crowd was generally in a good mood. The Christmas season in South Philly could have that effect on people. On the other end of the spectrum, there were those individuals for whom the festivities only managed to highlight their loneliness and desperation. A normally harmless drunken regular had taken the mistletoe from an arch separating the bar from the dining room and affixed it to his belt buckle, then began to thrust it at every cocktail waitress who passed by. It was funny the first couple of times, and the girls took it in stride, smiling at the silly prank. God knows they had been subjected to much worse. But then he began going up to tables of young ladies, and Mikey overheard one of them yell, "Pig!"

Mikey came around the bar and gently escorted him back to his stool as he slurred, "But it's a *trudishin*," in a weak defense.

The jukebox was playing Darlene Love's "Christmas (Baby Please Come Home)," and Mikey wasn't going to allow this guy to ruin his favorite Christmas song, so he deposited him on his stool and placed an overturned shot glass in front of him, signifying a drink on the house. "And put that mistletoe back where you found it," he said as he returned to his post behind the bar.

Scotty arrived around 4:00 p.m. and took a seat at the end of the bar. Ever since Mikey had extended his offer of friendship, and by extension, the protection of the High Noon, he had migrated from his quiet table to a stool at the bar.

"How's it going, Scotty?" Mikey said.

Scotty leaned forward on his forearms conspiratorially and in a low tone answered, "Good, Mikey. Just a few more finishing touches and... well, let me just say, it's my opus. No one will ever know the difference. Certainly not that crumb."

"Nice work, my friend," Mikey said. "Just finish it up, and I'll handle the rest."

Mikey thought about it as he mixed Scotty's White Russian. Could he really pull it off without tipping off the Duke? Things had been heating up over at the Bamboo Inn, and he swore he detected the yellowish tint of a bruise beneath Veronica's eye the last time he saw her. The idea of the Duke putting his hands on her, in any fashion, could drive him into a rage, so he distracted himself with the busy work of tending bar. The menial tasks and mindless banter distracted him just enough to get through another day. Once or twice a week, he would find precious solace in her arms, and it seemed like the time in between wasn't life at all, just a passage of time filled with the inconsequential rituals of sustenance.

Except for *the plan*. The plan gave his life meaning. It propelled him forward, got him out of bed in the morning. He had accumulated enough wealth to sustain his present lifestyle in perpetuity, but he sensed there was something greater out there for him, a larger, more beautiful world beyond the confines of his South Philly fiefdom. All he needed was for Scotty to finish the painting, and he would figure out a way to make the switch.

Like everyone else in South Philly, he had heard the rumors about the Duke strong-arming Anthony DiNobile out of the painting. It was hard to separate the truth from legend, but the story went that the Duke had trumped up some nonexistent sleight, manufacturing a rumor that DiNobile was moving in on the Duke and aligning with one of his rivals. It was all nonsense, and DiNobile initially dismissed it as such. It was only when the Duke threatened to drag DiNobile's son, Nick, into the fray that he finally caved and turned over the painting, Rembrandt's *A Lady and Gentleman in Black*, which had been stolen in the Isabella Stewart Gardner Museum heist in March of 1990.

DiNobile had long been rumored to be in possession of a few of the stolen paintings and had reinvented his Passyunk Avenue restaurant, Caffè Vecchio, as a kitschy homage to Renaissance art, with beautiful reproductions of the Old Masters' works lining the walls and name-sake dishes like "Botticelli Bolognese" on the menu. It was either a crafty cover—who would harbor a trove of priceless art and dare to surround himself with reproductions—or a ballsy thumbing of the nose at the myriad law enforcement agencies seeking their recovery.

Maybe it was a little of both.

# Chapter Forty-Five

# WHITE LIES

Grace had just finished her manager's shift at the Tiki when Jess, the new girl, rushed in, flustered and apologizing for her tardiness. Kim still hadn't surfaced, and all the news about the cocktail waitress from Surfside had Grace worried, so she was just thankful Jess had shown up and wasn't the latest *Local Woman Missing*. She smiled at Jess and said, "It's okay, sweetie. We're a little slow. Go get yourself together, and I'll wait for you." Grace didn't have any children of her own and sometimes felt like the Tiki girls were her adopted children. She sat with Ronnie as they waited for Jess, and they caught up on some Tiki gossip. Ronnie knew best to steer the conversation away from Nick and what he was up to in Philly.

"I've been meaning to ask, have you seen our friend Julian around?" Ronnie asked.

"Julian? Who's that?"

"You know, Mr. Mysterious with the Patek and the fancy cigars. He used to come in when Kim was on. Come to think of it, I haven't seen him since . . ." He caught himself and let the sentence trail off.

"Since Kim quit on us?" Grace wouldn't allow herself to consider any less savory possibilities. "Wait, you mean the well-dressed gentleman who used to sit over there?" Grace gestured to a spot halfway down the bar on the ocean side. Her imagination began to run wild. "No, come to think of it, I haven't seen him in quite a while."

"Oh well. You know how it is around here; people come, and people go. I remember having regulars who never missed a day in years and then all of a sudden—poof!" Ronnie gestured in the air above his head like a Vegas magician.

Grace's phone vibrated once in her pocket. Hope lived in the moment between reaching into her pocket and looking at the text. She'd have been lying if she said she wasn't hoping it was Nick, saying he was on his way to the airport. She would pick him up, and he would take her to an extravagant dinner. They would have drinks by the ocean, then they would make love and . . .

It was Arjun.

*Hi Grace. I need to see you please. Thanks. Arjun.*

She was disappointed, but happy to hear from her young friend. *How adorable*, she thought. Always so mannerly in the way he identified himself, as if she hadn't saved him as a contact the first time they met. She texted him back, and they made a plan to meet at the Chick-fil-A.

"I'm out of here, Ronnie. You need anything before I leave?"

"I'm good, beautiful, go get some rest."

*I wish*, Grace thought as she gathered up her belongings. She was halfway off her stool when Dave walked up behind her, giving her a start.

"I'm sorry, Grace, I didn't mean to startle you. I was just coming over to say hello."

"That's okay, Dave. Here, take my seat." She stood up and blew a kiss to Ronnie, hoping Dave would take the cue and let her slip out before—

"How's Nick?" The philosopher was great at quoting Marcus Aurelius. Taking social cues, not so much.

Ronnie rolled his eyes as he wiped the bar.

Grace didn't hesitate for a minute. She lied. "He's great, Dave. Just got off the phone with him. He said to say hello. He should be back in a day or two."

He smiled like he knew something. *Had he spoken to Nick?* She dismissed the idea and wrote the smile off to the man's quirkiness. She gave him a quick wave, meant to cut the conversation short, and hustled off before he could misinterpret and commit any further social faux pas. She didn't dislike Dave necessarily, and she forgave her little white lie as one meant to save him from any further embarrassment.

As she walked away, she heard him say to Ronnie, "Who's the new girl?"

* * *

Arjun was already sitting at their table at Chick-fil-A. He looked even thinner and shabbier than the last time she saw him, if that was possible, and her heart broke a little. She forced a smile. "Hello, Arjun. I'm so glad you texted me. It's great to see you!" She *was* glad to see him, but she hated how overenthusiastic she sounded. He kept his head down but raised his eyes to greet her and smiled ever so slightly.

"Are you hungry?" she asked. He nodded so slightly Grace wasn't sure he did, but figured he had to be. "Good, because I'm starving." Another lie, but this one was worth it, she thought, as it got a genuine laugh out of the boy. "I want a deluxe sandwich meal *and* nuggets. How about you?" She planned on picking at the nuggets and sending Arjun home with the leftovers. She ordered and returned with a tray full of food. "Let's dig in," she said as she clicked his cup.

The way he devoured his meal, Grace suspected that perhaps his text was simply a ploy to see her and have a good meal, and that was perfectly fine with her. She genuinely enjoyed Arjun's company and wished he would call her more often. When they finished, Grace felt okay about getting to the purported reason for their meeting.

"I saw the car again," he said.

"When?"

"The other night, outside my cousin's motel."

Grace hesitated before asking the question she hoped Arjun would answer yes to.

"Did you see Kim?"

"No. It was a different girl."

"Are you sure? What did she look like?" Grace realized she was leaning forward over the table, her hands inches away from his. She almost reached for him, but decided to back up instead.

"I'm sure. This girl was pretty like Kim, but it wasn't her. This girl had blonde hair."

"What was she wearing?"

"A red shirt. That's all I could really see before they left."

*Local Woman Missing.* The chyron scrolled by in Grace's mind, and she tried to remember the news story. *Did it say the girl was a blonde?*

"Did you notice anything else, anything at all?"

Arjun shook his head, then reached into his pocket and placed something onto the tray. "No, but I found this. He threw it out the window as they drove away."

Grace picked it up, rolling it between her fingers as she examined the glistening wrapper and the ornate band.

A cigar.

# Chapter Forty-Six

# CHERCHEZ LA FEMME

All eyes turned to Nick. He laughed nervously, assuming Angelo was mistaken or perhaps this was some elaborate misdirection on the old man's part. He pointed at his chest while pleading ignorance.

"Me? I hardly remember the guy. I must have been about seventeen when he disappeared, and he was a few years older than me, as I recall. Besides, I never set foot in the High Noon. Some ancient beef my father had with the original owner." He turned to face Ralph. "What was the guy's name?"

"Sal. Salvatore Di Cicco. He was married to a real hot number, Roe Gallo. I think that's what the beef was about, either that or a game of Ziginette. It was so long ago, I doubt they even remembered why."

"*Cherchez la femme.*" Nick tossed the phrase out into the room like a hand grenade.

"You mean the song?" Ralph asked. "Dr. Buzzard's Original Savannah Band, right Nicky?"

"Nice, Ralph. Good song. But I was talking about the phrase itself. It literally translates to 'look for the woman,' but it means more than that. It means that if you want to solve a mystery, get to the source of any controversy, chances are you'll find a woman at the center of it all. It's from the Dumas novel *The Mohicans of Paris*."

"I won't argue with that," Angelo said, seemingly satisfied that Nick was living up to his billing. "But I need you to think a little harder. You see, Fortuna reached out to us, says he wants to meet, negotiate a deal."

"Okay," Nick said. "Sounds great. Problem solved. I don't understand where I come in."

"That's the mystery, kid. Fortuna says the only way he does the deal is if he meets with you at the Caffè and you broker it. Sorry about all the other commotion, but we needed to get your attention."

"You could have just called," Nick quipped as Gary rolled his toothpick from one side to the other, and Joey cracked his knuckles.

"Eh." Angelo leaned forward, cane between his legs, one hand resting atop the other. "I'm not much for phones. My way is more effective."

"Okay, whatever. It's water under the bridge as far as I'm concerned. But I can't vouch for Angie. She's a bit feisty, if you hadn't noticed."

"So was her grandfather," Angelo said. "I think that's why I have a soft spot for her."

"You knew Biagio?" Ralph chimed in.

"He was my best friend once." The old man seemed to soften up a bit at the mention of Biagio's name.

"What happened?" Nick asked.

"Lots of things. The usual. Petty grievances that over the years turned into grudges." Angelo stared down at his hands and turned them over like he was holding the answer in his upturned palms. "But I guess if you had to sum it up..." He looked at Nick. "How do you say it?"

"Cherchez la femme." Nick extended his glass as he answered.

Angelo clicked his glass and reciprocated the toast.

*Who the hell was Mikey Fortuna, and why was he insisting on meeting with me?* Nick thought.

Cherchez la femme.

He reflected on the phrase as he started to piece it together.

# Chapter Forty-Seven

# THE SWITCH

**South Philadelphia**

**1991**

Scotty finished the painting a few days after the New Year. Mikey decided he would make the switch on Super Bowl Sunday, figuring the Duke would be occupied with the game and the festivities over at the Bamboo. Super Bowl XXV was scheduled for January 27th, with the Giants matched up against the Bills.

Mikey and Veronica began to finalize their escape plan. It took Mikey a week to inch the white van up from parking spot to parking spot until it was situated in front of the Duke's house on Juniper Street. The plates were stolen, and he hoped that some nosy beat cop wouldn't take notice. Scotty's reproduction of *A Lady and Gentleman in Black* was stashed in the back of the van in anticipation of the switch, which was scheduled for 6:13 p.m. to coincide with the kickoff. Mikey had been freezing his ass off in the back of the van since

6:00 a.m., pissing in a jug and starting the engine every few hours just long enough to get a little heat going.

The plan was for Veronica to leave at 11:00 a.m. for her shift at the Bamboo Inn. The Duke had built a bar in his basement where he occasionally held court and met with certain people he didn't wish to be seen with at the Bamboo. He had a print of *Dogs Playing Poker* hanging behind the bar, which was more consistent with his taste in art than the masterpiece stashed behind the liquor shelf. Veronica instructed Mikey on how the shelf-mounted corkscrew unlocked the hidden door—rotate 90 degrees counterclockwise and raise the handle—allowing the shelf to swing open on its hidden hinges. She had watched the Duke open it once while she was folding clothes in the laundry room. He hadn't noticed her as she peered through the slats of the laundry room door.

It took her months to muster the courage to try it herself. It was only after she had been emboldened by Mikey's arrival in her life that she resolved to discover what the Duke valued so much that he'd built a secret compartment behind his bar to conceal it. She expected to find stacks of money, which would come in handy, as she had already begun plotting her great escape with Mikey. Instead, all she discovered were stacks of cassette tapes and a rolled-up canvas that appeared to be in exceptionally bad shape. She had unrolled the canvas and taken Polaroids of everything. She gave the pictures to Mikey, and he shared them with Scotty, who studied them like a treasure map, which is precisely what they were.

Mikey found everything just as Veronica had described it. He made quick work of switching the canvas with Scotty's forgery, taking a moment to admire the man's handiwork. The replication was near perfect, not that a troglodyte like the Duke would ever notice the subtle differences. Mikey could never have dreamed it would go on to fool the Italians years later—at least for a while. Mikey secured the canvas with the same twine that held the original. He eyed the stack of TDK cassette tapes neatly arranged in the corner of the alcove. He was about to close the door when he made an impulsive decision and pocketed one of the tapes. It was risky, but his instincts told him that whatever was on the tape might come in handy one day.

The Duke had been recording his basement meetings for years, friends and enemies alike, especially since those roles were so fluid and interchangeable. It was his insurance policy. When everything went to shit, and inevitably it would, the tapes would be his final ace. The two stacks had been of even height, so when he opened the hidden door to add another cassette to his collection, he quickly noticed that one was missing. It had to be Veronica, he thought, and vowed to teach her a lesson she would never forget.

Over the following days, Veronica felt so light it was like she was walking on air. The switch had been made. Their plan was coming together. Even the Duke's never-ending insults seemed to bounce right off her. After all, in a few short days, she'd be free of him and the neighborhood forever. She spent as much time as she could at the bar, and when the Duke was there, she snuck back home. She was only taking a few things when she and Mikey left. "Just what you absolutely need," Mikey had said. "I'll buy you everything else when we get there." It was supposed to be a complete fresh start, and shedding the weight of her belongings would make her lighter still, like she could take flight at any moment.

She allowed herself to imagine her new life with Mikey, free from the clutches of the Duke and his endless insults and degradations. She was overcome by a sense of serenity as she glimpsed the salvation waiting for her on the West Coast and in Mikey's arms. His love was like a force field of gentleness that shielded her from all the ugliness of the bar, the neighborhood, and the men who had come before him. They had all taken from her, demanded of her, and ordered her around, leaving her feeling weary and drained. His love was unlike anything she had encountered in her life. Mikey had asked for nothing. Instead, he gave of himself. Not trinkets, but real attention and care. She had blossomed under his attention.

*So this is what everyone meant when they spoke of true love*, she thought as she tended to some last-minute details around the house before her exodus. Before Mikey, she had convinced herself that true love was just a convenient story people told themselves, like Santa Claus, or praying to St. Jude, the patron saint of hopeless causes. She had given up praying to him long ago. And then one day, Mikey Fortuna walked into her bar. Now there was something she could give to *him*, and she nearly burst with joy as she savored how happy he would be when she told him he was going to be a father.

She balanced the laundry basket on her hip as she pulled the chain on the bare bulb that illuminated the narrow stairway to the basement laundry room, taking comfort that this was likely the last load of clothes she would ever wash for her oppressor. Such was her loathing for him, she avoided even having their clothes mingle together in the washing machine.

She felt a push in the middle of her back and shot forward with a velocity that propelled her all the way to the concrete landing at the bottom of the stairs. The laundry basket, which she gripped reflexively as she took flight, initially cushioned her fall. But in an odd twist of physics and fate, it caused her to somersault forward as if she had launched off a springboard. Veronica landed upside down, her head and neck absorbing the brunt of the impact.

It wasn't clear whether the Duke was trying to kill her. There were certainly more efficient and tidier ways. Perhaps he just thought it would be satisfying to see her topple down the steps. Then she would get up, bruised and, more importantly, humbled. But now he had a body to deal with. He called the one person he could trust in the cover-up—his sister. Veronica was still breathing when she arrived. The soon-to-be Sister Mary Rita deemed that to be a complication neither she nor her brother could risk. A throw pillow fetched from the sofa did the trick in short order.

He dropped her off at the emergency entrance of St. Agnes without so much as an explanation. The statement drafted by his attorney set forth a narrative of the sister finding her at the bottom of the basement steps with dirty laundry scattered all about. The Duke was in such despair, his counsel related, his grief prevented him from staying with her until she was carried into the hospital. With little to support foul play other than a cloud of healthy suspicion, balanced against the word of a postulant about to take her vows and enter the convent, the Duke was cleared after the coroner ruled it to be an accident instead of the homicide it was. A sad mishap had snuffed out the life of a beautiful woman . . . and her unborn child.

Mikey was already in LA when he got the news. He saw right through the Duke's bullshit story and seethed as he plotted an elaborate revenge. The scenarios he created in his mind were so exquisite in their infliction of pain, he couldn't settle on just one. He stayed awake for days, finally falling into a fitful sleep on the flight back to Philly. By the time he landed, the feds had moved on the Duke—not for Veronica's death, but for a long-brewing racketeering indictment. This was somewhat fortuitous for the Duke in that it spared him (for the time being) a slow, gruesome death at the hands of Mikey. For Mikey, his revenge would have to wait a couple of decades, during which time his hatred only grew larger and more malignant as it spread to every facet of his life. Even more than the memory of his love for

Veronica, it gave him a reason to go on. It's what he lived for. The Duke was held without bail at his detention hearing, but was granted permission to attend his wife's funeral.

In a final act of disrespect, the Duke had opted for a closed casket at the viewing, which was held at Monti Funeral Home. This despite the pleading of her mother, and the funeral director's assurances that she would look just as beautiful in death as she did in life. Mikey knew the real reason; the Duke wanted to deny him a final opportunity to kiss her face. He skipped the official wake, opting instead for a private visitation courtesy of his old friend Sam Monti, who, despite the Duke's instructions, had preserved Veronica as close to her mortal beauty as was humanly possible. It was Sam who broke the news to him that Veronica had been pregnant.

Just after midnight on the evening before the viewing, the undertaker led Mikey to the parlor where he had situated Veronica's open casket. "Take all the time you need. You can let yourself out when you're done. I'll be in my office if you need me," Sam said as he closed the double doors to give Mikey his privacy.

"Thank you," Mikey muttered weakly as he kneeled at the coffin. "This is all my fault," he whispered in her ear as he kissed her for the last time. His hand rested over her midsection, where his child had been growing only days before. He let out a cry of grief and rage that filled the parlor and chilled even Sam, who had long ago grown accustomed to such outbursts.

The following day, flowers began to arrive from seemingly every flower shop in Philadelphia, as well as a few of the counties. They soon filled the narrow parlor, and even after Sam had filled the adjoining parlor, which was luckily vacant, flowers continued to arrive until they flowed out the front door and onto the sidewalk. Each arrangement bore the same card with the same inscription.

***All My Love, Always and Forever. M***.

It was rumored that Mikey spent more than twenty thousand dollars on the elaborate displays, with each florist trying to outdo the other. The following day, two US Marshals accompanied the Duke to Holy Cross Cemetery, standing on either side of him as he stood at the head of the grave. Mikey looked on from a distance, and for a moment, they locked eyes. It would be the last time the Duke would see Mikey Fortuna... until the day he stood over him twenty years later, cutting his tongue out with a dull knife.

A search warrant had been executed at the Duke's home seeking evidence of racketeering. Some firearms had been recovered, but they had miraculously missed the compartment hidden behind the bar. Once it became clear the Duke was likely to spend a long time in a federal penitentiary, interested parties became more than a little insecure with the safety of *A Lady and Gentleman in Black*. It was decided that the Rembrandt would be safer on another continent, and as is often the case with priceless stolen art, it was exchanged as collateral for another stolen work in return. The Italians agreed that Caravaggio's altarpiece, *The Nativity with Saint Francis and Saint Lawrence*, would be safer in the States, far from the prying eyes of the Carabinieri Art Squad.

Two ships set sail. One from Palermo, the other from the Philadelphia Marine Terminal. A consortium consisting of certain interested parties representing New York and Philadelphia concluded there was no safer place for the storage of the Caravaggio than the Convent of the Divine Sisters, where it would remain locked away in a basement under the careful watch of Sister Mary Rita. Back in Palermo, Maurizio Messina Denaro took possession of the Rembrandt, displaying it only on special occasions and for Christmas Eve ceremonies, unaware his prized treasure was a forgery.

The original *A Lady and Gentleman in Black* remained with Mikey in Los Angeles. He displayed it openly in his penthouse apartment as a quality reproduction. Numerous Renaissance and Baroque reproductions surrounded it on either side, giving it cover and never raising an eyebrow among the guests Mikey hosted at countless parties and get-togethers. Many complemented him on his collection, but none imagined it was the real thing. He had even gone so far as to affix an engraved badge below it that read:

***A Lady and Gentleman in Black***

***Rembrandt van Rijn***

***Original stolen from the Isabella Stewart Gardner Museum***

It was the perfect cover—displayed in plain sight, its disappearance recited reverently.

On some nights, after all the guests had left and the penthouse was empty, Mikey would sit alone before the painting. The story behind Rembrandt's masterpiece was heartbreaking. A couple had commissioned the painting, which originally depicted three figures: the husband, the wife, and, between them, their young child. It is believed the boy died soon thereafter, and the mother, overwhelmed with grief, requested that he should be painted over, the memory of their loss too much for her to bear. X-rays had later confirmed his presence, covered over in black paint, but still stubbornly asserting his existence.

On those nights, Mikey stood gently touching the spot between the couple where he imagined the boy rested for eternity... and cried for the child he would never hold.

# Chapter Forty-Eight

# AMANDA

The body was discovered in an overgrown lot behind a liquor store on Oakland Park Boulevard. It was a rough area, rampant with drug dealing, homelessness, and sex workers.  An aid worker saw what looked like a human foot sticking out from beneath a palm frond. The worker was handing out food and toiletries to the residents of a homeless encampment. She went from tent to tent, offering services and rousing the occasional fentanyl overdose victim with the Narcan she carried with her.

She was tending to a woman who was bent over at an impossible angle, suspended in a pose that seemed to defy gravity. She managed to rouse the woman and provided what scant comfort she could. As she kneeled to leave a sandwich and toiletry bag for her, she caught a glimpse of what appeared to be a bright dollop of flesh peeking out from the underbrush. The underside of the girl's heel stood out like a brushstroke of lead white on a canvas of palm frond green. The worker cleared the palms and debris that had been hastily arranged to cover the girl's body. It was not the first time she had discovered a body, not that it ever got easier, but something about this scene seemed different.

Even in death, against this sad backdrop, in the midst of all this human suffering, the young woman was beautiful, dressed in a cute red top, with a face that was both sad and angelic. She checked for a pulse, even though it was clear the girl was dead, and, finding none, dialed 911. Sirens approached in the distance. Time stood still as the worker knelt beside her. She was overcome with emotion as she contemplated that these were the last moments this young woman would likely spend in the presence of someone who cared about her, other than the well-meaning first responders. She found an odd peacefulness in that moment, despite whatever evil forces had brought this woman here. The worker reached for her hand. It was cold and stiff, but she gripped it firmly. With her other hand, she brushed back the hair from her face and stroked her head gently. "My name is Amanda. I wish we had known each other." She began to shake and cry as she heard the first responders crunching through the brush behind her as they approached. "I want you to know that I see you, that you mattered, that you are loved."

An EMT touched her shoulder and gently helped her to her feet. "Are you okay, miss?"

"No," she responded. "I don't believe I am."

# Chapter Forty-Nine

# A DIFFERENT SETTING

"You okay with this, pretty boy?" Gary was rubbing Nicky's shoulders like he was working the corner of a heavyweight championship fight.

Nick thought about it for a second before responding. "Do I have a choice?

Gary didn't have to pause for reflection. "Fuck yeah. You always got a choice."

"Fate leads the willing and drags along the reluctant. I think Seneca said that."

"Whatever the fuck that means," Gary huffed.

"I don't know exactly, but my friend Dave would say I should just embrace my fate. You know, *amor fati*."

"Amor who? Listen, slick, you always got a choice in this life. I don't know some fancy Latin phrase for it, but I believe you make your own fate. That's how I live *my* life."

"I suppose you're right, big man."

"Right or wrong, *I'm* the one gonna be back in that kitchen with a .38 shit go sideways. Where Dave gonna be?"

Nick raised a glass of Crown Royal in response. *Guess I can't argue with that*, he thought as he knocked back half the glass.

Angelo and Ralph were seated at the back corner table, underneath a reproduction of Caravaggio's *David with the Head of Goliath*. David's eyes are downcast, while Goliath's severed head possesses a blank stare. Nick recalled his father telling him that Caravaggio painted his own face onto the disembodied skull. At the time, Nick thought it a silly thing to do; he was beginning to understand. The two men were hashing out the ground rules for the upcoming meeting. Ralph had Dmitry standing by on an encrypted app for his seal of approval for any deal that was reached. The Russian would be arranging any exchange, as well as the transport, given that he owned a fleet of container ships based in the Port of Oslo. He was also the common denominator between Angelo and Ralph, and now, apparently, between Angelo and Mikey Fortuna. *Why am I not surprised*, Nick thought.

Joey brought two espressos over to Ralph and Angelo, then took his place on a barstool, one foot resting on the crossbar, the other on the floor. He sat at a 45-degree angle to both Ralph's table and the front door. An ankle holster peeked out from the hem of his black jeans.

Nick sipped a Peroni and pretended to watch the stocks scroll by, gauging the never-ending struggle between fear and greed. Greed seemed to be ahead today. The jukebox was turned down low, and the gentle strains of Sinatra's version of "Dindi" lent a sense of calm to an otherwise tense setting. The song transported Nick back to a rainy afternoon in an Atlantic City bar many summers ago. Such was his trance that when the bell above the front door jingled, he turned, half expecting to see Angie walking in.

He was met instead by the gaze of a man he didn't immediately recognize, but sensed he had met before, albeit in a much different setting.

# Chapter Fifty

# BESPOKE

Grace didn't recognize the brand emblazoned on the cigar band. She was pretty familiar with all the Padrons, Fuentes, and Davidoffs favored by Nick and the guys at the Tiki. A quick internet search revealed a finely curated line exuding sophistication and exclusivity. The band she held was from the Salomon Collection from Didier cigars. *At fifty dollars a stick, it better be something special,* she thought. She immediately texted Ronnie and asked him to meet her at the Tiki.

The news about a cocktail waitress found dead behind a homeless encampment had begun to spread, and the "Breaking News" teased across the Tiki's TV screens asked whether a serial killer was hunting beach bar waitresses across the Fort Lauderdale area. Grace stared long enough to be sure Kim's picture wasn't the next to be featured. When it wasn't, she was able to let out her breath in relief for the time being. She wondered how long her sense of relief would last, as no one had heard from her in weeks. Grace had reported her missing, but the police didn't seem terribly concerned about some waitress who had apparently flaked out and failed to show up for work.

Ronnie was waiting for her, sipping a Corona at a table outside the perimeter of the Tiki and overlooking the ocean.

"This is my favorite table," Grace said as she kissed Ronnie on the cheek and took a seat. It occurred to her that this was the first time she'd sat at this table without Nick sitting next to her.

"I know that." Ronnie smiled. "That's why I held it for you." He nodded to a new waitress, tapped his Corona, and flashed two fingers. She retrieved two Coronas and placed them on their table, along with the bar menus that Grace knew by heart, given that she had created them. Grace hadn't met the new server yet and decided she would wait to introduce herself. This way, she could get an honest preview of her personality. She seemed attentive and sweet enough, but Grace couldn't shake the fact that she resembled Kim.

"So," Ronnie said, "whatcha got for me mami?" Grace reached into her handbag and tossed the cigar band onto the table. Ronnie picked it up and unfurled it a bit, as it still retained the shape of the cigar it once dressed. "Looks like about a fifty-eight ring gauge," Ronnie guessed.

"It's a sixty," she said. "The internet is a beautiful thing. It's a Salomon from Didier. You ever see one of our customers smoking these?"

Ronnie reflected for a moment. "I can't say for certain. It's a premium stick."

"Bespoke is what I think they prefer to call it. It's expensive, that's for sure."

"Twenty?" Ronnie asked.

"Try fifty," Grace answered.

Ronnie let out a low whistle. "Too rich for my blood."

"That might be true, but not for a few of our regulars."

"What are you trying to say, Grace?"

"I'm not saying anything. I'm asking. Who around here would smoke a cigar like this and have interacted with Kim?"

"Look, Grace, I'm not ready to start accusing people over a cigar brand."

"I'm not there either, but humor me for a minute. Let's call it a game."

"A game? We're talking about people's lives here."

"What about Kim's life? No one seems to care about that."

Ronnie looked hurt. "That's not fair. I care. You know that, or you wouldn't be here talking to me."

"You're right. I didn't mean it like that. Of course you care. We both do. But the police don't, so let's just call it a game of logic. What do you call it? Deductive reasoning."

"Like a process of elimination, right?"

"Exactly," Grace said as she clinked his bottle and plunged her lime down the neck of her beer. "A process of elimination."

"Okay, cool. I'm down with that. I mean, most of our guys smoke whatever stogies they can get their hands on. The younger guys smoke those horrible, flavored cigars, so that would rule most of them out."

"Yeah, I bought one for Nick once. I think he smoked it not to hurt my feelings, but I noticed he let it go out about a quarter of the way through." Grace paused and looked out at the ocean. Saying Nick's name out loud reminded her of his absence.

"How is my boy?" Ronnie said gently.

"You know, for once, I'm really not sure."

"I'm sorry, beautiful. I didn't mean to—"

Grace cut him off. "I'll tell you one thing I am damn sure of. If he doesn't get his skinny Italian ass back here soon, I think a certain Puerto Rican is gonna be driving a certain pissed off Colombian to the airport."

"Noted." Ronnie nodded and clinked her bottle.

"Now, back to my question. Who around here would smoke this cigar?"

Ronnie had the answer, but he hesitated. It was a heavy accusation after all. "I know who you're thinking, Grace, I think you just need me to say it, to confirm your suspicion. So fine, I'll play along. I want to be clear that this is a guess, mind you, but I would have to say the guy with the Patek and the Loro Piana shirts—Julian.

"Good. That's who I thought too," Grace said.

"Whoa, let's slow down. I said it was a guess."

"Come on, Ronnie. The watch? The shirts? You said yourself, he uses a thousand-dollar lighter. And now, since Kim's been missing, he's conveniently absent? I bet he drives a Rolls-Royce."

"That doesn't prove anything and you know it."

Grace placed the band back in her bag, knocked back what was left of her Corona, and stood.

"Where are you going?" Ronnie asked.

"To the valet stand. I have a question for Jose. You coming?"

Ronnie stood. Corona dangling at his side, he covered his brow with the other hand and squinted at Grace, who had the sun at her back. "Do I have a choice?"

"Of course. You always have a choice. You can come with me now or..."

"Or what?" Ronnie played along.

Grace smiled as she playfully grabbed him by the arm. "Or you can live to regret it."

Ronnie downed his Corona and tossed it in a trash receptacle as he walked with Grace toward the valet stand.

Jose was jockeying a Mercedes G-Wagon into the front row as Grace and Ronnie arrived at the stand.

"You guys ready to leave?" Jose jogged toward them.

"Not yet," Grace said. "Mind if I pick your brain for a sec?"

"I can't promise anything, but sure, fire away." Jose sipped a spring water and wiped his face with a towel.

"Parked any Rolls-Royces lately?" Grace asked.

"A few. More during the height of the season, but yeah, a couple a week."

"Any regulars?" Ronnie asked.

"Ralph is here on Thursday."

"No, not Ralph," Grace added. "This is a two-tone number, maybe a Spectre?"

Jose paused a moment before responding. "Well, there is one guy. Not sure of his name, but he insists on the front row, then tips five dollars. Imagine belonging to the Royal Palm Club and being so cheap."

"Does he wear a Patek?" Ronnie asked.

"I don't think so, more of an Apple watch guy if I recall correctly."

"Julian?" Grace asked.

"Julian?" Jose laughed. "No way, I know Julian. He drives a Toyota RAV4. And he tips fifty minimum. My guys love him."

"Wait." Ronnie chuckled. "Julian drives a RAV4?"

"You'd be surprised," Jose said. "Half these guys driving Bentleys and Rolls-Royces are stretched thin. We've even had them repoed right off the lot. But guys like Julian, they got that stealth wealth thing going on. Nothing flashy, you can just tell. They got that quiet luxury vibe." Just then, a BMW XM pulled up, and Jose excused himself. "Gotta go, guys. Let me know if I can do anything else for you."

Grace and Ronnie exchanged a puzzled look.

"So, I guess we were wrong," Ronnie said.

"Maybe. It doesn't prove or disprove anything," Grace answered.

Jose jogged back from parking the BMW. "Hey, I just thought of something. The guy with the Spectre? I remember him picking up one of the Tiki waitresses once. It seemed a little strange, but you know how it is around here. Not much surprises me anymore."

"Not Kim?" Grace asked.

"I can't say for sure, but it's possible."

"Do you remember his name?" Ronnie asked.

"I don't remember his name, but he's Nick's friend. That's the only reason we put him on the front row with those cheap-ass tips. In fact, hold on one second." Jose walked behind the stand and rummaged through a plastic bin. He handed an object over to Grace.

"What's this?" Grace asked.

"The cheap son of a bitch handed me this coin once instead of a tip. Said I should keep it in my pocket and reflect on it every day."

Grace turned it over in her hand and held it up so Ronnie could see it as well.

Ronnie read the inscription out loud. "Memento Mori. What the hell is that supposed to mean?"

"Something about remembering that you are mortal and you're gonna die, so live every day accordingly. That's what he said anyway. I tossed it in the bin and haven't looked at it since. You can have it."

Grace and Ronnie shared a knowing look.

"One more thing," Grace said. "You mentioned he belonged to the Royal Palm Club. How do you know that?"

"Sticker on the windshield. Fancy-ass coat of arms with a barcode beneath it to open the gate."

"Motherfucker," Ronnie said. "I think I'll take my car now, Jose."

Jose grabbed Ronnie's keys from the board and went off to retrieve his car.

"You coming?" Ronnie asked Grace.

"Absolutely."

# Chapter Fifty-One

# EDEN ROC

**Miami Beach**

Dave turned onto Collins Avenue and pulled into the driveway of the Eden Roc. He had reserved a penthouse in the Nobu tower section of the resort. The Nobu Hotel was an even swankier portion of the storied resort, a somewhat classier neighbor to the occasionally raucous Fontainebleau—what one would refer to as quiet luxury. The valet's broad grin upon his arrival dimmed noticeably as he eyed the five-dollar bill that had been pressed into his palm with all the earnestness of a C-note. He mumbled something under his breath about cheap motherfuckers as he sank into the driver's seat of the two-tone Spectre and drove off.

Dave had planned on driving down to Cudjoe Key. He had a friend who let him crash at his bungalow on occasion, an old Florida affair, complete with jalousie windows and wicker furniture. But the traffic on 95 South was even worse than usual. He was in the mood for a little pampering before secluding himself in the bungalow, where he would lie low for a few months while things blew over, contemplating his next move, constructing a new persona, and settling on a new hunting ground.

He checked into his room, flopped onto the bed, and surfed through the local news channels looking for some mention of the waitresses. He should have been relieved when no updates were reported, but was strangely disappointed instead. A familiar restlessness rose up in him, a sensation that he couldn't stand to be alone with his thoughts. He craved distraction. Something to observe other than his own reflection in the bathroom mirror. Someone to look down upon. Someone to pass judgment upon. Dave changed his shirt, pocketed his room key card, and headed down to the lobby bar, where he could lap up a few cocktails while scouting for crippled prey.

"Would you like to see a cocktail menu?"

What a stunning specimen. She was tall and sleek, and her hair was pulled back in a way that accentuated her eye shadow, or maybe it was the other way around. Either way, she was certainly different from the hassled, humidity-plagued cocktail waitresses that populated Dave's previously favored hunting grounds. She resembled one of the Lamborghinis that seemed to occupy every inch of Miami—bright, bold, and capable. **MELISSA** was etched on her name tag in bold, businesslike script.

"I'll just have a Martini, please. Stoli Elit if you have it."

Melissa smiled and commenced a graceful routine that was equal parts mixology and ballet. By the time she placed the carefully constructed drink in front of him, Dave had already made his assessment. The faint smile as she shot a glance at the barback, the cold efficiency with which she took his credit card and opened a tab, the economy of her movement behind the bar, all suggested a mastery born of experience. She had self-confidence in bunches and gave off no sign of the desperation Dave thrived on. *She simply won't do.* Once he ruled her out, Dave resigned himself to finishing his drink and heading over to Ocean Drive, where he might find more suitable prey.

He asked for the check, and she presented it with what he interpreted as a knowing smirk. He penned in a paltry tip and tossed in a coin from a collection he carried around with him for just such occasions.

*Memento Mori.* She mouthed the coin's inscription as Dave headed out the door. *Remember you will die.* That was the rough translation Google provided.

"Mind if I have a look at that?" The woman had walked over from the other side of the oval bar. She had been watching their interaction between the pyramid of liquor bottles and made her way around as soon as Dave walked off. She was beautiful in an understated way, with very little in the way of makeup and sunglasses that concealed her eyes. A bit dark for indoors, but not necessarily out of place in the swanky setting.

"Here you go," Melissa answered. "You can keep it if you like. That guy gave me the creeps. Can I get you anything?"

"No," the woman said. "This will do just fine." She placed the coin in her handbag and slid a twenty across the bar.

"Thanks. My name is Melissa."

The woman slipped off her glasses, folded them into a case and extended her hand. "Anna," she said. Her eyes were steely, with a Medusa-like intensity that suggested the sunglasses were for the benefit of everyone else in the room.

Anna walked out to the valet stand. The hundred she had tipped the valet upon her arrival assured that her car was waiting for her on the front line. She flipped down her visor and applied some lipstick as she waited for Dave's car to be brought around. She watched him pull out, then followed him down Collins Avenue from a safe distance.

# Chapter Fifty-Two

# SPREZZATURA

Mikey opened the door slowly and stepped into Caffè Vecchio. The song playing from the jukebox ended as if on cue as he walked in, lending a dramatic touch to an already charged moment as the room fell silent and all eyes turned to the stranger.

Joey walked over first and introduced himself. He flipped the Open sign to Closed and placed the *Members Only* placard in the window. "Everyone's here now, so I'm going to lock the door. Is that alright with you?" Joey asked in a respectful but perfunctory way.

"Of course." Mikey smiled like he understood perfectly. He put out his hand to Joey.

"Mikey Fortuna."

"So I've been told." Joey took his hand firmly and smiled back. "Joey Musante."

Nick and Ralph stood at the bar waiting for the guest of honor. Angelo stayed seated at his table in the back.

"I feel like I know this guy," Nick said to Ralph.

"Me too," Ralph answered. "But not from here, from the Tiki."

Mikey walked over to the bar. He had a nonchalant elegance in the way he carried himself, understated yet with an undercurrent of opulence. Sprezzatura was the word that came to mind. Mercifully, the jukebox started up again. Tony Bennett's "The Shadow of Your Smile" continued the mellow soundtrack, but did little to defuse the tension in the room.

"I know what you're thinking," Mikey started, but Ralph put up his hand, cutting him off.

"Before we get into all that, let's get you a drink. After all, you're a guest here, and well, we already have our drinks. Isn't that right, Nick?"

Ralph waved Angelo over, and the old man got up slowly, making his way over to join the group.

"That's right. Besides, I think I'm gonna need something stronger." Nick tapped his Peroni bottle with the back of his fingernail, and Alberto appeared behind the bar to take their order. He poured three shots of 1942 and an anisette for Angelo.

"To your dad," Mikey proposed, in deference to the deceased proprietor.

The four of them raised their glasses and knocked back their drinks. Nick signaled for four more, and Alberto complied. This time, Nick took the lead as they raised their glasses.

"To our guest, Mikey Fortuna." Before their glasses reached their lips, Nick amended the toast. "Or is it Julian?"

"Touché." Mikey smiled and knocked back his tequila. "But why don't we all take a seat. I've got quite a story to tell you, and I think it's gonna take a while."

They took a seat at a corner table, and Alberto brought over a massive charcuterie board, San Pellegrino, Aqua Panna, and opened two bottles of Amarone. Mikey took a deep breath as he placed his hands flat on the table. After all the time that had passed and everything that had transpired, he hardly knew where to start. His head hung forward noticeably as he let out an audible sigh. Angelo reached out and placed his hand on top of Mikey's, like he was reading his mind.

"Why don't you start at the beginning? That's usually the best place."

Mikey nodded. He took a sip of his Amarone, and it gave him a warm feeling that was just enough to encourage him. "Sorry about the Julian thing." He was looking at Nick and Ralph. "I gave up the identity of Mikey Fortuna almost thirty years ago, right after everything happened with Veronica. By the time they found those bones on the farm, he was already a ghost, so I just went with it. I know it sounds crazy, but with Veronica gone . . . it didn't feel right that he should continue to exist." The man's voice softened considerably at the mention of her name.

"That's not so crazy," Nick spoke up, sensing the man's pain and looking to let him off the hook so he could continue his tale.

"Thanks, Nick. I appreciate it." He took a large gulp of his wine and began. "I guess you can say it all started with a sketchbook. A sketchbook and a pimple ball."

Gary took a nearby barstool, and Joey spun a chair backward and took a seat a few feet from the table, leaning forward with his forearms crossed over the chair back. Mikey told the whole story in painful detail, from his baptism at the High Noon Saloon, to his penance at the Bamboo Inn, to Mikey Fortuna's supposed death, and his rebirth as Julian.

"This sounds like a Hollywood screenplay," Ralph said.

"Not exactly," Mikey countered. "Fiction is obliged to stick to possibilities. Truth isn't. That's how Mark Twain put it anyway. Besides, I can prove it."

"How's that?" Ralph asked.

"For starters, I'm the guy with the paintings . . . both of them." He looked across at Nick as he reached into his breast pocket. Joey subtly slid his hand down his leg toward his ankle holster. "Plus, I have this." Mikey placed an old cassette tape case down on the table. It was a blank TDK case with a date written in black marker on its edge—**March 25, 1990**, one week after the Gardner heist.

"I don't think we have anything to play that on," Nick said.

"No need, besides, it's too old to risk playing. I copied it to an MP3 file a while back." Mikey queued up a file on his phone and turned up the volume. "The Duke had a habit of taping people. Mostly down in his basement, but this one sounds like it was recorded at the Bamboo Inn. Guess he thought he could use them as an insurance policy."

"Then why didn't he?" Ralph asked.

"I've asked myself that same question quite a few times over the years. I've come up with a few possible explanations. First, maybe somebody else got to them before he could try. Second, he decided it wasn't worth it and just took his medicine, thinking he had a priceless masterpiece to come home to. Third, and I've come to believe this is the most likely explanation, he tried, but there was nothing of any real value on the other tapes. You know, just some low-level shit from years ago, way past the statute of limitations, no bodies. The only recording that would have given him any leverage was this one." Mikey tapped twice on the cassette case. He picked up his phone and looked at Nick for a long moment before starting the recording.

"Prepare yourself," he said, then pressed play.

The recording was a bit muffled, but a man's voice came through clearly enough. He asked a question that was soon answered by a second man on the recording. The voice was louder and clearer than the first. It rose up like a ghost from the phone's speaker and filled the room.

Nick nearly fell out of his chair.

# Chapter Fifty-Three

# DENROY

Grace and Ronnie pulled up to the front gate of the Royal Palm Club and Resort. Ronnie's beater didn't have a fancy coat of arms on the windshield, but Ronnie had something even more exclusive—Ralph Cappello's date of birth and member number. All the guys in the Tasker Morris crew used Ralph's membership number for access to the club and charged food and drink to the tab. They squared up monthly at the unofficial board meeting at the Dunkin' Donuts on Federal Highway. It was usually so jumbled up that after an hour or so of faux scrutiny and good-natured ball busting, Ralph just picked up half and everyone else whacked up the balance equally.

The gate rose, and they were greeted by Denroy. The valet was a friend of Frankie Stone Crab and drank for free at the Tiki. He had a beaming smile that explained why his face was the first one guests encountered at the club.

"What's up, my brother?" Denroy gripped Ronnie's hand in a soul shake and embraced him in a power hug. He bowed to Grace, and they exchanged a kiss on both cheeks. "How is my dear uncle Frank? I haven't seen him lately."

"He's in Philly with Nick," Grace said. "He'll be back soon."

"Good. We miss him around here. He's a better man than all these mummies put together." Denroy turned to cast a critical eye toward the club looming behind him.

Ronnie nodded in agreement. "That's for sure. Speaking of mummies, you seen Dave around?"

"Who's Dave?" Denroy asked.

"Drives a two-tone Spectre."

"Lots of them around here," Denroy answered.

"This guy claims to be a friend of Nick," Grace added a sarcastic note to the word *friend*.

"That motherfucker?" Denroy raised a hand to his mouth. "Excuse me, Grace."

"That's okay, Denroy. I couldn't agree more."

"He checked out yesterday. He was staying in a long-term rental in the bungalows. Walked around here like he was some big shot, talking down to everybody like some half-assed philosopher. Gave all the girls the creeps."

"That's him alright," Grace said. "Any idea where he was headed?"

"Nah. Pulled out of here in a hurry. Didn't even leave a tip, just gave my guy some corny-ass coin."

"Like this?" Ronnie pulled the Memento Mori coin from his pocket.

"Mother—" This time, Denroy caught himself as he eyed the coin.

"Fucker," Grace finished for him.

They took A1A back to Fort Lauderdale. Ronnie tried a little small talk to break the solemn mood, but the inevitable reality of the situation had become apparent. Dave was in the wind, and the chance that Kim was still alive somewhere had become more remote. Grace mindlessly scrolled through her Facebook feed to kill the time. It was a habit she was trying to break, but she needed some mindless distraction to take her mind off the worst-case scenario. And then the worst-case scenario popped up on her feed.

**Woman's Body Found Behind Warehouse.**

Grace clicked on the post. It opened up to a *Sun Sentinel* article about the discovery of a woman's body in a weed-strewn lot off Powerline Road in Pompano Beach. It was an industrial area populated with gas stations, warehouses, and a few gentlemen's clubs sprinkled between. The article went on to say the woman's identity had not been established, but speculated she might be a sex worker. No further details were provided, and a quick Google search turned up no other articles.

"What's wrong?" Ronnie asked as they pulled up to the entrance to Grace's condo building. She showed Ronnie the article and hunted around the bottom of her handbag for a tissue.

"It's Kim," she said.

Ronnie finished reading the article before answering her. "You don't know that. It could be anyone. She could be anywhere. She could have gone back north, could have relapsed and put herself in a rehab."

She sniffled and dabbed at the corner of her eyes with an old, bunched-up tissue. "I guess you're right." She forced a smile as she got out of the car and turned to blow Ronnie a kiss before walking through the sliding doors.

Neither of them noticed the man sitting in a parked Mercedes as he snapped pictures of Grace with his iPhone.

# Chapter Fifty-Four

# DMITRY

**WINSTON CIGAR LOUNGE**
**VIA ROMA, WORTH AVENUE**
**PALM BEACH**

Dmitry carefully heated the foot of a Padron 1964 Anniversary Series torpedo. He held the flame of a torch lighter at an angle, meticulously spinning the stick and toasting the cigar before placing it to his lips and puffing it into ignition. The lounge wasn't open for business yet, and Luigi, the host, was flitting about, prepping mixers, cutting limes, and filling lighters with butane. There was a knock at the door, and Luigi paused his preparations to walk over and open the door a crack to address the would-be customer. It was only fifteen minutes before opening, and the man seemed insistent.

He was a corpulent man of indeterminate Asian descent, dressed in a fashion-forward blend of Palm Beach couture sprinkled with Miami street wear, topped off with a red-banded Richard Mille watch that screamed newly minted tech centimillionaire. Luigi closed the door, leaving the man outside, and turned to Dmitry, who was by now enveloped in a glorious cloud of smoke. Dmitry took a quick look at the man through the glass door and shook his head in an almost imperceptible gesture that Luigi recognized as disapproval. Luigi instructed the man to come back in fifteen minutes. The man's face registered a mix of disappointment and effrontery.

"Look," Luigi told the man. "Come back in fifteen minutes and your first stick is on me, or don't come back ever. It's up to you."

The man looked down at his RM in a perfunctory gesture meant to buy him a moment and save some face. He made the calculation that he couldn't afford to be shut out from the social structure of the club. He smiled and gave a friendly wave to Luigi. He nodded to Dmitry, and Dmitry nodded back. The man walked off to get an espresso and kill some time.

Dmitry had been tracking a rumored sighting of a Nazi looted painting, *Portrait of a Lady*, rumored to have been spotted in a real estate listing in Argentina. It was a portrait of Countess Colleoni by Giuseppe Ghislandi. It was one of many works of art plundered by the Third Reich during World War II. Dmitry was a ruthless businessman who moved in the gray area of the art world, but he had a passion for tracking down Nazi looted art and reuniting it with its rightful heirs. He subscribed to a code that tolerated murder under the right circumstances, yet recoiled at fascism. The lead seemed solid, and he had reached out to an operative in South America to have a closer look. He would ordinarily have used Anastasia, but she was on an equally sensitive assignment in Miami, so he sat waiting for a man to arrive at the lounge. He would provide the man with funds and instruct him to report to Signature Aviation, a fixed base operator at Palm Beach International, where he would board Dmitry's G600 for the flight to Buenos Aires to connect with their operative on the ground.

He puffed on the Padron between sips of Pappy Van Winkle, and by the time the ice rock had melted in his glass and the cigar burned down to the band, the man had come and gone. Now, Dmitry set to attend to the more pressing issue, the recovery of both the stolen Rembrandt and the missing Caravaggio altarpiece. He opened an encrypted messaging app on his phone and sent a text to his man in Philadelphia asking for an update.

At Caffè Vecchio in South Philly, a phone pinged, indicating an incoming message.

# Chapter Fifty-Five

# PRODIGAL IN THE TAVERN

Mikey reached into his pocket to silence a secondary phone. His primary phone sat on a linen tablecloth before him, broadcasting a voice from the past.

*"Are you sure you want to do this? I mean, you have options here, you know what I mean? All you have to do is say the word, and I'll pull the plug on this whole thing."*

The voice was a bit gravelly; it belonged to an older man and carried the weight of authority and self-assurance. The accent was vaguely Brooklynesque.

The responding voice was the one that froze all in attendance and hit Nick in particular with the weight of a sledgehammer to the solar plexus.

*"No way. As much as I despise this cocksucker, I can't risk it. If it was just me, I'd say fuck it, let the chips fall where they may. But I can't put it past this prick to go after my Nicky. And I can't risk not being around to make sure that*

***doesn't happen.*** "The man cleared his throat in a distinctive manner, triggering memories that brought Nick to the verge of tears.

It was the voice of Nick's father, Anthony DiNobile, with all his inflections and colloquialisms brought back to life. And he was on the verge of giving away his most prized material possession, all in an effort to protect something he valued even greater. The room began to spin, and Nick reached out to grip the table, fearing he was about to pass out. Even Ralph rested his head in both hands, elbows on the table, as he leaned forward and listened intently.

Meanwhile, Tony DiNobile peered down at all assembled from his appointed position, captured in the reproduction of *Prodigal in the Tavern*, the painting situated above the jukebox. His old friend Virgil, the mad painter of Rittenhouse Square, had captured him in a perpetual salute, arm extended with a drink, smiling broadly. For years, he sat silent, but now he had found his voice.

"Stop," Nick ordered.

Mikey complied, and everyone in the room seemed to understand. It was all too much, and while a part of Nick rejoiced at hearing his father's voice, he needed some time to compose himself and sort out the implications. His father had turned over *A Lady and Gentleman in Black* to the Duke to ensure Nick's safety; that much was clear. The Duke had recorded the interaction in case things went south and he needed some corroborating evidence to back up his story to the feds. He hadn't counted on Mikey Fortuna snatching the tape, and certainly didn't suspect the painting had been switched out with Scotty's forgery.

"Did you know anything about this?" Nick was looking at Ralph when he said it.

"No way, kid. I'm as shocked as you." Ralph shrugged and turned his palms up to the ceiling.

"What about the other voice. Does anyone have any idea of who it might be?" Nick was addressing the room.

"I never could figure that one out," Mikey responded.

"Don't sound like nobody I know," Gary spoke up.

A chair made a scratchy sound as it was pushed back from the table. Angelo braced one arthritic hand on the table and the other on his cane as he thrust himself up to a standing position, although still bent over considerably at the waist. "I know who it is." The old man reached into his breast pocket for a handkerchief. He blew his nose loudly, without any apparent concern for maintaining appearances, a luxury afforded by his age and position.

"Well?" Nick was impatient and disregarded the deference ordinarily afforded to the man on account of his age and position.

Joey was squirming on his stool and seemed to be itching for something to pop off.

"I would know that voice anywhere, even though I haven't heard it in years." Angelo blew his nose one more time before answering the question everyone in the room was hanging on. "It's my old friend . . . Biagio Romano."

"As in Angie's grandfather?" Nick asked.

Angelo nodded. "The very same."

# Chapter Fifty-Six

# THE NATIVITY

**Oratorio di San Lorenzo, Palermo**
**October 17, 1969**

The boys managed to steal a ladder from Giuseppe, the painter. Antonio promised himself that he would find a way to return it when they had finished the job. It was Friday night, and they entered the church just after 10:00 p.m. They knew they wouldn't be disturbed, as Francesco, the caretaker, would be reliably drunk by then, stumbling home through the streets of Palermo. As remarkable as it might sound, the church doors weren't even locked. They had been altar boys at the Oratorio in their youth, and as such, were intimately familiar with its layout and history.

The altarpiece, completed by Michelangelo Merisi da Caravaggio in 1609, featured Saint Francis and Saint Lawrence worshiping the Christ child in the manger. Antonio, only seventeen years old, had marveled at the painting his whole life. He would kneel in a pew, struck by Caravaggio's vision of the Blessed Mother. In most other religious paintings and sculptures, Mary was depicted in an ethereal, otherworldly fashion, clothed in a flowing robe, arms extended in beneficence, her head covered in fabric, and sometimes surrounded by a halo. In *The Nativity*, Caravaggio simply painted her as a beautiful young mother, indistinguishable from the contemporary women of Palermo. Therein lay the genius of Caravaggio, and as Antonio stood there, knife in hand, about to slice the painting from its frame, he gazed upon her visage and begged her forgiveness for what he was about to do.

Giorgio had no such crisis of conscience. He leaned the ladder alongside the painting with efficiency. He gestured upward with his chin, indicating that Antonio should ascend with the knife while he held the ladder steady. Giorgio was the larger and less nimble of the two, so it had been decided that Antonio would be the one to do the actual climbing and cutting. He complied and took his time, cutting as delicately as a surgeon. Giorgio chided him to hurry, but with each slice, Antonio felt as if he were plunging his knife into the heart of the Blessed Mother. He wiped at the corner of his eyes with the back of his sleeve and nicked his forehead with the knife. A trickle of blood joined with the tears already streaming down his face, and a drop of the mixture plunged to the marble floor, like water turned to wine.

Giorgio had negotiated a sale to a local chieftain in advance, and the boys were going to split the proceeds. Antonio planned to use his share to take Maria, his girlfriend, to Philadelphia, where his uncle had promised to house them and provide him with work. He justified the theft as a necessary evil, a way to start fresh in the land of opportunity, where Maria would be safe, and the child she was carrying, his child, would be an American by birth.

They rolled the painting up in a carpet, which they also stole, and walked out the side door of the Oratorio without so much as a peep. Giorgio insisted they leave the ladder, as it would draw suspicion and prove to be too unwieldy for the two of them to carry along with the rolled-up carpet.  It was now after 2:00 a.m., and the streets of Palermo were deserted. They weaved their way through the narrow, twisty streets along Via Lungarini and past the Giardino Garibaldi. It was pitch-dark, save for a dim light emanating from the window of a Caffè, casting a strange shadow of the two boys upon the opposite wall. Antonio glanced at the shadow. They looked like two graverobbers carrying a body freshly plucked from its place of eternal rest. The image stuck with him for the rest of his short life. The only prayer he had left was that God's fury be visited upon him alone, and that Maria and his child would be spared his just punishment.

His punishment would arrive swiftly in the days that followed, at the end of a blade brandished by his childhood friend Giorgio, as the chieftain looked on approvingly. God granted his final prayer, and Maria, joined by her mother, managed to escape to America with the small pittance Giorgio had given her.

Six months later, a child was born at Pennsylvania Hospital. His mother would come to tell him the story of his father, a good, brave man who sacrificed everything for the two of them. She would also tell him a folktale about a stolen painting that would have sounded unbelievable if it were not true. Maria named him Antonio Michelangelo, but his friends in their South Philly neighborhood would come to call him Mikey.

GLORIA IN ECCELSIS DEO

# Chapter Fifty-Seven

## THE CONVERSATION

Nick still hadn't recovered from hearing his father's voice from the grave. He had spent the better part of his adult life grappling with the enigma that was Anthony DiNobile. Every time he thought he had learned everything he could about his father, another revelation would drop.

"Are you okay?" Ralph had walked over to the table and had his hand on Nick's shoulder. "How about we take a break?"

Nick reached up to his shoulder and patted Ralph's hand reassuringly. "No, I'm good. Let's get to the bottom of this. In fact, can we have the room to ourselves?"

Ralph glanced over at Angelo, who shrugged his shoulders. Mikey nodded his assent.

"Okay," Ralph said. "We'll be in the back if you need us." He turned and waved his arm as if it took a great effort. "Come on, guys, let's give these two lovebirds some space. Maybe Beto can whip us up some of those birria tacos." He draped his arm around Angelo's shoulder, and they left Nick and Mikey alone in the dining room.

"Stick?" Mikey reached into his breast pocket and placed a leather three-cigar holder on the table. He slid out two sticks and pushed one across the table to Nick.

"Thanks." Nick picked it up and inspected the band on the robusto-sized cigar. *Montecristo Habano.* "Nice stick," he remarked. "Can't say I've ever smoked one though."

"Cuban; they're all I've smoked for years. This one is called the Edmundo."

Nick used the cutter Mikey provided. It notched a perfect V-shaped cut across the cap. Mikey preferred it to a straight cut. So did Nick. He heated the foot of the cigar before lighting it, and as the smoke billowed around him, the band triggered a memory of the Dumas novel gifted to him from his father on a Christmas morning many years ago. The implications of Mikey's choice of cigar began to resonate. He excused himself to retrieve an ashtray from behind the bar.

"How about a bourbon to go with that?" Nick asked as Mikey lit his cigar.

"As long as you're joining me, why not?"

Nick placed two glasses on the bar. "Single large rock?"

"Neat for me," Mikey answered.

Nick placed a single rock in one glass and poured a measure into both. As he wiped his hands on a towel, he felt his phone vibrate. He reached into his pocket and opened a text message from a number he didn't recognize. It had a 718-area code. When he opened it, a photograph of Grace appeared. The picture was taken outside their condo building. She was smiling and brushing her hair back from her face in that casual way Nick found so endearing. One of many small gestures and mannerisms he adored in her but never mentioned. He considered them his secret treasures. He overcame his initial shock and, oddly enough, was fixated on how beautiful Grace appeared, even in what was undoubtedly a hastily snapped pic she wasn't aware was being taken. The message was clearly meant to be a subtle threat. Nick tried to shrug it off, but the message was nonetheless effective.

He looked up to see if Mikey was watching him or had detected him reaching for his phone, but "The Count of Monte Cristo" seemed to be preoccupied with retrohaling a plume of smoke from the Edmundo. Maybe it was the affront of someone sending him a picture of Grace and the threat inherently conveyed, but Nick found himself making an impulsive choice that went against all his principles. He reached into a box on the shelf beneath the register and felt around for the .38 he knew Joey kept there. He gripped the revolver and clumsily jammed it beneath his shirt, in the waistband next to the small of his back. It felt cold against his skin, and he hoped his belt was tight enough to keep it in place as he walked the drinks over to the table, returning to the bar only briefly to retrieve the ashtray.

"So, what shall we drink to?" Nick inquired once he had settled back into his seat.

"I heard you guys had some kind of proprietary toast around here. In fact, I overheard your friend Frankie Stone Crab propose it once at the Tiki."

"I can't say I recall. Then again, maybe I'm mistaken. After all, you were going by Julian back then."

Mikey placed his glass back on the table for a moment, interrupting the toast. "I'm sorry about that, Nick. Believe me, it wasn't personal. But now that the Duke is gone and I've accomplished what I set out to do all those years ago, there's no longer a need for subterfuge. Besides, I genuinely enjoyed watching you. Dmitry once told me that we were two sides of the same coin. I'm starting to think that might be true." He raised his glass once again. "What do you say we start fresh?"

"Okay. So I guess we're drinking to your revenge?"

"Revenge is its own elixir; it needs no toast. How about we drink to something even more fulfilling?"

"How about redemption?" Nick raised his glass but did not clink Mikey's yet.

"Sorry, Nick. I don't believe that's possible for me any longer, and I make a habit of never drinking to something I don't believe in. But something tells me maybe you do."

"The jury's still out on that, but I read a novel once that said, 'The sum of all human wisdom is contained in two words: Wait and hope.' Anyway, I think that's how it went. I'm pretty sure you know the book. So, your choice. Let's drink to something you do believe in."

Mikey didn't hesitate. "That's easy; to a father's selflessness." He clinked Nick's glass a bit roughly, as if emphasizing the importance of the toast.

Nick fell silent. Maybe Dmitry was right. Perhaps this man was more like him than he realized, and in this crazy universe, was it so hard to believe they had lived parallel lives? He reciprocated with a gentle clink and drank enough to feel the burn.

"So," Nick said, "about the paintings."

Mikey smiled. "What's your hurry? I've looked forward to meeting you for a long time, and we're finally getting to know one another. At the risk of sounding naïve, I was actually hoping we could become friends. Would that be the strangest thing?"

Nick considered it for a moment. "Yeah, it actually would. Besides, that all depends."

"Depends on what?"

Nick reached into his pocket, opened the picture of Grace on his phone and showed it to Mikey.

"Isn't that a picture of your wife? She's beautiful, Nick. God bless you guys. May I ask, why are you showing me this?" Mikey sounded sincere, and there was nothing in his reaction to seeing the picture that betrayed complicity.

"Someone sent me this a few moments ago. It appears to have been taken today, and it doesn't look like she knew it was being taken. I guess it's supposed to be some kind of message to me that she's being followed. You wouldn't happen to know anything about that now, would you?"

Mikey looked disappointed. "Is that why you put that thing in your waistband?" Nick squirmed a bit. "It's okay, Nick. I'm not offended. You're right to be suspicious. I guess I would have done the same thing. Two sides of the same coin, remember? But to answer your question..." Mikey placed his hand on his heart. "On the soul of my Veronica, I have no idea who took that picture or what they want. I'm a direct person, in case you hadn't noticed. I have no need to play little games. Ask me anything you like, and I'll tell you the truth." Mikey leaned back and placed his palms on the table like he was getting ready to submit to a polygraph test.

"The Duke. Was that you?"

"Right to the point huh? Good for you."

"Can I get you gentlemen anything?" Alberto walked over to the table timidly, hands folded in front of him.

"Another bottle of Amarone, please," Nick answered for both of them.

Alberto moved quickly and returned with a fresh bottle. "I'll be in the kitchen if you need anything else. Just holler." Mikey peeled off a hundred. Alberto looked at Nick. He nodded that it was okay, and Alberto accepted the bill and retired to the kitchen.

This time, Nick led the toast. "To Veronica."

The sound of her name coming out of someone else's mouth stunned him for a moment, and Mikey realized that her name had resided mainly in his own thoughts for decades.

"Thank you, Nick. That's very thoughtful of you." They drank, and Mikey picked up where he had left off. "As far as the Duke, let's just say he didn't get nearly what he deserved. It was quite the piece of performance art, though, if I do say so myself."

"And the nun?"

Mikey smiled. "No comment on that one. Make of that what you will, but for what it's worth, she was even worse than the Duke. I would suggest to you that her disappearance is no loss to humanity."

"Jesus Christ." Nick took a sip of his Amarone. "Wait. Ralph told me that back in the day, you were against putting hands on another person, even in the boxing gym. What the hell happened?"

Mikey shrugged. "The same thing that happens to all of us. The same thing that happened to you, I would venture. A sequence of cruel events that causes us to abandon our first innocent things and head down a path of survival. Once you choose that fork in the road, you become capable of anything."

"The best revenge is to be unlike he who performed the injury. A great man once said that."

"That's a cute saying. Let me ask, how's that working out for you?"

"Honestly? Sometimes good, other times . . . I wonder if maybe your way isn't better."

They drank and smoked, and Mikey filled in the blanks on his early life, the soul-shattering loss of Veronica, and his transformation into Julian.

"So what was it for you?" Nick asked. "You know, the innocent things you mentioned."

Mikey considered for a moment before responding. "It was many things, but if I had to nail it down to just one, I guess I'd say it was my sketchbook. You see, when I was a kid, before there was anyone to judge, I loved to draw."

"What type of things did you draw?" Nick nudged him like a therapist.

"Eh, nothing special. A little bit of everything I guess. I started with a bowl of fruit, because that's what I thought you were supposed to do. Eventually, I started drawing people I saw in the neighborhood, guys on the corner, drunks stumbling out of the bar." Mikey chuckled before finishing. "Even a few nuns. But mostly, I drew pictures of a girl from the seventh grade."

Nick seemed to really enjoy his answer. "What happened? Why did you give it up?"

"I had a few teachers who encouraged me, but then I fell and scraped my knees."

"I don't understand," Nick said.

"It's kind of a long story. I'll tell you some other time. Who knows, maybe we'll finish this conversation one day back at the Tiki Bar. I really grew fond of that place. Anyway, what about you? What did this fucked-up neighborhood steal from you?"

Nick knew the answer, but hesitated. It was a painful subject that continued to haunt him. With each year that passed, it became increasingly likely Nick would never get around to writing the book that was burning inside him. He decided to be candid with Mikey, as it seemed he was being pretty honest with him.

"I guess reading. You know, literature, novels, poems, everything... and writing. That was my first passion, and somewhere along the line, I'm not sure exactly when, I gave it up. And I've been vowing to get back to it for as long as I can remember."

"Passions can be tricky like that. You start out thinking you have all the time in the world, until the years pass and all the time in the world turns out to be pretty fucking short. And then one day, you buy a pint of half-and-half and wonder if you'll outlive the expiration date."

Nick nodded in agreement.

"Well, maybe after we settle our business, you can finally get around to it."

"I didn't realize we had all that much business to settle. I barely know what I have to do with this whole mess. All I really want to do is wrap this up and get back to my bar. Oh, and thanks for that image; I'll never look at a carton of half-and-half quite the same. I think from now on, I'll start drinking my coffee black."

"Funny you should mention the Tiki." Mikey touched up his stick on one side, as it had begun to burn unevenly. He ran the lighter along one side, then took a drag and blew the smoke out his nostrils in a masterful retrohale.

Something about the way he mentioned the Tiki made Nick a little sick to his stomach. "What do you say we focus on the paintings? That's why you're here, right?" Nick had texted Grace when he first received the picture to make sure she was okay. He checked his phone, and she still hadn't texted him back. His anxiety gave him some added urgency in wrapping the conversation up with Mikey, although in all honesty, he was enjoying it a great deal.

"Yes, the paintings. That's mainly why I'm here, but it isn't the only reason."

"Okay, let's start with *the Nativity*. Where do I fit in?"

"You don't. That's already been settled between Dmitry and the Italians. I'm just here as a middleman and to assure Angelo that it's already on a container ship headed across the Atlantic. It was in pretty bad shape, basically cut into two pieces, but not as bad as some had represented, partially eaten by rats and pigs and such. That was just an old wives' tale. There's already a team of world-class restorers waiting for its arrival and ready to use all their powers to bring it back to its former glory."

"And then it will be returned to the Oratorio in Palermo?" Nick asked, but he already knew the answer. There was no way the Italians would ever give it up again.

"Factum Arte did a masterful job with the reproduction hanging over the altar of the Oratorio. I've seen it, and it's quite beautiful. Almost indistinguishable from the original. Although I think Scotty would have done even better."

"How *is* Scotty these days?"

"Not so good. He's in an assisted living facility in Scottsdale. I visit him whenever I can, and he wants for nothing."

"I'm sorry to hear that. He was always a good guy."

"To Scotty." Mikey raised his glass. They drank, and Alberto magically appeared to refill their drinks.

"That brings us to the Rembrandt," Nick said. "It's all that's left."

"Not exactly. First of all, the Rembrandt belongs to me. I stole it fair and square. And Veronica paid for my foolishness with her life."

"It belonged to my father first," Nick countered. "You heard the tape."

"I wouldn't be here if I didn't think you should be compensated, Nick, and Dmitry agrees. Besides, I didn't know your father well, but the way he sacrificed the painting for your safety—well, let's just say it touched me deeply. You see, I never got to meet my father, but my mother did tell me a story once."

Nick knew he had very little to negotiate with. He would have preferred the painting be returned to its rightful place, back at the Gardner Museum, in the empty frame that yearned to be made whole again.

"That painting belongs back at the Gardner. I don't pretend to know you, but after all you've been through, something tells me you agree. I know Scotty would."

"It doesn't matter if I agree or not. You and me, we're pawns in this game. Two fleas arguing over who owns the dog. Guys like Dmitry, they fly at an altitude where the air is so thin, there's almost no turbulence at all, and as a result, they move more efficiently. What you or I want is of little consequence. Besides, you know Dmitry. Underneath all that bluster, he's still an art lover at his core. He'll probably keep it for a while, display it in one of his mansions or on his Yacht at the Monaco Grand Prix, and then return it to the Gardner in some grand display of philanthropy."

"So why are you even here? Why all the drama with Joey and Angie? Was all of that really necessary?"

"That wasn't my call. You know how these things go: people get nervous. They revert to their baser instincts and stick with what worked for them for years, what got them to where they are. I'm just a middleman, Nick, that's all I've ever been. And I always deliver, that's why *I'm* still here."

"So then what's left to be done? I mean, as much as I've enjoyed our conversation and the cigar, what else is there to talk about? I feel like this could have all been resolved without me."

"Not all of it. Not between us."

"What the hell does that mean? Have I done something to you I'm not aware of?"

"Of course not. If anything, it is I who has infringed upon you. I'm intrigued by you, Nick. Two sides of the same coin, remember? Let me ask you something. What do you want out of life?"

Nick took a long look at Mikey, trying to gauge his sincerity, to determine whether he was toying with him or had a genuine interest in his answer to an unanswerable question. He rose from his chair slowly, so as not to alert the man by any abrupt movement. The snub nose poked his spine. He had forgotten about it for a minute and suddenly felt foolish for his impulsive choice. He walked over to the jukebox, figuring it would buy him some time to sort out his thoughts.

"Any requests?" Nick asked.

"Not really. I'm sure you'll think of something appropriate."

For no discernible reason, a song popped into Nick's head— "Not on the Outside" by the Moments. It wasn't a song he had heard recently, and it had no particular relevance to the setting, but Nick figured it would do. There was a certain freedom he associated with moments like this, when he was operating on pure instinct. The combination of the alcohol and the jukebox allowed him to make whimsical choices he only wished he could replicate in everyday life. And it occurred to him... he'd never played a wrong song in his whole life. Nick cued up a few more songs to fill the time, resolving he would settle affairs before the last song in the set was over.

"Nice song," Mikey said as he returned to the table. "I don't think I've heard it since my days at the High Noon. It kind of took me back there for a moment. Has that ever happened to you?"

"Only every day of my life." Nick took a long, satisfying draw of the Montecristo.

"Have you given any more thought to my question?"

"It doesn't matter how long you think about it. There's no real answer. A man wants things out of life; he gets them, and then suddenly, he needs new things, or more of the same things. Either way, he's screwed. The best I can come up with is to learn to want what you already have."

Mikey seemed exceedingly pleased with Nick's answer. "How about what you once had?"

"That's trickier. You can't recapture the past. You should know that better than anyone."

"That might be true, but running from it is no better."

"I'm not running from anything," Nick answered.

"Are you sure about that? What sent you to Florida all those years ago?"

"Probably some of the same things that turned you into a ghost, I suppose. That's the tricky thing about life; it's lived forward but can only be understood in reverse."

"Well, I'm done haunting people now, and I'm ready to resume my old life, or at least a reasonable facsimile of what used to be my life. I'll never get over Veronica, that's something I just have to live with, but you still have a chance. After all, aren't you the one who believes in redemption?"

"Redemption isn't something you can readily seek out. The best you can hope for is that one day it comes looking for you."

"Well, maybe today is your lucky day."

"You'll have to forgive me for saying this, but it doesn't exactly feel that way."

"No, I suppose it doesn't, so let me be direct. How would ten million make you feel?"

Nick did his best to mask his shock. "What would I possibly do with ten million dollars? Besides, that sounds a bit unfair to you, and my experience is that one-sided deals rarely end well for all involved."

"You could fix up this place for starters. Don't get me wrong, I personally find it charming, a little slice of old South Philly, but it could use a few updates. Besides, maybe you should hear out the other side of the bargain before you form an opinion about what's fair."

"First of all, we like Caffè Vecchio just the way it is. That's why people come here. That's the way my father intended, and I'm not about to second-guess him. I made that mistake too often when I was younger. It's not missing anything."

"Sure it is. It's missing the most essential ingredient of all. And you'll forgive me, but I'm sure your father would agree. It's missing a DiNobile. It's missing you, Nick."

"I'm here right now, ain't I?"

"For the moment you are, sure. And then you'll go back to Florida and the Tiki, and the Caffè won't be the same without you. You're hiding, Nick. Believe me, I know what it's like to run away from yourself. It leaves a hole in you that no amount of money or women can fill. You want to talk about redemption? Well, here's your chance. It's time for you to come home."

Nick put his elbows on the table and made a peak with his hands. He tapped his fingers together a few times. Martha and the Vandellas' "I'm Ready for Love" played on the jukebox, the third verse, the one where the tone of the song shifts from one of excruciating longing to one of boundless possibility. He couldn't believe what he was about to do, but he knew down deep that Mikey was right. So he responded instinctively.

"What are the terms? Actually, hold on a sec. I want everyone here before we settle this. This affects them too." Nick signaled for Alberto and asked him to bring everyone else into the dining room.

Ralph and Angelo sat at the table. Gary and Joey hung back on the periphery, but still in earshot. Frank had arrived and stood behind Nick to one side, his hand on his nephew's shoulder.

Mikey spoke first. "The Tiki. I want to buy it. I'll keep it just the way it is, and you and the guys would have VIP privileges for life."

"Fuck that," Frank spoke up, but Nick raised his hand. He held Frank's hand tight to his shoulder and patted it reassuringly with the other.

"It's okay, Unc. We're just talking here." He turned back to Mikey. "Go on. Something tells me there's more to this."

"What makes you say that?" Mikey laughed a little, betraying that Nick was onto something.

"You know, the whole coin thing, two sides?"

"Yes, the coin. Indeed." Mikey leaned forward. "It's a bit personal, Nick. Is that okay?" His eyes moved about the room, taking in everyone in attendance, which by now also included Alberto and Beto, the cook.

"It's okay. I don't have anything to hide from anyone here. Say what's on your mind."

Mikey cleared his throat. "It's the girl, Nick."

"Cherchez la femme," Angelo muttered under his breath, mangling the pronunciation.

"Grace?" Nick was about to leap out of his seat, and for the first time, he was glad to have the .38 handy.

"Of course not." Nick settled back, and Mikey picked back up after a moment's hesitation. "It's Angie. We had quite the talk earlier. She's an amazing woman, Nick, but let's face it, life hasn't been easy for her either. She wants to come with me, make a fresh start. I just didn't want to do this deal, and then you find out later and feel some kind of way about it. If it doesn't sit right with you for some reason, I'll honor your wishes, and we can still do the deal. I just didn't feel right about keeping it to myself."

The room fell silent.

Beto retreated to the kitchen.

Nick thought he was ready for anything, but he hadn't expected that.

"Joey, play something, will ya." Frankie peeled off a twenty and handed it to him. The room stayed like that, frozen, until Teddy Pendergrass broke the silence with "You Can't Hide From Yourself." Alberto opened two bottles of 2010 Tommasi Amarone della Valpolicella Classico and set to placing wine glasses on the table, filling them as he went.

After a while, when all the glasses had been filled, Nick spoke in a firm, determined tone. "Angie doesn't belong to me. She never did. But I appreciate you telling me. It's what a gentleman would do. But aren't you a little old for her? Besides, I thought Veronica was the only woman for you."

"She is Nick. And she always will be. You're misunderstanding. This isn't romantic in the least. You see, I couldn't save Veronica, but maybe I could help Angie in some small way. I would be her benefactor. Strictly platonic."

"And she's on board with this?"

"She is."

Ralph and Angelo both nodded in approval.

"Just a word of advice though. I've known Angie for a long time. Don't make the mistake of believing she belongs to you either. She doesn't belong to anyone, and she plays the game better than either of us."

"You see, that's where you're wrong. Want to know how I can be so certain? I used to *be* you, Nick. And then a long time ago, I figured out that the only way to win the game is to stop playing it. And I haven't played it ever since. I find it a nuisance, white noise, like some meddlesome soap opera playing in the background. I've learned to tune it out, as I have all things, if you'll excuse the expression, that are beneath me.'"

"So, you're saying Angie is beneath you?"

For the first time in the conversation, Mikey hesitated. Nick couldn't say for sure, but it appeared Mikey was enjoying the challenge. After a moment of reflection, he answered. "No, she is neither beneath me nor my equal. But she's had a rough trip, clinging to you all these years, and I'd like to help her. Simple as that."

"Had I known all this, I might have held out for eleven."

"I don't know about that. If we're talking about the same girl, maybe it's you who should be paying me."

It was a good line. Nick raised his glass in recognition.

"It's time to let her go Nick," Mikey said.

"She's a good girl, Mikey. Look out for her. I never really could."

"No, she's not, but that's okay. I'm not such a good guy either. Besides, there will only ever be one woman for me, and she paid for my foolishness with her life. I'll never forgive myself for that. The part of me that could love unconditionally also died that day, and I'm okay with that."

"You know something? I'm genuinely sorry to hear you say that, though there have certainly been times in my life when I probably felt much the same way."

"And then what happened?"

"I waited for a long time. And hoped a little while longer. Then Grace came into my life. But to be honest with you, I did my best to fuck that up too."

"And now?"

"And now fate brought you through that door. I guess I shouldn't be surprised. My whole life has been a series of unlikely coincidences that, when all strung together, seem incomprehensible, so why even try?"

"And to what do you attribute that, my friend? Please don't say God."

"I honestly don't know. Nor do I really care. God? Sure, why not? But I'll leave you with this: something my father told me a long time ago, and I don't think I fully appreciated it until this second. He told me in this very dining room, 'There are only two ways to live your life. One is as if there are no such things as miracles.'"

"And the other?"

Nick took a sip of the Amarone and smiled. "As if everything is a fucking miracle."

Mikey didn't immediately have a retort for that, and for the first time in the conversation, Nick thought he might have actually gotten through to him.

Angelo broke the silence. "This has all been very entertaining, but where does this leave us?"

Mikey recounted the terms of the deal, much of which Angelo was already aware of, but summarized for the benefit of Ralph and the crew. The recitation had the same effect as a binding contract. Their cumulative honor secured the deal, but the implicit weight of their probable reactions to any breach is what cemented it. *The Nativity*, or what was left of it, would make its way back to the "rightful" owners in Sicily. Angelo and Mikey would split a predetermined commission. The Rembrandt would be transferred to Dmitry, and whatever deal he had with Mikey was between them. Nick would receive ten million for his troubles, which he would whack up among the crew. Title to the Tiki would transfer to High Noon Holdings South, LLC., and the Tasker Morris boys would retain lifetime VIP privileges. Mikey extended his hand to seal the deal.

Nick felt his phone vibrate and retrieved it from his pocket, leaving Mikey hanging and the room on edge. It was a text from Grace.

*Just landed. Getting in an Uber to the Caffè. You better be there.*

Nick was never happier to receive a threatening message from her, and it gave him an idea. One final nuance to the deal.

"I have one more condition . . ."

# Chapter Fifty-Eight

# MIAMI VICE

**OCEAN DRIVE
SOUTH BEACH, MIAMI**

Dave decided to take a walk along Ocean Drive for old times' sake. It was a far cry from its '90s glamour days and had mostly devolved into a scattering of chain-style watering holes and restaurants with plastic-coated picture menus thrust into your face as you walked by. The girl who approached him as he passed one such restaurant made a vague promise of free drinks in an accent that might have been Albanian. He declined abruptly. She was brash and rude and the opposite of the type of woman he was trolling for. Besides, she was a Miami 6 at best.

He finally gave up and ducked into the Clevelander for a quick beer before he returned to his room at the Eden Roc and moved on to exile in the Keys. He ordered a Miller Lite and took a sip. It was warm, and he decided his visit would be even briefer than he'd anticipated. The Clevelander was one of the last true spring break haunts. Since the city had cracked down so aggressively, the traditional bacchanalian fest had been all but gutted by increased police presence, checkpoints, and astronomical parking rates. It had worked. Arrests were up, crime was down, and Fort Lauderdale residents feared the party would move north to them.

He was about to ask for his check when he noticed the woman at the end of the bar. She was wearing an oversized T-shirt emblazoned with *Miami Beach* that she must have bought out of either necessity or desperation from one of the cheap T-shirt shops on Ocean Drive. Dave figured she had overstayed her beach day and was wearing her bikini underneath. She also wore a baseball cap, flip-flops, and oversized sunglasses, none of which detracted from an underlying beauty that refused to be covered up.

She had ordered one of the frozen drinks the strip was notorious for, probably something corny like a Miami Vice, and the bartender asked if she wanted to upgrade to a rum floater. Dave took close notice that she appeared to lack the confidence to refuse. When her bill was presented, she scrambled into a small purse, taking out crumpled-up bills one at a time and smoothing them out on the bar. It became clear that she was coming up short, and the bartender was becoming impatient. She was digging in her purse, now extracting coins. She bit her lip nervously as she mumbled an apology. Dave saw his opening.

"Excuse me," he said to the bartender. "I got it." He placed two twenties on the bar. The floater, service charge, Miami Beach tax, and State of Florida tax pushed the drink north of $25.00.

"No, you don't have to do that," she said sheepishly, but the look of relief on her face suggested she was hoping he would. "I was meeting my girlfriend here. We were supposed to be on a girls' vacation, but then her boyfriend called her, all jealous about something she posted on Instagram, so now she cut her trip short. We have two more nights at our Airbnb, so I figured, fuck it, I might as well stay by myself."

"Sounds perfectly reasonable to me," Dave said. "How's that drink?"

"Pretty good," she said as she slurped an impressive gulp through her straw. She smiled proudly after swallowing it down. "I'm Anna, by the way."

"Dave."

They shook hands. Dave bought her two more drinks and tolerated one more lukewarm Miller Lite as they made small talk, which consisted mainly of Dave pretending to listen intently as she told him about her excruciatingly boring life back in Pittsburgh. For all her annoying banter and cringe-worthy mannerisms, she displayed a quality that Dave valued above all others: vulnerability.

He offered to give her a ride back to her Airbnb, which turned out to be in one of the still sketchy areas of Wynwood, and she readily accepted. Dave ogled her the entire ride over as she continued to drone on about her ex and her job, which she insisted she had been fired from unfairly, and about all the other painful minutiae that constituted what he concluded was a pathetic existence. At least it passed the time until they arrived at her Airbnb.

"Make yourself comfortable," she said as she filled a tea kettle and placed it on the gas range. "Sorry, I don't have any liquor, but let me fix you a tea."

"I'm okay," Dave said.

"Oh, come on. I accepted your hospitality. Allow me to pay you back for everything you've done. Besides, it will relax you, I promise. I'll just freshen up a bit while you enjoy it."

Dave relented. The kettle whistled, and Anna prepared his cup.

"I'll be right back," she said as she spun on her heel and walked into the bedroom. "This won't take long." She pulled her T-shirt over her head before she shut the door behind her, allowing him a glimpse of her bare back.

Dave took a sip of the tea. "Not bad," he remarked to himself, taking another sip.

The drinks from the Eden Roc and those lukewarm Miller Lites must have caught up with him, as he found he had lost track of time. For a minute, he thought maybe he had fallen asleep for a while, except he couldn't tell if it had been for two minutes or two hours.

"Hello, Dave." Anna was standing before him. Except that she looked different. The sunglasses and ball cap were gone. So was the cringeworthy personality. Her demeanor was stern and not the least bit vulnerable.

That's when he first realized he couldn't move or speak. He tried to summon his legs to move, then his arms, then his fingers, all without success. He tried to talk, but his lips and tongue felt like they no longer belonged to him.

"I know what you must be thinking right now, but don't be alarmed; I assure you, you'll still be able to feel pain." She flicked open a tactical blade he hadn't even seen her holding and sliced his arm in one deft move. "See?"

She was right, he could still feel pain. Dave tried to cry out but was unable to.

"I'm not going to lie, Dave. This isn't going to be quick." She unrolled a leather case of various tools and blades, placing them on the coffee table in front of her. She used one of the blades to cut off his shirt, and that's when he noticed the propane torch she must have retrieved while he was sleeping. A tear rolled down his face.

"Oh, good, you can still cry. You see, I haven't mixed this particular cocktail for quite some time. In fact, it's the first time I've tried it in the States. My father taught me how to make it many years ago in Kyiv, and I'm a little rusty."

Dave would have screamed now if he could, and somewhere in his head, he did.

"Oh my." Anastasia put her hand to her chest as if she were clutching an invisible string of pearls. "I almost forgot." She reached into her pocket and pulled out a coin. She held it up directly in front of Dave's unblinking eye. "Memento Mori. I'm pretty sure you know what that means." She wedged it into his frozen fist.

Sweat poured down Dave's face. His eyes managed to open a bit wider as Anastasia fired up the propane torch and adjusted it to a narrow flame.

"Darling," she said as she approached. "You look so . . . vulnerable."

Three hours later, she gathered her tools and slipped out of the Airbnb she had rented under an alias. She didn't text Dmitry until she had arrived at Miami Executive Airport, and then only two words.

***It's done.***

# Chapter Fifty-Nine

# MOON OVER FORT LAUDERDALE

**Veronica's Tiki Bar**
**One Year Later**

Mikey had settled into his role as proprietor of the Tiki, which he renamed after Veronica. Angie had also settled in nicely enough, even joining Ronnie behind the bar for a few shifts. A few people would occasionally still call him Julian, a slip-up he generally resolved with a friendly smile, a firm handshake, and a jovial hint: "My friends call me Mikey." He had to remind himself from time to time that he was a host and each visitor was a guest, although he would never fully let down his guard. Ralph continued to be a regular patron, and the Stone Crab was like a piece of furniture.

Tonight marked the monthly full moon party, and a decent crowd had assembled for the festivities. Mikey hung back a bit, sitting at a table on the periphery that had become the unofficial owner's table. He mostly held court there with some of the Tasker Morris crew, the conversation alternating between current events and reminiscing about the old days. The calendar promised a super moon, a full moon that occurs during perigee, when the moon's orbit brings it closest to Earth. Some of the patrons wandered down to the water's edge to take pictures of the extra-large orb with their phones, but they would all be disappointed with the results. There was simply no substitute for experiencing it in real time with the naked eye. They would have been better served by simply sitting in silence and allowing its magnificence to wash over them.

Angie was bartending, but had taken a smoke break and was sitting on a stool next to the beach chair hut. She sat with her legs crossed, one arm crossed over her midsection, the other propped up at the elbow, cigarette dangling between two fingers. Her eyes were on the horizon, and as the moon began to crest, it illuminated one side of her face more prominently, making her look like Caravaggio's *Saint Catherine of Alexandria*. As the moon rose above the ocean, she seemed to fall into a trance, as if she were struggling to recall a memory from long ago.

Mikey watched from a distance. He took a sip of his Eagle Rare bourbon, his left hand resting on a black sketchpad. The textured surface felt reassuring and helped transport him to a more innocent time. A postcard stuck out from the top of the pages. Mikey used it as a bookmark but kept it one page ahead so as not to smear his drawings. He opened the sketchbook to a fresh page and looked at the postcard. It was from the Isabella Stewart Gardner Museum. It depicted Rembrandt's *A Lady and Gentleman in Black* back in its original frame. Mikey's prediction had been correct, and after a nearly yearlong underground tour, Dmitry had finally returned the painting to its rightful home to much fanfare, even donating the reward money to a youth arts program in Boston.

This particular postcard bore a hand-cancelled "B. Free Franklin" postmark from the Ben Franklin Post Office in Philadelphia. It read:

To Mikey,

Never forget

Everything is a Miracle.

Nick

Mikey started to sketch Angie's face, realizing he could no better capture the riddle of her gaze than the iPhone crowd could hope to capture the mystery of the moon.

Still, he sketched away.

# Chapter Sixty

# MOON OVER SOUTH PHILLY

**Caffè Vecchio**
**Also One Year Later**


Nick sat at his father's old corner table, where he now held court most nights of the week. The restaurant practically ran itself, what with Gary managing things in the back of the house and Grace taking over most of the hostess duties. Ralph and Frank dropped in from time to time, and when January rolled around, Nick and Grace headed back to Florida for a couple of months. His bones just couldn't tolerate that deep cold any longer. Mikey Fortuna made a big production about rolling out the red carpet for him, and he played along for a bit, trading stories and playing some songs, but he had given up drinking, other than the occasional glass of Amarone, and his heart just wasn't in it anymore. Besides, Vecchio was home now, and while he felt as if he still had plenty of good years ahead of him, he hoped that when his time came, he would leave the earth right where he sat.

The busboy brought over some bread and olive oil. "Can I get you anything else?" he asked.

"No thank you, Arjun. How's everything going?"

"Everything is great. I start Drexel in the fall."

"How's the apartment?" Nick asked.

"I love it. Thank you so much."

Grace had agreed to relocate to Philadelphia on one condition—that Arjun come with them. Nick was happy to agree and had taken a genuine liking to the boy. They fixed up the apartment above the Caffè, where he would be close to Nick and Grace. Arjun was a mathematics prodigy and was accepted into Drexel's mechanical engineering program, where he intended to pursue a concentration in aerospace engineering. Or as Frankie Sone Crab would put it, "Kid's a fucking rocket scientist."

"There's a super moon tonight. Have you seen it?" Arjun asked.

"Not yet, maybe later." Nick knew about the super moon but, for some reason, had been avoiding it.

"Okay, don't wait too long." Arjun smiled as he rushed off to bus another table.

Nick took out a small Moleskine notebook from his pocket. Grace had bought it for him when they first moved back and suggested he start keeping a journal. It seemed a bit silly at first, but eventually, he began to write about things that felt as if they had been trapped inside him for decades. Sometimes he would read parts of it to Grace, and it felt pretty good.

Nick absentmindedly looked out the front window, and there it was—the super moon. He felt himself transfixed and on the verge of lapsing into one of his old spells, the ones that usually precipitated nostalgia-fueled benders supercharged by alcohol and music, until he found himself with a regret-filled hangover that made his head feel like a snow globe swirling with cherry blossoms. It was at that moment, on the precipice of ruin, that Nick realized the moon was no longer there. Another heavenly body had stepped into his line of sight and eclipsed it.

"How's it going, DiNobile?" Grace was leaning over the table with that mischievous smile that still made his heart skip a beat.

"I'm good, just writing down a few thoughts."

"Oh really?" Grace teased him.

Just then, Arjun came running over, phone in hand. "You're not going to believe this, but I just got an email from Drexel; I'm receiving a private scholarship to cover whatever Drexel doesn't pay, including room and board."

"Oh my God, Arjun, that's great news." Grace hugged him and kissed him on the cheek. "Who's it from?"

"That's the funny thing. I don't even recall applying for it, but apparently it's from something called the Tasker Morris Foundation." He turned to Nick. "Have you ever heard of it?"

Nick shrugged. "No idea. Don't be quitting on us now."

"No way. I love it here," Arjun said before heading over to clear another table.

Grace stood with her arms folded, staring at Nick with a mixture of amazement and admiration. "You're a good man, DiNobile."

Nick cleared his throat and brushed a piece of dust from the corner of his eye. "No, I'm not," he said. "But I'm trying to be."

"Hold that thought. I'll be right back. There's something I need to do."

Grace walked over to the jukebox, and Nick followed her with his eyes; she was as beautiful to him as ever. Above the jukebox, next to

*The Prodigal in the Tavern* that depicted Tony DiNobile as the prodigal, hung a new painting. It was the last condition Nick had insisted on; Scotty's forgery of *A Lady and Gentleman in Black*. Nick focused on the empty space between the two figures, where Rembrandt had painted over the child to soothe a mother's grief. Nick could never get that story out of his head, but now, for the first time, the space didn't seem so empty anymore.

Grace returned and sat in Nick's lap, her arms wrapped around his neck. Her song began to play: "I Believe in You and Me" by the Four Tops.

"How'd I do, my love?" Grace asked.

"You did great, baby, just great."

"Good," she said. "So then kiss me."

And he did.

# EPILOGUE

**NICK DINOBILE**

If I'm being honest with myself (Is anyone ever truly *dishonest* with themselves? I mean, down deep, don't we always know the truth?), I guess I always knew I'd end up back at the Caffè. Back where it all started, where all the hurt began. I thought I was letting go of attachments and breaking the cycle of suffering when I first left, but part of me was always on the run, in perpetual motion like a rogue shark. I was running from ghosts that had way more endurance than I did, and lately, I was feeling exhausted. Those ghouls had been snapping at my heels for decades. They'll always win in the end. That is, unless you turn and face them—fight them, or hug them, or laugh at them. Whatever it takes to confront the dragon. Notice I didn't say *slay*. I'm not sure slaying is necessary, or even possible.

For me, that meant grappling with my father's legacy and embracing all his complexities instead of continuing to bristle at his memory. Because, as it turns out, I think we have a lot in common after all. That's what Gary was always trying to make me realize all these years. That's what the paintings whisper to me as I sit at my father's table, sipping an espresso, communing with the art he had assembled, and I continue to add to.

Thank God for Grace. I never would have been able to figure these things out without her support. I'd still be swimming in circles in that vast, cold ocean, afraid to stop lest I perish. Don't get me wrong, I'm still pretty fucked up. You don't flip a switch on years of denial and simply shut off the trauma like the light in the Caffè window at closing time. Because just when you think you're past it, that you can finally breathe, the universe throws you one last curveball.

I still get down to Florida, especially after the first snowflakes fall. They're beautiful when they first begin their descent, but I just can't handle the cold anymore after all the years away. So when the tiny white crystals raced at my windshield, and I found myself flipping on the intermittent wipers during a mid-December drive down the Atlantic City Expressway, I pulled over at the Frank Farley Service Plaza, grabbed a coffee, and booked a flight for the next day. Both Ralph and Frank had been inquiring about when I planned to visit. Lately, something about their calls and texts suggested there was more to it than a simple desire to catch up and reminisce. I pulled out of the rest stop and immediately felt lighter for having booked the flight.

I drove to a cigar lounge on Tennessee Avenue in the Orange Loop section of Atlantic City. It was an oasis of calm in an otherwise rough area. I kept a locker there stocked with some hard-to-get cigars, a bottle of Blanton's, and, at Big Gary's insistence, a Smith & Wesson .38. I was off the hard liquor, and I hadn't touched the .38 since I put it there, but I still enjoyed a cigar with a double espresso. I picked up a box of Rembrandts from the El Septimo Sacred Arts Collection. It came in a gorgeous red lacquered box with an image of the master's *Return of the Prodigal Son* emblazoned on the lid, so I couldn't resist. I placed five of the sticks in a Ziploc bag for my pending trip and put the box in my locker.

When I landed in Palm Beach the next day, I Ubered to the condo Grace and I had purchased after selling our place in Lauderdale. After Mikey Fortuna took over the Tiki, I tried to cut some ties to the Lauderdale area and start fresh. The condo in Boca was close enough for me to stay in touch with the Tasker Morris guys and visit the Tiki when I was feeling a bit nostalgic, but still preserve a little distance. Grace had given me some good-natured grief about my sudden trip. Her mother was in for a visit, so she couldn't join me. After a few playful jabs, she decided her heart wasn't in it, so she settled for a gentle kiss and a not-so-gentle fist to my midsection. I got the message. *Fair enough*, I thought.

Frank picked me up in the RAV4 he had extracted from Mikey as a last-minute concession on the eve of settlement. Mikey had just smiled and tossed the keys onto the table. It was a slick move by Frankie the Stone Crab, and a classy move by Mikey. We made some small talk on the ride over. Frank drove us along the beach and flicked a few Marlboro butts at the oceanfront mansion gates along the Hillsboro Mile as he chain-smoked his way south. There was no sense in complaining, so I just cracked my window and fiddled with the radio as the Stone Crab brought me up on the latest gossip. He was rambling nonstop about various goings on and petty grievances. I've known Frank all my life, so it wasn't difficult to figure out that his rapid-fire delivery was a half-hearted attempt to keep me from asking any questions. There was something he didn't want to tell me. I turned off the radio and interrupted him, waiting for the inevitable curveball to break over the plate.

"What's going on at the Tiki?"

Frank fumbled with a pack of Marlboros to buy himself some time. "Maybe you should just talk to Ralph when we get there."

"Well, we still have fifteen minutes or so, and I'm talking to you now."

Frank turned the radio back on and took a deep drag of his Marlboro, buying himself a few more seconds before responding. "I've been hearing some talk about Mikey possibly putting the Tiki up for sale."

"Possibly? It's either for sale or it isn't."

"Okay, likely. Probably. Maybe definitely." Frank wasn't good at keeping a secret once I pressed him. "Just please don't tell Ralph I told you. He wanted to talk to you first. He made me promise."

"I'll remember not to ask you to make any promises." I couldn't help taking a playful swipe at my uncle.

"Thanks, Nicky."

When we got to the Tiki, now renamed Veronica's, Ralph hadn't arrived. It took me a while to wade through the crowd of regulars eager to say hello and buy me a drink, all of which I politely declined. I scanned the crowd for any sign of Ralph, but truthfully, I guess I was also checking to see if Angie was there. There I was, back for a hot minute and already telling white lies to myself. I can't really say if I was relieved or disappointed by her absence.

Once I got through the crowd, I found a spot close to the beach and was pleased to see my old friend Ronnie Cruz behind the bar. He smiled broadly and placed a club soda in front of me.

"What's up, *jefe*?" He raised his arm and clapped my hand in a soulful grip.

"All good, my friend. Better now that I'm with you. Anybody around?" It was an open-ended question, and Ronnie answered by shooting a worried glance toward the beach.

I followed his gaze down to the edge of the property, where the Tiki meets the sand. Mikey was standing at the top of the stairs leading down to the beach, leaning against a pillar. A woman stood on the other side of the pillar, wrestling with a small child as she attempted to rinse him off under the beachfront shower. It looked like she was losing the match. I wasn't sure what Mikey was wrestling with, but from the looks of it, he didn't appear to be doing much better. He was looking out at the horizon as the SS *United States* made its final voyage from its berth in Philadelphia, under tow by a tugboat, her engines having been silenced long ago.

She resembled an aged starlet of the Golden Age of Hollywood, being pushed around a nursing home in a wheelchair. After over a decade of raising millions to preserve and convert her to something approaching her previous glory (a hotel or a museum), the Conservancy had finally concluded she was best suited for sinking. The once proud vessel had become obsolete, and the efforts to save her, while noble, turned out to be an exercise in futility. In her afterlife, she would support organisms that would latch onto her skeleton, providing shelter and nutrition for larger sea creatures. Not very sexy, but probably better than a tourist trap.

"How's it going, Mikey?"

He turned toward me with a jolt and a stern look on his face. That hard look morphed into a smile as soon as he realized it was me and not some crypt keeper from his past showing up to settle an ancient debt. I recognized that look well, having spent most of my adult life with my head on a swivel.

"Nick!" He grabbed me in a bear hug, and the sketchbook wedged under his arm fell to the ground in the process. I bent down to pick it up for him. It was opened to a random page, and for a split second, I glanced at a sketch of a woman who looked an awful lot like Angie. A quick electric jolt travelled through my body. I might have healed myself to an extent, but I still couldn't control my nervous system from reacting to the sudden shock of seeing her face, even if it was just a sketch. I quickly snapped the sketchbook closed, not mentioning the sketch. It was the gentlemanly thing to do. Besides, in all fairness, I wouldn't want him reading passages from my journal either.

"You look good, Mikey." And he did; tan, well dressed as always. Maybe a little grayer at the temples, or perhaps it was just the contrast with his bronzed complexion.

"Eh, I've put on a few pounds." He patted his midsection. "It's this place, I guess."

"Is that why you're selling it?"

He recoiled a bit at my question. "Right to the point, huh? You always were pretty direct. It's one of the many things I like about you." He extended his arm to put it around my shoulder, but I pulled back. "Come on, Nick. Let's go to the bar, and I'll tell you everything you want to know."

I allowed him to put his arm around me, and he guided me over to my old table. It felt strange sitting there as a guest, like running into an old flame with her new boyfriend. I ran my fingers over the surface. The sun-drenched and salt-sprayed lacquer had given way to the bare wood beneath. It didn't feel all that different from the bar at Caffè Vecchio.

"So what's the deal, you're selling the Tiki?" I asked as soon as he took his seat. Ronnie interrupted us for a moment to take our drink order. I stuck with the club soda, but it wasn't easy.

"It's not what you think, Nick. If it were just the Tiki, I would offer it back to you. A developer wants to put a tower here, but they've assured me they'll maintain retail space on the ground level for a restaurant, so there will still be an oceanfront bar here."

"A restaurant bar? That's bullshit, Mikey. That was never the deal. Besides, Tasker Morris has a right of first refusal. What the fuck happened to you? I thought we had an understanding. Not just about the Tiki, but about everything."

"I know, I know." Mikey put his head down, looking a bit dejected. Even his Loro Piana shirt and Patek Perpetual Calendar couldn't mask the inexorable reality—he was getting older. "I'm just tired, Nick. And you know me, I could never turn down a good deal. And believe me, this one is incredible."

"Do I even know you? I thought maybe I did. But how much fucking money do you really need?" I snapped. "I don't think that's what this is about at all. So why don't you level with me? After all, I've always been straight with you."

He looked up at me with a reluctant smile as he ran his fingers across the marbled cover of the sketchbook. "You're right. It's not the money. I mean, it is a little bit, but..."

"Fuck the money." I'd had enough of this dance. "Tasker Morris will match any bona fide offer. And by the way, if your buyer thinks they're gonna build some monstrosity here, they've got another thing coming. We'll bury that plan in zoning with so much red tape and political pressure, they'll run back to Dubai or wherever the fuck they're from. Ain't that right, Ralph?"

Ralph and Frank had walked over during my rant. Ronnie dropped off our drinks and beat a hasty retreat, sensing the growing tension.

"Absofuckinglutely." Ralph lit a Padrón as he took a seat. Frank puffed out his chest, doing his best to conjure up the Stone Crab of old.

"Let me finish," Mikey said.

Ralph put out a meaty hand and gestured toward me in a way meant to signal that I should settle down a bit. I complied.

"I'm just restless, guys. It was good for a while, but I can't stay in one place for too long. I was going to give you the opportunity, but—"

"Stop," Ralph said gently. He put a hand on Mikey's shoulder and angled his head down, peering over his glasses so he could look him dead in the eyes. "There's something you're leaving out."

Mikey took a sip of his bourbon and put up his hands in surrender. "Okay, okay, you're right, it's not just the money. I need to get out of here. I feel like a caged animal."

"And?" I pressed him a bit.

"It's Veronica. I just can't stand being here, thinking about what could have been. This should have been *our* life. And lately, well, God forgive me, sometimes I think about joining her."

I looked out at the ocean. The ship that had broken the transatlantic speed record continued to creep along reluctantly, her tow cable dragging her to a watery grave. She glided from left to right before me and would soon be out of sight for eternity. I thought about the danger of attachment and how difficult it can be to let go gracefully, even when every fiber of your being is telling you it's the right thing to do.

I couldn't help feeling bad for Mikey, and this time it was me who gestured to Ralph to take it easy on him.

Mikey had been through a lot in his life, and I'd hoped he had come out the other side. But I knew better than anyone what he must have been going through—some shit just changes you. I mean, he had already risen from the dead once, so I guess I couldn't fault him for not coming up with an encore. I tempered my remarks, as I was certain this man would never again know true love, at least during this lifetime.

"Okay, I get it. Thanks for leveling with me." Ralph said. "But that's no reason to do something crazy like selling the Tiki out from under us and burying it under some concrete tomb. And it's certainly not a reason to do something even crazier."

"I know." Mikey seemed different now that everything was off his chest. "I wasn't thinking straight for a minute. I'm sorry, Ralph. Of course, I'll sell it back to Tasker Morris."

"And at a fair price?" Ralph added.

"A fair price." Mikey raised his glass.

"What about Angie?" I couldn't help asking.

"I did everything I could for her, but it turns out she's just as restless as you and me. Last I heard, she went to Palm Beach with some guy she met on Las Olas, and they're living at The Breakers."

I smiled and shook my head a little. I'm not going to say it didn't sting to hear it, but it was nothing like the jolt of electricity I would have felt years ago. I guess I'll take it. After all, what other choice do I really have?

Ronnie walked over with another round. My club soda was now conspicuously absent, and a bourbon had taken its place. He had also poured one for himself. We all raised our glasses.

"You have the honors, Mikey." I deferred to the guy with the broken heart. I had learned that kernel of drinker's etiquette many years ago, at the Caffe.

He paused for a moment, and I was worried he would propose a toast I couldn't get behind. But in the end, he did the right thing.

"To the Tiki," he said, and we all clinked glasses. "Long may she live."

"To the Tiki." We all echoed the toast and drank. I had given in. The bourbon felt good, good and dangerous. I guess sometimes that's the best part.

Ronnie raised what was left in his glass to me. "Welcome back, boss."

I paused for a moment, as I hadn't really thought that part through; things were happening so quickly. I raised my glass and stared out at the horizon. The ship was gone. My mind must have been playing tricks on me, but at the water's edge, through the afternoon haze, I thought I saw a beautiful woman who looked an awful lot like Grace. Mikey was looking in the same direction, at the same woman, but I'm sure his mind saw someone else, someone from long ago. *Two sides of the same coin*, I thought. We all sat in silence for a moment, each one of us a survivor of his own personal shipwreck, marooned together and finding shelter under the shade of a tiki hut.

"Play a few songs, will you, Ronnie? And get me a Peroni to back this up."

I drained what was left of my bourbon as Ronnie fired up some of the old tunes. The first selection kicked in, "Standing in the Shadows of Love" by the Four Tops.

Ralph snapped his fingers as he shuffled back to his seat, my Uncle Frank kissed me on the cheek, and even Mikey had a smile on his face.


THE END

# Acknowledgements

Nick has had quite the journey over the course of three books, and this one certainly had some twists and turns I wasn't expecting. Hopefully, the kind readers who have taken the trip with us feel the same. I'm always excited when the characters do and say things that surprise me, and I believe that is when writing is at its purest. Writing Redemption of the Prodigal was a challenging endeavor, so I'd like to thank the readers, because the joy I experience from anticipating your laughs and tears is what keeps me going when the writing gets tough. So, to the person holding this book, thank you. None of this is possible without you.

Thank you, as always, to Elizabeth E. White for her exacting yet compassionate editing. Any errors are mine and not hers.

Thank you to Christian Storm for the exciting cover. In the end, the story ended up mirroring the cover, another unintended surprise!

*Redemption* had me revisiting the street corners, bars, and haunts of my South Philly youth. I owe a debt of gratitude to all the guys I shared those years and beers with. I won't name them because God forbid I forget somebody! I will, however, single out my oldest and dearest friend, Michael Marinucci, for his unwavering loyalty. I thought about him more than he can imagine during the writing of the *Prodigal* novels. Thank you Michael, for always having my back and wanting what was best for me, even when I was too foolish to realize it.

A very special thank you to the Honorable T. Francis Shields for his constant encouragement and support.

Thank you to Coby Frier and all the guys at the Tennessee Avenue Tobacco cigar lounge in Atlantic City for giving me a place to reflect and find inspiration. I wrote a good deal of the Ducktown and Orange Loop chapters while sitting there and sipping bourbon. Thank you all for your brotherhood and encouragement. Thank you also to John Exadaktilos for making me feel welcome at the Ducktown Tavern.

This book is dedicated to my grandmother, Santa Ruggio. The quiet daily sacrifices she made for her family made our happiness possible.

This book is in memory of my dear friend, Anthony "Radar" Risoli for always encouraging me. I still hear you whisper to me in the palm trees.

Thank you to the kids, Nicky, Santino, and Sophia. Having children who look up to me keeps me humble and accountable, qualities that are good for any author.

My wife, Christine, is my single most important reader, editor, and cheerleader. These books belong to her as much as to me. Thank you, my love. I believe in you and me.

Nick has certainly evolved throughout the novels. I hope you have enjoyed his sometimes-tortured journey and transformation. The first-person epilogue is my personal gift to the readers. Please let me know how you liked it. His journey is far from over, and as I write this, the characters are starting to speak to me again, demanding yet another adventure. Because, as I'm sure you've come to realize, there is always another stolen painting to be recovered.

# About the author

Michael Caudo is a Philadelphia attorney and novelist whose work blends crime, art, and the complex loyalties that shape us. Raised in the tight-knit neighborhoods of South Philadelphia, he draws on lived experience to explore themes of love, loss, and family through the lens of crime fiction.

Redemption of the Prodigal is the third novel in the Prodigal Trilogy. Each book can be read as a standalone thriller.

# Also by Michael Caudo

RETURN OF THE PRODIGAL
REVENGE OF THE PRODIGAL


For exciting updates about the world of Nick Di Nobile and the Prodigal crew, join us in the Prodigal Cabana Club at caudobooks.com. You'll be the first to learn about events, giveaways, bonus material and updates about the Prodigal Series.

caudobooks.com
Instagram: @michael_caudo_author
Facebook: @caudobooks

9 781737 298885